Edward S. Gould

John Doe and Richard Roe

Episodes of life in New York

Edward S. Gould

John Doe and Richard Roe
Episodes of life in New York

ISBN/EAN: 9783337399511

Printed in Europe, USA, Canada, Australia, Japan

Cover: Foto ©Andreas Hilbeck / pixelio.de

More available books at **www.hansebooks.com**

JOHN DOE AND RICHARD ROE;

OR,

EPISODES OF LIFE IN NEW YORK.

BY

EDWARD S. GOULD.

AUTHOR OF "ABRIDGMENT OF ALISON'S EUROPE;" "THE SLEEP RIDER;" "THE VERY AGE," A COMEDY; ETC., ETC., ETC., ETC.

NEW YORK:
Carleton, Publisher, 413 Broadway,
(LATE RUDD & CARLETON.)
MDCCCLXII.

THIS VOLUME IS INSCRIBED TO

THE HONORABLE GEORGE GOULD,

ONE OF THE JUSTICES OF THE SUPREME COURT OF THE STATE OF NEW YORK,

BY

HIS BROTHER.

CONTENTS.

JOHN DOE AND RICHARD ROE.

CHAPTER I.

As you cross the Park diagonally between the City Hall and the Hall of Records, you observe a crowd of men on the steps, and around the steps, of a square, brown-stone, four-story building—which, to be precise, has one front on Chambers-street and another on the Park.

You inquire, " What's the matter there? What's the excitement? Is anything up?"

Nothing special. At least, nothing unusual. That building has its own uses and its own history.

The apartments on the ground-floor, left side of the hall, are occupied by the collector of the city taxes and his deputies. He annually handles some ten millions of what was the people's money. His bureau is a sort of maelstrom toward which flow streams of coin from every imaginable point of the compass. I should like to know the fractional subdivision of NNW. by NW. a little W., or any other nautical line, whence and along which money does *not* find its way into the strong-box of this functionary! A meteorologist will tell you about *due* north, due east, and so on: but here the *dues* are not confined to the cardinal points: it is perpetually *due, due, due,* from all points—cardinal, sacerdotal, and geometrical. What becomes of all this money after the collector has absorbed it, is little to our present purpose.

Cross this ground-floor hall to the right, and—if you can gain admittance—you see a dark, dingy, carpetless room, filled with long wooden benches and wooden-bottomed chairs, which, in turn, are filled by men and women, who may have seen better days, but whose days, just now, seem to be none of the brightest. Who are they, do you ask? These are witnesses in attendance. Some of them have "attended" for two or three days past, with a mixture of resignation and impatience; some have just arrived, and wonder they are kept waiting at all, for their subpœnas say "nine o'clock precisely," and the city clocks are all banging out "ten" at that instant; and others, having important business elsewhere, are preparing to "leave," and take the consequences. Suddenly a bell rings, and a door opens into an adjoining room, rather better furnished, and somewhat better lighted, through the length of which run two long tables, connected at the further extremity by a curve, around the outside of which are seated something less than twenty-four respectable citizens, known for the time being as the Grand Jury. I presume you know what a Grand Jury is—or should be; and we will pass on to the next floor above.

On this stage, or story of the building, sits the Supreme Court in its various departments—Circuits, Chambers, Special Term and General Term; *terms* intelligible enough to the initiated, but the precise definition of which is here pretermitted.

Ascend a second flight of stairs, and you come bolt upon the entrance to the rooms of the District Attorney—an officer whose duties in part precede and in part follow the action of the Grand Jury; an officer of high trust and great power; a man who can "put through" indicted offenders on the right or the wrong side of justice very much as he pleases, and without any particular reference to the merits of the case; a man, in short, who is able to do more than any man *ought* to be able to do, unless he is perpendicular in personal and official integrity.

Cross *this* hall, and you find yourself in the arena where the District Attorney's ministerial functions having terminated, his executive duties begin; where our Recorder and City Judge alternately preside; where criminal law is the rule of action, and where *justice* is very unequally distributed among miscellaneous offenders. We call this the Court of Sessions.

Toil up one more flight of stairs, and the signs tell you that you are in close proximity to the several departments of the Marine Court—a court of various and somewhat anomalous jurisdiction, but a court where old sailors will find very few *marines*, should they happen to be looking for them.

Now, after this hurried glance through the brownstone building with two fronts, you will not be much at a loss to understand why so many people, in small knots and large groups, are crowded around it. Jurors, witnesses, parties, counsel, and miscellaneous spectators, are there; and when you add to those, more or less of all who have to do with the collector of taxes, you perceive that the varieties of our male population are there tolerably well represented.

This brown-stone building with two fronts is named the "New City Hall." We will step into it for a few moments. This is the floor, or story, appropriated by the Supreme Court, and this room is its "Circuit, Part One." Here, too, is a crowd of men, with their hats on, who seem to be talking against time, for the court "opens" at ten o'clock, and it is past that already.

Time does not pass very rapidly when one is waiting; and, as we are spectators, we seem to have been looking about, studying physiognomy and architecture, for at least a quarter of an hour; my watch, however, shows that it is but twelve minutes past ten. Suddenly a knocking is heard, hats are taken off, men seat themselves, a respectable-looking citizen is seen on "the bench," and another citizen, not quite so respectable-looking, stands at the end of "the bench," remarking, in moderately loud tones:

"*Hear ye! hear ye! all tpmnqromtttssjkiabret kkllmdoifhhhabcdefghijklmnopqrstuvwxyz* * * ———"

I am not quite sure what that man said, but probably other people understand him, for you see they have come to order. This proceeding is called "*opening* the court," and it has the effect of *closing* a great many people's mouths.

The business of the day centres around "the bench," where the judge is seated at an elevation of two feet, listening to half a dozen men in front of him, who seem to be all talking at once. They poke up papers, and take back papers, and read papers; while the judge, with great blandness and no little skill, keeps them both busy and in suspense. This thing has lasted about twenty minutes, and, for all that a spectator can see, nothing has been accomplished; when the judge announces that he will "call the calendar," and the standing men lapse into chairs to listen.

"John Doe against Richard Roe."

"In that case, if the court please," remarks an eminent lawyer, "there has been a great difficulty in finding witnesses on both sides, and we would like the case to be reserved, specially."

"I can give no preferences till I get through with the calendar. John Doe and others against Richard Roe."

"In that case, if the court please," remarks an eminent lawyer, "a demurrer has been entered, and we want time——"

The judge, it seems, also "wants time," and without waiting to hear the eminent lawyer, he proceeds:

"John Doe and others against Richard Roe and others."

"Ready for the plaintiff," remarks an eminent lawyer.

"If the court please," remarks an eminent lawyer, "the principal counsel for the defendant is now engaged in the Superior Court."

"Is he trying a cause?"

"He is trying a cause, if the court please."

"John Doe and several others against Richard Roe."

"Ready for the defendant," remarks an eminent lawyer.

"If the court please," remarks an eminent lawyer, "we are not prepared to try that case, and would like to have it go over for the term."

"If the court please," remarks an eminent lawyer, "we have been here through three entire terms, ready to try this case, and every time have been met by my learned friend with the same excuse. If the gentleman presses for further delay, I shall move that the complaint be dismissed."

"I presume," remarks an eminent lawyer, "that this honorable court will not listen to the base insinuations——"

Rap, rap, rap, rap, of the judge's hammer, announces that this honorable court will listen to *no* "insinuations."

" *Why* are you not prepared, Mr. Roe?"

"If the court please," responds the eminent lawyer, "we have several reasons. My learned friend well knows——"

"If the court please," interrupts the eminent lawyer on the other side, "I know nothing of the kind."

Rap, rap, rap, rap, again informs the learned friends that the honorable court will not listen to this form of debate.

"As I was saying," continues the eminent lawyer for the plaintiff, "my client is at this moment sitting on the jury in the Common Pleas, in the well-known case of Doe *versus* Roe; the testimony is not yet concluded, and there are five eminent counsel——"

"Cannot this case be tried in his absence, Mr. Roe?" inquires the judge.

"Impossible, if the court please," responds the eminent lawyer; "my client is his own principal witness, and no one else is fully conversant with the facts."

"If the court please," replies the eminent lawyer for

the defendant, " this is the seventh time this case has been called; we have always been ready; we have no less than three witnesses here from Boston, who have been called here solely to testify in this case; and I am prepared to show that my learned friend's client managed by collusion to get himself impanelled on the jury——"

" I do trust," interrupts the eminent lawyer for the plaintiff, " that this honorable court will protect my client from the aspersions of my learned friend——"

" Gentlemen, I cannot listen to all this. Do you state, Mr. Roe, that your client is an important witness in this case, and that he is now sitting as a juror in a case actually on trial in the Common Pleas ?"

" I do so state, if the court please," replies the eminent lawyer for the plaintiff; " and I will make an affidavit to that effect, if my learned friend insists on it."

" That can hardly be necessary. Mr. Doe, I must pass this case for to-day."

Mr. Doe scowls, grumbles, and retires, notifying his three Boston witnesses that they can *go.*

" John Doe and a great many others against Richard Roe."

" Ready for the plaintiff," says an eminent lawyer.

" If the court please," rejoins an eminent lawyer, " we are not prepared to try this case. My partner, Mr. Roe, is engaged in a case in the Superior Court."

" Is the case you speak of actually on ?"

" It is, if the court please."

" If the court please," says the plaintiff's eminent lawyer, " I would like this case to be specially reserved for to-morrow. This is the fourteenth time I have been here with my witnesses, twenty in number, and every time my learned friend on the opposite side has been engaged in some other court."

"It is a hard case, Mr. Doe; I will see what I can do. I must first go on with the calendar. John Doe and a great many others against Richard Roe and a great many others."

" Ready for the defendant," says an eminent lawyer.

" If the court please," rejoins an eminent lawyer, " we are not prepared to try that case. Mr. Roe, who has had sole charge of it from the beginning, is now engaged in a case actually on trial in the United States Court."

" I suppose I must pass it, then, Mr. Doe?"

" If the court please," replies the defendant's eminent counsel, " this is positively the twenty-third time I have been here with my witnesses—three from Chicago, two from Baltimore, and one from Cincinnati—and in every instance my learned friend on the opposite side has been engaged in some other court."

" I really have no option, Mr. Doe. I cannot order a trial to proceed when counsel are absent. John Doe and so forth against Richard Roe."

" Ready for the plaintiff," says an eminent lawyer.

" If the court please," rejoins an eminent lawyer, " it is with the utmost concern that I announce to my learned friend on the other side, that Mr. Roe, my colleague, who has had exclusive control of this case, is now trying a case in the Marine Court."

" Then I must pass——"

" If the court will indulge me for one moment," interrupts an eminent lawyer; " my client is on the eve of departing for Europe; he has been here with his witnesses from different parts of the country, more than twenty several times, and in each instance my learned friend on the opposite side has offered this identical, *verbatim*, excuse."

" What is your motion, Mr. Roe?"

"If the court please, that this trial proceed," answers the defendant's eminent lawyer.

"I am sorry I cannot oblige you, Mr. Roe. The rule is fixed that the court cannot order a case on when counsel are absent."

Do you find this tedious, my good sir?

I must confess, I find it rather monotonous.

Ah! you think you have heard the same thing several times repeated? Well, you are not far wrong, though the cases all represent different parties and different causes of action. Yet, tedious as this may seem to a spectator, and annoying as it must be to the various parties in interest, the precise counterpart of all this may be witnessed five days in every week, in every court-room of this metropolis, every month of every year. It involves the loss of time and often the loss of something much more important than time, to hundreds of people who are compelled to resort to the law for a defence, or a recovery, of their rights. On that point, as you will readily see, I might enlarge indefinitely.

The foregoing account of a day in court is sufficiently accurate in details for all practical purposes.

The only essential variation from what is there of constant occurrence, is, that in place of the bad Irish in which every New York lawyer addresses the judge, good English is here substituted. The lawyers all say, "may it please *your honor;*" "if your honor please;" "your honor ruled, or decided, so and so:" each of which expressions is vulgar Irish, and not English at all. Paddy from Cork, who is the veritable author of the phrase "yer honor," carries the thing rather further than the lawyers do: he applies it to every man, lay or professional, whom he considers his superior. But it is *his* language, to whomsoever applied, and not the language of educated men.

The error among men who should know better owes its continuance, probably, to a vague misapprehension that "honor" is in fact *a title*. It is not so. "Majesty" is a title. "Highness," "Excellency," "Grace," "Lordship," "Lord," are also titles. And therefore "*your* majesty," or "his majesty;" "your" or "his" highness, excellency, grace, lordship, and "my" lord, are correct English terms. But "honor" not being a title in any possible sense, "your" and "his" honor are mere vulgarisms.

How the objectionable phrases ever came to be so generally adopted by men of education, is neither here nor there. That question is foreign to the purpose. Those who choose to go into it, will never get beyond, nor above, the Paddy aforesaid: and if any professional man will venture to cite Paddy as actual authority in a philological court, he will find himself ruled out.

Judges of Courts, State and United States Senators, Representatives to Congress, and some other officials are by courtesy designated " the honorable;" but that is a mere prefix, an epithet, an adjective; it is not in any sense a title. Nor, therefore, can the process of manufacturing it into a substantive—honor —make *that* a title.

Would it not be better, hereafter, for the educated members of the profession to speak English when addressing the presiding officer of a court?

CHAPTER II.

RICHARD ROE was about forty-five years of age, six feet high, and well proportioned. His face was nothing particular. Neither was his dress. He would pass in a crowd, without attracting attention by his appearance. He differed, externally, from no one of ten thousand men, excepting in his walk, which was a kind of shuffling gait, suggestive of profit to his boot-maker. He barely raised his foot from the ground at the beginning of a step, and the latter half of the step was a slide, or scrape, admirably adapted to the frittering away of sole-leather.

Richard was what is called a man of standing in the community. He lived in his own house, drove his own horses, figured in all the published lists of charity and benevolence, and had the credit of expending fifteen or twenty thousand dollars a year: hence, he was supposed to be wealthy. Moreover, he responded audibly, sang loud, and knelt low, in church; and, as he paid liberally toward building the church, owned a square pew, was a member of the vestry, carried around the plate with more unction than any of his colleagues, and was particular to attend the weekly evening lectures of the church— and to tell of it—he was supposed to be righteous, much.

Again, Richard was a man of large charity; not

of the pocket, but of the heart. Scriptural charity. The charity that thinketh no evil of any man, unless any man's evil had touched Richard personally. For example, if the confidential manager of a money-corporation, or the trustee of an estate, or any person who had custody of large sums of other people's money, proved to be a defaulter to the extent of millions, so long as Richard was not himself a loser by the default, he could never find it in his heart to proscribe the thief. He would speak gently of the robber. He would take him by the hand—if nobody was looking on.

Richard was, or had been, the president of a great many incorporated companies—as Coal, Railroad, Insurance, Banks, and what not? and the fact of his having once enjoyed the confidence of so many stock-holders and boards of direction, clearly showed that he was a man of great executive ability—at least, such would have been the inference in men's minds, if any of those incorporated companies had chanced to prosper under his management. Nevertheless, he had the reputation of great shrewdness and forecast in the investment of money. His judgment was supposed to be, or to have been, a little better than his neighbors' in such matters, and he was often the first man applied to, for private information about the good things that were lying about the market, waiting to be snapped up by early birds. His connection with so many corporations gave him peculiar facilities for knowing the nooks and corners where worms lay hid, and many were the friends made glad by being allowed to come into such pickings "on bottom principles." Richard was remarkable for the moderation of his own views, in such cases. After getting

his friends fairly "in" an enterprise which made fortune a sure thing to those who would only hold on,
he was sure to sell himself slyly "out" to the last
applicant for a paltry fifteen or twenty per cent.
profit—the said fifteen or twenty per cent. advance
being, in fact, the " bottom principle " on which the
last applicant's predecessors had all been "let in."

The strict impartiality of Richard in thus letting
people into good things was another feature of his
well balanced character. He made no distinction
between rich and poor, friend and foe. He treated
all alike. A relative who had but a few thousands
stood the same chance for eventual profit as the out-
sider who was rich : and Richard pocketed his little
twenty per cent. from the former as calmly as from
the latter—but always with the solemn assurance to
each that each was let in on bottom principles.

Richard was a model man in his own family. He
rose up early, sat up late, and ate the bread of care-
fulness. He was punctilious about family prayer.
Of a morning, that might be set down as a sure
thing, as it was his main dependence for the day.
He relied on it as confidently as on winding his
watch. The latter made him all right in interests
temporal ; the former, in those eternal. For no man
knew better than he that a good long family prayer
of a morning is like a large deposit in the bank at
ten o'clock : it provided for any incidental tricks
which, in the burden and heat of the day, he might
find opportunity to practise on his customers. The
prayer was so much to his credit in the Books above :
it furnished a fund of grace to draw on ; and a
balance to credit there, as elsewhere, secured him
against being overdrawn. To omit the morning

prayer, would have been almost as bad as to neglect his watch or his bank account. As to evening prayer, although his thirst for that service was not less parching than for the morning service, impediments·would present themselves. The cares of this world, arising from the deceitfulness of riches, despite all his precautions, would now and then interfere with that season of refreshment. But Richard was equal even to that disappointment. It never crushed him. He would look placidly around the room and remark that accidents must sometimes happen in the best regulated families. But whenever the service took place, the edification was great. Richard's fluency in prayer was prodigious. He never stuck for a word, and it must be acknowledged that his word was generally the right one. If any man was ever heard for his much speaking, that man was Richard Roe. He was, at times, as some people thought, rather familiar in his form of address to the Deity. He occasionally impressed his audience with an idea that, somehow or other, he stood on remarkably good terms with the Power he was ostensibly supplicating; and that he asked for things in a way that might perhaps prevent anybody else, who should so ask, from obtaining them. Certain it is, that, for a bruised and broken reed, he exhibited an astounding quantity of backbone in family prayer.

Richard, like all pious and conscientious men, was sensitive to the opinions of others as touching his walk and conversation. If a thing of questionable propriety was proposed in his family, his first thought was, not whether the matter was innocent and proper in itself, but what would Doctor Perkins and Deacon Brown think or say of it? He was very solicitous about the *appearance* of evil. He knew he was all right, but he wished other people to know it. He was unwilling that his good should be evil spoken of. He was for a long time time perplexed about drawing the line between permitted and forbidden public amusements. The secular lecture seemed to be all right; the unmitigated theatre was perhaps all wrong. Concerts and the opera were safe middle ground. But "Niblo's" tried him sadly. A large portion of his circle patronized Niblo's, and it was *very* embarrassing to be inquired of by half-and-half people in society, why he did not take his family to see the Ravels? It is generally believed that he whipped the devil around the stump, by allowing the members of his family to go to any place of amusement on invitation from serious people.

Richard had persuasive ways, adapted to winning golden opinions from all sorts of persons. For instance, religious persons. Put him into a party of church-going ladies and gentlemen, and, before he has been there twenty minutes, all the ladies and half the men will be perfectly convinced that Richard Roe is the only really pious person in the room.

Richard affected fine books, fine furniture, and fine pictures. His actual knowledge of such matters was very limited. But he made up for that, by paying extravagant prices: for it is worthy of remark, that while in his business he screwed farthings out of both rich and poor, and in his charities he made shillings do the work of dollars, he was not only free, but foolishly lavish, in home expenditures.

Thus, his furniture was costly, but ill assorted; his books were trashy, but well bound; his pictures were daubs, but richly framed. He was fluent, however, in designating the merits of his pictures. But he never quite comprehended the difference between depth of shade and breadth of shade, depth of coloring and breadth of coloring, transparency, perspective, relief, fiddle-de-dee and so on.

Richard's physiognomy was peculiar in one feature: his upper lip was an eighth of an inch too long—which is considerable in a man's lip, though not much in a carving knife. The lip was also flabby and meaty; and, moreover, to those who knew the man well, it was what sailors would call a "tell-tale" on Roe's veracity. When Roe had a point to carry, or to defend, he put on what he intended to be a benignant and persuasive smile, though the thing often turned out to be a sorry grin: and whenever, hereaway, he was telling the truth, the big upper lip would answer the helm, and go the way that the under lip did. But when Richard was lying, the big lip, as if it were a talisman placed there by Providence to betray him, became suddenly rigid and impracticable. It would quiver under the impulse of the tiller-ropes, but it would not move to the right hand or the left. In short, it would not join in the smile. And hence, by watching the upper lip of Richard Roe when he was getting up a persuasive smile, any one could tell at once and unerringly whether he was lying.

This detailed account of Richard Roe, banker and church-member, however tedious to read, is indispensable to remove a popular prejudice. A great many people, even among the more cultivated classes, entertain a belief that Richard Roe is a myth. But they are deceived. Richard Roe is no myth. He knows it. His family know it. His friends, if he has any, know it. His enemies—and he has plenty of them—know it. His debtors know it. Every one who has had money dealings with him knows it —to his cost. No, indeed! Richard Roe is no myth.

CHAPTER III.

The family were out of town for the summer; and, as a matter of course, certain details of housekeeping were attended to negligently—if, indeed, they were attended to at all. For example, the clocks were wound up at odd times, after having run down in their own time: and that is the reason why the clock on the bedroom mantlepiece of the house No. 713 Queer-street, now struck twelve, when the hands on the index indicated two o'clock. Two o'clock P.M. was in fact the hour.

The clock happened to be a fast striker: so fast, that the striking reached the ear in a confused and continuous ring, unless you were on the alert and watching for it. And, consequently, the striking of this clock was often mistaken for the ringing of the door-bell, especially if the occupant of the room was in a brown study. That was the fact in the present instance. He started from his chair, ran toward the head of the stairs, and in the extremity of his surprise and agitation accidentally let off a mild oath:

"Who the h— is that?"

It proved to be nobody.

"Pshaw!" exclaimed the gentleman, provoked with himself for having been frightened, yet gratified that after all there was no occasion for fright, "it's only that infernal clock. Why don't they let the noisy thing run down?"

Sure enough. Why don't they let it run down? But rather, why should the striking of a clock, or the ringing of a door-bell, give such a shock to a respectable citizen?

The truth is, the man was in trouble; at least, doubt; at least, perplexity. He had a thing to do which he feared to do, and feared to leave undone. It had been on his mind for weeks. He had delayed his action in the premises until delay became decidedly dangerous. The very last chance was now flitting rapidly away.

He resumed the seat from which the clock had startled him: looked vacantly *at* the clock: looked at a portrait hanging above it: and thence his eyes wandered slowly along the wall and up to the ceiling. Finally, he closed them. They might as well have been closed the whole time, for all the service they had rendered. The entire man was absorbed in thought; and his physical functions, if they acted at all, did so mechanically.

At length he aroused himself; and, by his promptness, seemed likely to make up for lost time. He took his watch, porte-monnaie, and sundries from his pockets; took off a ring from his finger; replaced a diamond breast-pin with a pearl button; placed these valuables in a drawer of a dressing bureau; locked the drawer; and dropped his bunch of keys into a vase on one side of the clock. He then put in his pocket a roll of something in brown paper that seemed to be heavy for its size, took from the table a pair of double green spectacles, which he also pocketed; and thus, with nothing about his person but these two articles and some loose silver change, he rang his bell and walked down stairs.

"Bridget," said he, as the girl answered the bell, "I am going to Long Island, and shall not be home until to-morrow morning."

"Will you be in to breakfast, sir?" inquired the girl.

"Yes. Probably." And he was quickly in the street, on his way down town. He took his course through the Fourth Avenue and the Bowery, where nothing seemed to attract his attention but the apothecaries' shops. These he eyed carefully as he passed along; and, at length, finding one empty of customers, he walked in.

"I want," said he to a man in attendance, "an ounce or two of chloroform."

"For inhaling?" inquired the man.

"Eh—yes; for inhaling," said the gentleman. "I didn't know that there are two kinds."

"You have a physician's prescription, I presume?" said the careful apothecary.

"Certainly," answered the gentleman, with great readiness and confidence, although he did not produce it. That was, in fact, a part of the business that he had not contemplated nor provided for. But a gentleman of his position and appearance was not likely to be disobliged by a Bowery apothecary: the man would take the gentleman's word, of course. Indeed, as the shopman was already busy in preparing the vial, probably he would not recur to the prescription. The vial was speedily filled, corked, labelled, and papered.

"How much?" inquired the gentleman.

"Four and sixpence.   And—the prescription, if you please," answered the apothecary.

The gentleman had thrown down the change and extended his hand for the vial; but the apothecary retained it.

"We are obliged," said he, "to be very particular. We never deliver things of this kind to strangers without an order."

"It's very odd!" said the gentleman, who had been eagerly diving into one after another of his pockets to find what never was there: "it's very odd!   Doctor Jenkins gave me the paper this morning—pink paper, too, as I remember—I must have left it on my table.   Well.   I am going directly home.   Let that boy jump into the car with me, and I'll send it back by him and pay his fare."

This was plausible, and in the ordinary course of things.   Therefore the apothecary, though apparently with some reluctance, assented.

"I say, Tom," said he to the boy, "mind you hurry back, now."

The first car that came along proved to be rather full of people.

"My lad," said the gentleman to Tom, "go forward there and find a seat.   I want to speak to the conductor."

Tom went forward quite contentedly.   The gentleman handed two fares to the conductor; and then, fortunately remembering that he had forgotten something, he stepped from the platform while the car was in motion.   Tom probably had a nice ride, and a nice time of it, looking for the gentleman when the ride was at an end.   But the gentleman was elsewhere, having been industriously pursuing an opposite course ever since he stepped from the platform.

When the gentleman reached Centre-street, he found the sunlight oppressive to his eyes; and, in a stealthy way, he put on his green spectacles. Yet other people found no difficulty about the sunlight, for the luminary had just then passed behind a cloud that was ominously dark, and threatened rain.

Everybody knows that the Tombs-front is on Centre-street, so that a few steps brought the gentleman in specs to the Franklin-street entrance, ground-floor, keeper's room.

The keeper knew the gentleman in specs; indeed, he knew him *by* his specs; for the gentleman had been there twice before, on the same errand, and each time had found spectacles necessary to protect his eyes.

"You are wishing to see Wilson again, sir, I suppose?" said the keeper.

"Yes," replied the gentleman; "I am going out of town this afternoon, and I understand his trial comes on to-morrow. I want to say a word or two to the poor devil."

"Yes, sir, certainly; very kind of you, I'm sure, sir," rejoined the keeper. "Here, Bill, show this gentleman to number thirteen."

Bill had already twice previously shown the gentleman to number thirteen, and was therefore in a manner acquainted with the gentleman. Besides, in walking through stone corridors, even with strangers, one likes to be conversable.

"Nice day, sir," hazarded Bill.

"Yes, yes. Rather warm, though. Looks like rain."

"Shouldn't wonder, sir. Rain, they say, is much a wanting. Eyes still troublesome, sir?"

"Eyes?—oh, yes; very."

"Specs must be a great relief to weak eyes; but not much use here, sir, a body might suppose. What with the specs and what with the clouds, it's rather dark just along here. Mind that pail, please, sir. This is number thirteen. Should I wait, sir?" unlocking the door, and partly opening it.

"No. I won't trouble you. I may be detained. Come back in half an hour, Bill, and here's a trifle to drink my health when you get a chance."

"Against rules, sir," muttered Bill, casting an eye up and down the passage, to ascertain if any one was witness to the gentleman's liberality; "much obliged to you, sir. I must lock you in, sir, but I'll be back in time."

And the gentleman was locked in, accordingly, and Bill withdrew. The prisoner, Wilson, was sitting on his bunk with a newspaper in his hand, although the cell was just then too dark for him to read the news.

Wilson was confined and about to be tried on an indictment for forgery. He had, some years previously, been a confidential clerk of the gentleman in specs. But that gentleman, either suspecting Wilson of dishonesty, or finding him too inquisitive as to the private details of the business, and too intelligent to be put off with evasive answers, managed, through indirect intriguing, to persuade a neighboring firm to make Wilson a very advantageous offer for his services: in short, to offer Wilson inducements, privately, to leave his employer. In this way, the gentleman relieved himself from the espionage of a troublesome clerk without (as he supposed) making an enemy of him. Wilson, for a time, got on very well in his new situation; but at last things went wrong, and he was discharged.

There has been a deal of discussion "in the books" as to the length of time needed to make a thorough-going rascal out of a previously honest man. Some contend that rascality grows slowly, like an elm; others, that one good opportunity brings it into immediate and full development, like a mushroom. Be that as it may, Wilson, being hard up for ready cash, had forged the name of his last employers on a bank cheque, which was well executed and readily paid. Subsequent imprudence, on his part, led to his arrest, the money was found in his possession, and he was fully identified by the teller of the bank as the person who presented the cheque.

The gentleman in specs had taken a deep interest in Wilson's situation—especially after their first interview, when Wilson informed the gentleman that whereas the gentleman had once suspected him of dishonesty, he, Wilson, had also suspected *him* of dishonesty, and had taken possession of certain papers in the gentleman's own handwriting, which very prettily proved Wilson's suspicions to be well founded: and that, as matters now stood, he wouldn't mind surrendering those papers to the gentleman, conditioned that the gentleman should get him out of his present dilemma.

"I began to fear you were not coming," said Wilson, as the gentleman took a seat on the only bench in the cell.

"I was detained at home by visitors," the gentleman replied; "but there's plenty of time. Plenty of time," he repeated in a doleful tone, " for what we have to do, and for me to be caught in doing my share of it. You will be a great gainer by me, this time, Wilson."

" Some little percentage of profit on your side, sir, *I* think," Wilson rejoined, sneeringly.

" Don't talk so, Wilson," said the gentleman; " pray don't talk so. You entirely misapprehend the nature of those transactions. I could show you that that was all fair between man and man. You have the papers, though ?" he continued, suddenly changing his tone. " Not that they are of any intrinsic importance ; but in the hands of third persons, and without my explanations, they might certainly be made to look suspicious. You have the papers ?"

There was no doubt about that. He had them, snug. A little rap with his left hand indicated the place where he kept them under his jacket.

" Oh," continued the gentleman, " you needn't be so cautious with me. You must place them in my hands at last ; and we haven't much time to lose."

" All right, sir, no doubt," responded Wilson ; " but, on whatever ground you put it, we must exchange commodities. I must take if I give."

" Pshaw !" replied the gentleman, impatiently, " don't affect punctilio now. You must trust me in the first instance from the very nature of the case. Besides, my interest in your future welfare ought to satisfy you that I shall carry through what I have begun. Give me the papers."

" It doesn't matter much," rejoined Wilson, after a pause. " I have them by heart, and I could reproduce them, word for word, if I find myself deceived.

The facts are the main thing, after all." And so saying, he placed the parcel in the gentleman's hands.

That individual carefully examined the papers; and, if Wilson had taken the trouble to note it, the temporary paleness, succeeded by a temporary redness, of the gentleman's face, seemed to contradict the valuation he had so recently put upon the parcel. The examination finished, he put the documents into a side pocket of his coat, and buttoned his coat up to his throat, with the air of a man who is sure he has done a good thing.—But if, in the masquerading prank which forms a part of his programme, he should become excited; and if, in his excitement, arising from the novelty and danger of his situation, he should become forgetful; and, in his forgetfulness, should omit one thing mechanically small, yet practically of greater magnitude than all the rest;—of what avail will be the sacrifice and the risk that the gentleman in specs is about to incur? A man who involves himself with culprits, and trifles with the law, needs to have *all* his wits about him!

"Now, Wilson," said the gentleman, with considerably increased confidence, "we will proceed according to the programme. Here is the money; one thousand dollars in gold. Where that will carry you, and what it will do when you get there, you understand without further explanation. We must now change clothes: or rather," he added, with a thrill of disgust as he took a survey of Wilson's tattered garments, "you must put on my clothes, and I will take possession of your bunk. (Another thrill of disgust; but there was no help for it.) You are about my height; not unsimilar in person; and these spectacles will go far to disguise your face; while the darkness of the storm that has now providentially come to our assistance, together with the improbability that so bold a design can be suspected, renders success sure. You will escape to a certainty."

" And you ?" inquired Wilson.

"Never fear for me : my plan is all right, when you are fairly out of the way," answered the gentleman. "Come ; hurry with your dressing, and then I have a few more words to say."

He put the vial of chloroform under the pillow of the bunk, divested himself of his clothes, managed to double the blanket of the prisoner's bed in such a way that he avoided contact with the sheets, and then laid himself down.

Wilson, with corresponding promptness, encased himself in the gentleman's apparel, which really fitted him to a hair. And when the hat and spectacles were mounted, the resemblance was so complete that the gentleman felt quite oppressed with a sense of his own surpassing cleverness.

It is useless to ignore a familiar truth. There is a moral effect in dress. A man well clad is twice the man he was in shabby garments. His deportment, his feelings, his very thoughts, are elevated as by the touch of a conjurer's wand. So, therefore, was it with Wilson ; and *so, reversely*, was it with the unclad gentleman—the gentleman wrapped in a prisoner's blanket. A sense of humiliation and degradation so pressed on him that he was near bursting into tears. He was so entirely overcome by his feelings that for a few moments he seemed to be incapable of carrying out what was so boldly begun.

" Wilson," he said, at length, " you are now about to leave the country forever. Of course, you will never think of returning. When you are once in safety, set about a thorough reformation in your character and conduct. Go and sin no more. Good bye. God bless you."

Wilson—not making allowances for what was passing in the distressed gentleman's mind, and by no means sympathizing with his depressed and altered tone—Wilson was at first inclined to laugh at this sudden transformation; but real passion has its power, as dress has, and it is not easily counterfeited. Seeing, therefore, that the emotion of the gentleman was genuine, Wilson took him by the hand, and, in all sincerity, bade him an affectionate farewell.

" My dear sir," said he, " I am afraid you will get into trouble here. I am, really."

The tone of genuine sympathy had *its* effect, in turn, and the gentleman replied with renewed firmness, " There's no sort of danger, thank you. My plan is what I call fireproof. Now, then, to simplify matters, and to dispense with your services in the assault we agreed on, I hit myself *thus*," he continued, rising in the bed and actually giving himself a blow with his fist between the eyes that set his nose to bleeding. "By Jupiter, that was a settler, though! I needn't have hit quite so hard. No matter. This vial, now" (feeling for it under the pillow)—" you take it out of the paper and uncork it. There. That will do. Set it on the floor where it will stand. Now, you know, you attacked me suddenly; knocked me down: put me into a state of insensibility with that chloroform; dressed yourself in my clothes; passed yourself off on the turnkey for myself, when he came to let me out: and then, boldly and deliberately walking away, you escaped."

"My dear sir!" exclaimed Wilson, with a burst of enthusiastic admiration, "this is worthy of Jack Sheppard! But about the chloroform? How will you manage? Suppose you should overdose yourself?"

"Don't you be unhappy about that!" replied the gentleman. "Do you think I am fool enough to use it, in fact? No, no. It must be here, to account for my position by and by, when the safe time arrives for making myself known. As for the sleep and the stupor, I can put on as much of them as the circumstances may require."

Then, looking about him, and beginning once more to appreciate the risk and the degradation of his position, he continued in an altered tone, "Make sure of your safety now, Wilson, and then consider your ways."

"But," inquired Wilson, whose mind, just now, was running on things physical rather than things moral, "how shall I manage the turnkey? he may recognize me by my voice."

"Say all you have to say to him in whispers," replied the gentleman, "and then he can't observe your voice. Tell him, the prisoner is asleep and don't want any supper. I gave him a fee as I came in, and he'll be civil, expecting another next time. All must go well now. What a condition, though, am I in! Good-bye, Wilson! Remember your childhood and its lessons; and the Sunday-school, with its experiences. Reform, Wilson. Turn from every false way. Be a good man. Pray for strength from on high—*there's Bill!*"

The turnkey accordingly unlocked the door, remarking that the time was up; but, as it was raining cats and dogs, the gentleman would probably sit awhile in the office.

"Hush!" said Wilson, in a mysterious whisper, "he's asleep. Quite down-hearted, too. He said not to bring him any supper. If he's asleep then, don't wake him. As for the rain, that's neither here nor there. I can jump into a car. Never mind me. I'll find my way out."

And he pushed on accordingly, favored by the darkness: bowed to the open door of the keeper's office as he passed it; and was out of sight around the corner before anybody could say, Jack Robinson.

The devotional mood of the incarcerated gentleman, so abruptly disturbed by Bill's return, was fast coming back upon him, as Bill retired with his late prisoner. The gentleman listened attentively for a few moments. All was still. All, therefore, was well. No news was good news in this case, if never in any other. A minute elapsed. Two minutes. Five minutes.

"Safe! safe! Heaven be praised! That Wilson is a good man at heart. He will escape ruin, and he will reform. His precious soul may be saved by this very means, and that end will justify those means. God be merciful to him, a sinner—and to me, a sinner! for he who saves a soul from death——"

"DAMNATION!"

And he leaped from the bed as if a scorpion had stung him. *Was* it a scorpion? *What* was it?

"That fellow has carried off those papers in the breast-pocket of my coat!"

CHAPTER IV.

THE newspapers of the following day had a genuine sensation article. It was the real thing, and no mistake. Wilson, the desperate and notorious forger, had escaped from the Tombs. And in such a bold, audacious, unprecedented, scandalous, infamous, outrageous, awful, terrible and incredible manner, the editors really wanted words to give adequate utterance to their horror. No man's life was safe. The temple of Justice was profaned by the rude hand and the strong arm.

One of our richest, noblest, most exemplary, and most pious citizens was stricken down at the very portals of the temple. It was time for the citizens to arise in their might, in the plenitude and the majesty of their power. Otherwise, our charter was nought. Our freedom was a fiction. Our character as a sovereign and an empire city was blown to the four winds.

Let not cavillers turn up their noses at the four winds. Let not critics derisively ask *what are* the four winds? There might be other winds. No editor would presume, officially, to deny that. For example, there is the wind that blows nobody any good; that, clearly, is not one of the four. Then, there is the wind that people *raise* when they are short of funds; that, too, is none of the four. Then, there are head winds, and fair winds; Boreas and zephyrs, and the wind that blows where it listeth. But, enough said about winds. No editor is going to be cornered on winds.

On the contrary, here is Richard Roe, banker and church member; a man whom all delight to honor; one of our oldest subscribers, too; a man all heart, all benevolence, all goodness; who has done more for our noble city than any other man (excepting, indeed, those who have done more than he)—this man, this friend to the poor, this pride of the rich, while actually sacrificing his duty to his family, and missing the cars, in order to speak a word of comfort to that fiend in human form, that robber of the widow and the fatherless, that vile forger, Wilson—was, by that same inconceivable villain, brutally assassinated in his, the prisoner's, own cell, while the good Roe was ministering unto him. Not, perhaps, quite assassinated, however. As the poet hath it, "not yet quite dead," not actually past the dread portal; but so near, that there was no fun in it.

The circumstances are substantially as follows. Mr. Roe called on the prisoner, a little before three o'clock, yesterday afternoon. Scarcely was he seated in the prisoner's cell, when he was struck in the forehead with a heavy iron bar, which bar has not yet been discovered. The blow was evidently intended to be fatal. Probably, its force was broken by Mr. Roe's hat; which, no doubt, was providentially on his head. But, not satisfied with that, this fiend in human form had provided himself with a vial of chloroform, and that fell and fatal poison was added to the murderous bar. Fortunately, respiration having been temporarily suspended by the iron blow, the poison was *not* inhaled, and the noble Roe is not dead, though his murderer has escaped.

While the illustrious victim of this fiend in human form lay senseless, Wilson stripped himself, stripped Mr. Roe, and arrayed himself in Mr. Roe's garments; and thus—literally, a wolf in sheep's clothing—he fiercely awaited the arrival of the turnkey, ready no doubt, to sacrifice *him* also, had the man imprudently recognized the monster in disguise. The turnkey, however, did not recognize him; but suffered him to pass as the personification of all the social virtues, which unfortunately he but too well represented.

When the hour arrived for dispensing the frugal meal known as the prisoners' supper, the turnkey visited the cell and found the supposed prisoner asleep. He made no effort to awake him, but placed the frugal meal on a bench, leaving the supposed Wilson to digest it at his leisure.

About four o'clock this morning, a disturbance and cry for help were heard issuing from Number Thirteen. The guard was mustered, the door was opened, the torches flung their flickering light along the frowning walls, and Number Thirteen became illuminated. There, in the precise condition in which he was born, stood Richard Roe, ghastly with wounds, weltering in blood, piteously inquiring where he was, and how he came there? At first, the officials of the gloomy prison did not appreciate the pertinency of the questions—for it is to be observed that, of all recognizable animals, a man stark naked is among the last. And for a prisoner who had been rusticating in Number Thirteen for some months, to inquire *where he was* and *how he came there*, did certainly, on the face of the thing, seem to be cutting it fat.

Naturally, therefore, the opening reply to these questions was one of those characteristic and colloquial banters, common enough as between prisoners and their keepers, but not exactly adapted to our columns. We never soil our paper with that sort of thing.

"But," answered the unfortunate Mr. Roe, in reply to this brutal profanity, which nothing could induce us to put in type, "I am not the prisoner Wilson; I don't belong here; I am Richard Roe, banker and church member; I called here yesterday afternoon to see Wilson; Bill, there, let me in; and I was attacked and robbed—don't you see my face and my very blood? and don't you smell chloroform?—there it is! that's the very vial itself."

Not to prolong these painful details, the truth, which is always mighty, and always prevails, slowly but distinctly came out.

A medley of clothes, just sufficient to enable Mr. Roe to be taken home in a carriage, was provided by the keeper of the prison; and just as our paper is going to press, we learn that Mr. Roe's physician considers the patient out of danger, though terribly shocked and weakened by the frightful ordeal he has passed.

It seems that Mr. Roe had left his office in Wall-street for the Hudson River train in Thirtieth-street, to join his interesting family at his country mansion on the banks of the Hudson, and stopped on his way for a few minutes' interview with Wilson, who was formerly a scholar in Mr. Roe's Sunday-school class, and more recently a clerk in Mr. Roe's office.

The result of his benevolent mission is before our readers.

Large rewards will doubtless be offered for the apprehension of Wilson; though we hear that Mr. Roe, with a kind-heartedness that will surprise no one who has the privilege of his acquaintance, has begged that no such step may be taken on *his* account. May Richard Roe soon find that rest, that calm, that quiet, that recuperation, in the bosom of his family, on the banks of the noble Hudson, which his life and conversation, his character and attributes, his wealth and worth entitle him to enjoy! And may that fiend in human form, who aimed this terrific bomb-shell at the peace of that family and the welfare of that noble man, experience the tortures of the doom he so richly merits!

The foregoing, without being precisely *verbatim* what the newspapers had to say on this interesting occasion, is near enough to literal correctness for all practical purposes.

Cynics have remarked, when a man of some note but questionable merit departed this life, that *dying* was the best thing that man ever did; inasmuch as, but for his death, the world would never have known a tithe of his good qualities. The meaning of which cynical remark probably is, that the inevitable obituary brought out the unsuspected secret.

There is a perpetual strife between newspaper editors in favor of deceased millionaires, which always ends in a printed catalogue of virtues that gratifies surviving mourners, amuses surviving acquaintances.

and *would* unutterably astonish the unconscious subject, could he but step back from the grave to read it.

The case of Richard Roe is not quite a case in point, because Richard Roe was not quite killed. But what the newspapers did, enables one to infer what, under other circumstances, they might have done.

Fortunately, or unfortunately, for Richard Roe, the summer is not over, and many of the readers of newspapers are out of town.

CHAPTER V.

IF there is one Americanism that clearly predominates over all other Americanisms, that one is a fondness for titles.

Titles of nobility, we have not. Lords, earls, dukes, barons, etc., are not to be found in our vocabulary. But we have military and naval titles in abundance. We have also generals, colonels, majors, captains, lieutenants, sergeants and corporals of our militia organization. We have, too, captains of ships, and all vessels; captains of police, of clubs, of newsboy-squads. We have, besides, governors and lieutenant-governors of States; judges of all manner of courts; attorney-generals, district-attorneys, mayors, aldermen, sheriffs; and of the interminable catalogue, how brief soever may be the tenure of office, the title never dies till the man does.

But this mass of titles has one merit: each, for the time being, means something. It means that the individual holding it is, or was, whatever his title indicates; and, excepting " captain," the indication is intelligible to the popular understanding. But the good people have managed to mystify one title to an extent that renders it unintelligible, if not ridiculous: namely, the title of *doctor*.

The " doctor " of whom we think first when the word is pronounced, and of whom we think most when we want a doctor, is the doctor of medicine. He is *the* doctor, *par excellence;* the doctor, proper; the traditionary proprietor of the title; the holder of it by right of the strongest; indeed, the only one who can claim the title by virtue of *fee* simple. In his case the title is convenient, descriptive, indispensable. It announces a fact—that the holder is a practitioner of the healing art. There is nothing ostentatious in it; no more than in "cobbler" appended to Joseph Crispin, or "weaver" to Nicholas Bottom.

But there are two other classes of men who seek, or receive the title of doctor merely as a title, without any definite signification whatever. Can any human being tell what a LL.D. or a D.D. *is?* Can any one recite the qualifications, the prerogatives, the duties, of a Doctor of Laws? Can any one tell what are the functions, or professional characteristics of a Doctor of Divinity—apart from the specialties of the "reverend" already conceded to him by the same usage that gives "doctor" to the physician?

Certain colleges and universities annually amuse themselves and the public by certifying that John Brown, person, or John Brown, parson, is something, or has done something which entitles him to be called Doctor—or, nicknamed Doctor—but what that something is, no one among all these institutions of learning has ever been able to say! There is, however, one thing to be said in extenuation of the LL.D. folly: its display is not always and necessarily inconsistent with the profession of its owner. Its assumption does not as a matter of course convict him of inconsistency.

But no such extenuation can be urged for the

Doctors of Divinity.   In every possible aspect, D.D. is a monstrosity.   It is meaningless, because it conveys no information ; superfluous, because all clergymen are " the reverend " *ex officio ;* and ostentatious, because it is a vainglorious " distinction without a difference."

Clergymen are our teachers; and, in that sense, they are all " doctors " philologically—*doceo, docere, docui, doctum ;* but their teaching is, and their example should be, patience, meekness, *humility.* They tell us of the vanity of the world, of the shortness of life, and of the unspeakable importance of eternity.   They would have us count all things but loss, for the excellency of the knowledge of Christ. Yet, nevertheless, if one looks at the number of clergymen who " attain " D.D., at their age when they attain it, and at their qualifications either before or after they have attained it ; one cannot but be struck at its miserable cheapness and insignificance ; while, also, one cannot but fancy that, corruptible as is the crown, it is a very prominent object in a clergyman's race.

No doubt, many institutions thrust this honor (?) unsought· on clergymen who have a well-earned reputation : but it is out of the question to suppose that a large number of D.D. diplomas are *not* painfully and laboriously sought by those who obtain them.

What a sad spectacle it is, in any printed list of clergymen, to see the lines sprinkled with D.D.'s as if they had been thrown out of a pepper-box! this good man with the cockade, and that perhaps better man without it.   For, considering how the D.D.'s are obtained, and *who gets them,* it is superfluous to suppose that they indicate any superiority over those who do not get them :

—All of which, by way of remark.

It may safely be presumed that-Richard Roe's clergyman was a D.D. Richard Roe knew the value of a title. He could not fructify under the exhortations of anything less than a Doctor of Divinity. If Whitefield or Robert Hall were preaching regularly in Richard's neighborhood, *Doctor* Perkins would still have been the man for Richard Roe's money. Necessarily, therefore, Doctor Perkins was Richard Roe's pastor.

Doctor Perkins had early learned that, in the biographical world, there are very few royal roads : none to high art; none to true fame; none, except by accident, to wealth; one, only, to happiness; several to notoriety. " Notoriety," he reasoned, " is not the genuine article; but it looks well in the newspapers, it passes current with the multitude, one can make sure of getting it—the other thing is up-hill work : here goes for notoriety !"

Once, somewhere, a notion was set on foot, that the primary duty of a clergyman was to do good to men —meaning men, generally. Perkins took a different view of the case, and strove for good to man individually—meaning one man; to wit, number one. And as he thus had a single object, he wisely resolved to limit his warfare to a single foe. Sin in the aggregate was a many-headed monster—he must be fought without ceasing : a man who undertook *that* must think more highly of his powers than the timid Perkins presumed to do. His humble abilities wouldn't venture to encounter anything more than the slavery question. No doubt, his congregation were sinful men and women—else, why were they there to listen? and why was he there to teach? No doubt, every individual of his flock was chargeable with a violation of some one of the precepts of the Decalogue, including always the supplementary precept of love to God and our neighbor. But Perkins couldn't do everything. He had always thought it better to do one thing well, than to deal superficially with many things. Not only so, that other sort of thing was the beaten track, and impressions [sensations] were not easily produced on beaten tracks. He would not dictate to his professional brethren. The field is the world. There is room for all. " Choose ye," he said to them, in imagination, " choose ye whom ye will assail: but as for me and my house, we will assail slavery, man-stealing, the chain and the lash."

It mattered little that the object of Perkins's artillery was a long way off. He would rifle his guns, he would elongate them, he would load them to the muzzle. And what powder failed to accomplish, faith should complete. Nobody had ever told him so, but he felt it in his bones that he was the right man for this sort of work. And he undertook it. And he did it. As a matter of fact, he was surprised to find how easily he did it. He disproved, he refuted, he overthrew, he abolished, he literally annihilated the " infernal Institution." He did this thoroughly; he did this repeatedly; he did this perpet-.ually. And it may be presumed that his congregation *did* as well as could be expected, under the circumstances. Like causes produce like effects. Mahomet was a man of one idea: Perkins was a man of one idea. Perkins was Perkins, and Richard Roe was one of his Profits.

Public anxiety had been greatly relieved by the successive newspaper bulletins which, on the day following the assassination, announced the gradual but doubtful escape of Richard Roe from death. The case did not seem to be quite clear. There was somewhat of mystification about it. But the high character and known wealth of the good banker caused all doubts to work together for his benefit.

The only man who couldn't be wholly deceived in the premises was doctor Jenkins. Being the family physician of Roe, he called without waiting to be sent for, and of course saw that " nothing was the matter " with his patient. Thus, at the outset, Richard found that the way of transgressors is hard : for while there was seemingly a necessity for making some sort of a confidant of his doctor, he perceived that making a confidant of a man without telling him anything, is difficult. On the one hand, letting the doctor into the true state of the case, was out of the question ; on the other hand, limited confidences are eminently risky. He therefore made what he considered " the best of it." He extemporized a rambling and inconsistent story, the only effect of which was, to show the doctor that Roe was endeavoring to deceive him ; but as the doctor was under a temporary pecuniary obligation to the banker, it was not his cue to betray his incredulity, and he pretended to swallow Roe's story as he sometimes pretended to swallow his own pills. He did it, too, with so good a grace that the interview terminated to Roe's entire satisfaction. Roe had obviously " done " the doctor, brown.

The other doctor, the D.D., was much more easily

" done." In fact, he " did " himself. He had been out of town (Doctor Perkins had) for some weeks previously ; he had read the newspapers ; he returned ; he flew to Roe's relief.

" My dear friend and brother !" he exclaimed, as he rushed into the parlor and caught his friend and brother in his arms, " how is all with you ? I have just returned from Wisconsin."

" Doctor ! Doctor ! how glad I am to see you," cried Roe, in the same overflowing tone.

Absence, and calamity in absence, operate on the lachrymal nerves when the separated and the afflicted are brought together, as uniformly as mustard or horse-radish. It was quite affecting !

" I have seen the newspapers," said the Doctor. " I have thought of you : I have *remembered* you, my brother."

" Ah, Doctor !" ejaculated Roe.

" True, true ! I see it, I feel it," rejoined his comforter.

" A night in prison, Doctor !" murmured Roe, with closed yet suffused eyes.

" Remember Paul and Silas, my brother," answered the Doctor in perfectly good faith. But Roe had an underlying sense of the ludicrous, and in spite of himself he smiled—upper lip and all. He was in trouble, but not the kind of trouble the good Doctor supposed. A man in earnest, encountering a man playing a part, jostles his friend at every turn without knowing it. There is about as much concord between them, as between two voices simultaneously singing different airs.

Clearly, the only way out of this corner was a change of the subject.

"Doctor," said Roe, "my nerves are so shattered, that we must talk of something else."

Nothing could have suited the Doctor better. He was all things to all men. And the thing really uppermost in his own mind, was the result of a controversy between himself and some conscientious members of his congregation; which controversy, he had absented himself purposely to avoid, leaving Roe and his party to carry on the war.

"How are our refractory members?" he inquired.

"Pretty well under," said Roe; "our young volunteers outflanked them handsomely."

"That was a nice bit of strategy," the Doctor replied, with a sly wink. "I hope no one suspects *me* of having had any agency in it?"

"No one," said Roe, reciprocating the wink, "but the friend who knows that you were substantially the *sole* agent."

"Hush!" cried the Doctor; "walls have ears. I know, my dear Roe," he continued, relapsing into the lachrymose tone with which he commenced the interview—for, now, *he* wished to change the subject—"I know that your thoughts are running on things personal and painful to yourself, and you needed a word to break the current."

"You are quite right," answered Roe. "'As iron sharpeneth iron, so the face of a man his friend.' This interlude has done me a world of good. You'll stay to dine? You must," he added, peremptorily, as the Doctor seemed to hesitate; "I'm all alone, and there's some of that blue seal on the ice."

"Ha! ha! Roe, you have such a way with you!" rejoined the Doctor, stretching himself on a sofa.

"Doctor," said Roe, stretching himself on another

sofa, "you have now been in person over that glorious country, the mighty west, where the fields are white to the harvest.   What is their true condition?"

"Superb! unrivalled! magnificent!" replied Perkins, enthusiastically piling up the epithets, as he called to mind what he had seen: "fields stretching out to the horizon, and sixty bushels to the acre reckoned as but half a crop."

Roe smiled benignantly on his ardent and animated friend, who in the excitement of recalling nature's wonders, had for a moment forgotten nature's God.   But Roe could make allowances.   He had himself been subject to worldly weaknesses.

"I referred, my dear, good friend," said he, "to the harvest of souls.   That is the great reaping field; and we, who have forsaken all for Christ, must not be unmindful of it."

The simple-hearted Doctor sank under the gentle rebuke of the sublimely devotional Roe.   But he soon rose to the surface.

"Alas!" said he, "the harvest is plenty, but the laborers are few: and, meantime, the enemy is sowing tares."   And he was proceeding to apologize for being so worldly-minded in Roe's presence as, at first, to mistake spiritual fields for wheat fields; but the banker magnanimously assured him that there was no harm done.

By way of another change of subject, and to reassure the good Doctor, Roe went on to speak of their fellow-laborer in the church, Henry Williamson.

"Williamson," said Roe, "is truly a brand plucked from the burning.   He tarried without till the eleventh hour, but the Lord knows His own time. Henry will be a burning and a shining light in our midst. He was telling me last Sabbath eve, what a glimpse he had of the promised land, in his private devotions. He was in his closet. The heavens seemed open to him, and the heaven of heavens was not hid from his view. And he thinks that he attained that sublime experience by fasting. I was able to corroborate that opinion. And as my heart warmed toward him, I related my own experience: for I, too, had fasted, and had a vision. It does not become me to say so—and I *wouldn't* say it to Henry —but my vision exceeded his, both in intensity and duration. But, then, Henry is a new beginner."

The good Doctor was too much devoted to the "infernal Institution," to care much about visions: and it was a great relief to him, that Philip here abruptly announced the dinner.

CHAPTER VI.

John Doe was a bachelor. He lived in a comfortable house. His family consisted of an unmarried sister, an unmarried niece, himself and the servants. His sister's name was Susan Doe. His niece's name was Jane Doe. His servants' names need not be mentioned, because servants are always changing places. The John of to-day is Peter to-morrow; and so on for the entire set. Additionally to these individuals, there was aunt Smith, a bedridden relative up-stairs, but not connected with this history except as an invisible supernumerary.

The old-fashioned, recently (in part) repudiated and always calumniated meal—tea—was still one of the institutions in John Doe's family. The fixed hour for it, was half-past seven on week-days and half-past six on Sundays. Breakfast is a meal of bustling preparation. Dinner is a serious meal; a meal of determined consummation. Tea is a recreation, replete with reminiscences. It is a "meal," however, only in conventional terms. People are expected to talk at a tea-table.

"Jane, my dear," said Mr. Doe to his niece, "will you hand that cup to your aunt? Peter has another bad turn to-day, and we must be our own waiters."

"I think," rejoined Miss Susan Doe, "that you will soon come to my conclusion about Peter—that his 'turns' should rather be called 'crooks.'"

"How do you mean?" inquired her brother.

"Crooks of the elbow," replied Miss Doe; "you are unwilling to believe any harm of Peter; but I tell you, he drinks. What about the tea, John?"

"Only to fill the cup," said Mr. Doe; "you have sweetened it on plantation principles; or, as our friend Roe would say, on Bottom Principles."

"For goodness' sake, don't quote Richard Roe," said the sister; "I am sick of seeing that fellow's name in the newspapers. Was there anything more about him to-night, Jane?"

"I believe not, aunt," Jane replied; "if there was anything, I overlooked it."

"No new developments, eh?" continued Miss Doe. "Do you know, John, I believe that whole thing is a humbug?"

"Not the escape of Wilson, surely," said Mr. Doe.

"Well—no," answered his sister; "I suppose we must admit that. But the iron bar that never was found, and the chloroform, and the clothes, and all that. Now, candidly, John?"

"I hardly know what to think," replied her brother. "It certainly is a very strange story. If I could imagine any motive on the part of Roe to favor Wilson's escape—but that is impossible."

"Impossible is a strong word," said Miss Doe. "Napoleon said it was not French. I remember when Roe's wife and I were at school, we agreed to be friends forever; but the word, in Napoleon's sense, proved not to be English."

3*

" She died, you know," said her brother.

" True," his sister rejoined, " but she outlived our friendship."

" By implication, then," Mr. Doe continued, " you think Roe *might* have had a motive ? Can you suggest one ?"

" No," said the lady ; " that's beyond my ability You, who are conversant with business relations and details, and know quite enough, I should say, of Roe : you might conjecture a motive. I'll warrant, Roe would conjecture one, if you and he could change places."

" The millstone through which he *couldn't* squint, must be a solid one, I grant you," said Mr. Doe ; " and the reputation in which he couldn't find, or make, a flaw, if he once set resolutely about it, must be a sound one. Roe ought to have been a lawyer."

" Roe a lawyer !" echoed the lady, with infinite scorn. " How can you couple his pettifogging mind with a profession in which our ancestors won so proud a reputation ? An attorney's jackal, he might be : a lawyer, never ! On my word, I believe the fellow is complicated in this matter somehow. Study it out for me, John."

" For that matter," answered her brother, " not for you only, but for Elizabeth, and myself, and all of us, if there's anything to *be* studied out, I would go to the bottom of it with all my heart."

" Is that confounded case never to be tried ?" said Miss Doe.

" I really don't know," replied Mr. Doe. " Roe shows his pettifogging cleverness there, if in nothing else. He has got that case put off more than twenty times. And I told Traverse, to-day, that, in view of that experience, I should say no man ever need be brought to a trial in New York, unless he chooses to be. Study out Richard Roe, do you say?" he continued; "I wish I could, that's all!"

"What's that, Margaret?" said Miss Doe to a servant who now entered the room.

"The medicine for Mrs. Smith, ma'am," replied the girl, holding out a vial.

"Did Tom bring it, Margaret?" inquired Mr. Doe.

"Yes, sir," said the girl, "and he is waiting to know if you would wish to see him."

"I do wish to see him," said Mr. Doe. "Tell him to wait in the parlor, Margaret."

Tom commenced business early in life and on a small scale. He was trained to the useful profession of begging; and as Mr. Doe's house was in his district, he made daily calls there for cold victuals. He was a bright, intelligent lad, and soon attracted the notice and favor of the servants, who used to reserve the best things for "little Tommy." One day, Mr. Doe himself, being in the kitchen to look after the Croton pipes, happened to see him. He was pleased with the boy's appearance, and especially pleased with his answers to some questions. He afterward called on the boy's mother, and the result was that he obtained employment for Tom in Mr. Scalpel's apothecary's shop, No. —, Bowery. Mr. Scalpel needed a boy for errands, to carry medicines as ordered, etc., and he engaged Tom the more readily from his being recommended by a gentleman of position and fortune, who, moreover, had an invalid relative at home requiring "any quantity" of doses which he, Scalpel, was now engaged to supply. It was a satisfactory arrangement, all around,

"Well, Tom, my lad, how are you getting on?" inquired Mr. Doe of his *protégé.*

"Quite pretty well, sir, and thank you, sir," answered Tom.

"Plenty of work, now, Tom?"

"Oh, yes, sir."

"And all well at home, Tom?"

"Mother's a little poorly, sir, since the warm weather; but Phebe is first rate, sir."

"And you like Mr. Scalpel?"

"Yes, sir, he's very kind in general; was a' little hard on me, though, for letting the gentleman slip with the chloroform."

"Chloroform? What about chloroform, Tom?"

Tom related the story, and added that he missed the gentleman in getting out of the car, and on his return Mr. Scalpel gave him fits.

Mr. Doe, quickened in his apprehension by the tea-table chat with his sister, began to cogitate.

"Who was the gentleman, Tom?" he inquired.

"I don't know, sir," Tom replied. "Stranger, sir. Never seen him before."

"Have you ever seen him since?"

"Once't, sir, in the evening, up hereabouts, crossing Broadway."

"What sort of man is he?"

"Tall, sir, I should say. Wears his whiskers so"— showing with his hands.

"Dark whiskers?"

"Rather dark, sir, and some grey."

"Did you see him, that day, after you got into the car?"

"No, sir; and that's what I told Mr. Scalpel. But he said I was so'gerin, and he give me fits."

"Tom, my boy, the next time you see that man, follow him and find out where he goes."

"But suppose I am carrying medicines, sir ?"

"Never mind medicines; never mind anything. Follow the man and find where he stops. I'll see Mr. Scalpel and make you right with him."

"Much obliged to you, sir, and I'll do it. And the next time you see Mr. Scalpel, if you please, sir, if you would speak about that extra half dollar a week ? I think, sir, he has forgot about it."

"I'll remember, Tom, and you shall have the half dollar."

"Thank you kindly, sir; and good evening, sir."

And Tom withdrew, not a little elated at the success of his visit.

"That sister of mine should have been a lawyer!" said Doe to himself.

Tom had repeatedly called at Mr. Doe's house with potions and plasters for aunt Smith; but as yet, he was unable to report any discovery of the missing gentleman.

Mr. Doe grew impatient.

"Tom," said he, one evening, " do you know where Queer-street is ?"

"Oh yes, sir," answered Tom, "I carry parcels there."

"There," rejoined Mr. Doe, "is number 713 on a piece of paper. Keep that in your pocket, and whenever you go past that house, look sharp at the door and the windows; and if you see that gentleman there, let me know."

On this hint, Tom made a report rather more to

the purpose. He had seen the gentleman twice't.
His clothes was not the same, but the gentleman was
the same, and no mistake.

"Stick a pin there!" quoth John Doe, to himself.

Personal identification is a nice point. Every
man's experience furnishes instances of mistaking one
person for another. Many trials in the courts have
become celebrated by the conflicting of evidence on
a question of identity; and many an innocent man
has paid a high penalty for resembling another man,
with whom he had no more to do than the man in
the moon. John Doe was aware of all this.

"I must get Scalpel to identify this customer,"
said he; "and yet, not in a way to lead him to suppose it's a matter of any importance. Thus far, he
merely blames Tom for negligence, and has no suspicion of anything wrong in the man. Let me see.
The church is Roe's fortress. We'll attack him in
the church. Jones's pew, as I recollect, is at right
angles with Roe's? and the Jones's are out of town,
as a matter of course."

Doe occasionally called at Scalpel's shop to look
after Tom's condition and prospects.

"By the way, Mr. Scalpel," said he, when he had
made the customary inquiries, "did you ever hear
Doctor Perkins preach?"

"No, sir," returned the apothecary, "he's rather
too strong for my fancy."

"I have a notion to hear him next Sunday," continued Doe; "And if you would like to go, just for
the curiosity of the thing, I will find you a seat."

"You are very kind, sir," replied the apothecary,
rather flattered with the offer; "I think I will accept
your invitation."

"Will you call for me, at my house, next Sunday morning, then ?" said Doe.

"Certainly, sir, and much obliged to you," answered Scalpel.

The apothecary presented himself accordingly; and, in due time, he was edified by one of those "peculiar" sermons which do so much good in northern cities.

After the services were over, Doe and Scalpel exchanged opinions in the usual way.

"Do you know," inquired Doe, "who that tall, heavy whiskered gentleman is, who sat alone in the middle aisle, near the pulpit ?"

"I don't know his name," answered the apothecary; "but he is the gentleman whom Tom missed in the cars that day."

"Quite sure he is the same man ?" pursued Doe.

"I was not sure," said the apothecary, "until we came out of church. I then took a better look at him; and what's more, he spoke to some ladies, and I recognized his voice."

"You thought Tom was a little tricky in that matter ?" said Doe.

"More or less, sir, I must say," replied the apothecary. "The gentleman couldn't keep watch of Tom in the crowd; it was Tom's business to watch *him*, and follow him when he got out of the car. However, it was a lesson to the boy. He has been very particular, ever since."

"He couldn't have run off to a theatre that evening ?" suggested Doe: well knowing that the affair did not take place in the evening; but intending, by his remark, to ascertain the apothecary's recollection of the hour when it did take place.

"By no manner of means, sir," rejoined Scalpel : "it was not in the evening at all, but in the afternoon ; about a quarter to three."

"In the absence of corroborating facts," thought Doe, on his way home, "this identification might lack weight. But combine with it the fact that Roe called at the Tombs at three o'clock that day, and remained there ; then put that vial of chloroform into the scale, and *my* inference is that—that—in short, that my sister ought to have been a lawyer!"

CHAPTER VII.

JACK AND GILL.

It is as true in real life as in novels, that young men and young women spontaneously fall into those ways and byways and pathways of attachment that lead to matrimony. And real life experience has this substantial advantage over the experience of romance: namely, that its personages manage to get through the byways and pathways without embarassing obstacles. The young people form their attachments; the old people give their approval; and the first thing you know, Brown carries around the cards.

The facility of the thing, as compared with novel-life, is really superlative. Of all the incidents of the every-day world, getting married is the most free from obstacles. If it were otherwise; if the candidates for matrimony in real life were subjected to the delays, the trials, the ordeals with which novel-writers surround *their* young men and women—why, the long and short of the business is, that nuptial ceremonies would cease to be performed.

In exceptional cases, and for good or bad reasons, the experience of heroes and heroines will obtrude itself into every-day life: but the general rule of real life is diametrically opposed to the rule of the novelist. Nor does the difference between the two terminate there. The persons themselves are as diverse as their biographies. The young men and women of novels are always beautiful in form and feature. They are intensely intellectual, highly accomplished for their station, and are positively overburdened with virtues.

To a practical mind, the tantalization of this, is that the novelist always closes his labors just at the moment when the happy couple begin theirs: and whereas one wishes to know how much more happily and usefully these paragons get on in life than humdrum human beings are able to do, one perpetually finds himself reduced to the privilege of guessing at it. People so highly endowed by nature and art *ought* to achieve very bright examples of domestic felicity. But do they?

Nobody can tell whether they do, or not. But if there should now and then be a failure in experiments on which so much preparation has been lavished, the sufferers might console themselves by reflecting that disappointments of that kind are not peculiar to imaginary people. For although the every-day women of real life are quite as worthy to be loved, and quite as likely to make homes happy, as the exceptional and imaginary women-of novels; it by no means follows that every woman in real life is just what she should be.

For example, what is termed a highly cultivated woman may be an " ornament to her sex " so long as she stands on the pedestal she has chosen. She may eclipse all her contemporaries in conversation with men of distinction, in foreign languages. She may shine in discussion with learned professors of the exact sciences. She may inform chemists, mineralogists, botanists, natural philosophers and geologists wherein they could popularize their books. She may make valuable suggestions to moral philosophers, metaphysicians, historians and poets. Her mastery of music may enable her to sing like Garcia and play like Ap Thomas. But it is very questionable whether in the capacity of a daughter, wife or mother, she would acquit herself creditably.

Again, the strong-minded woman may be an admirable politician. She may point out the blunders of all our public men, dead or alive. She may suggest valuable alterations in the elective franchise and trial by jury. She may propose important municipal regulations for our cities. She may change the plan of operations of the benevolent societies of the day. She may improve the church discipline, and dragoon her clergyman into more thoroughly doctrinal preaching. She may revolutionize the system of instruction in schools. She may discipline her husband (if she has one) on the same principle that she disciplines her servants. She may restrain all the mischievous proclivities, evil dispositions and bad habits of her neighbor's children. She may, in short, instruct everybody and *rule* everybody. But heaven help the family circle where she gets a footing in any of the aforesaid capacities—daughter, wife or mother! to say nothing of grandmother or aunt.

Plain, quiet, unostentatious people, whatever may be their rank in the social compact: people who form the majority of every community and have the good fortune to be remarkable for nothing: these people enjoy life and have the best of it.

On the other hand, people of distinction, mark, notoriety; people who make themselves conspicuous; who attract attention; who are admired, followed, imitated, flattered : these people pay a high price for their medals, and at the end they usually find them to be nothing but old brass.

As a matter of common experience, the enjoyments of the family circle depend very little on the beauty or the accomplishments of its members. Reciprocal affection, from which naturally flow kind disposition and accommodating temper—these are the substantials of domestic life; and without these, domestic life is all vanity and vexation of spirit.

A nice time we should have in this world, to be sure, if no woman could be loved who didn't come up to the regulation standard of the novelist! Hair as black as jet, or as yellow as gold, or as brown as a chestnut: forehead as white and pure and transparent as alabaster: eyes as bright as diamonds: eyebrows pencilled into a perfect arch: eyelashes an inch long: nose, aquiline, or roman, or grecian, or pug, only let it be "chiselled:" lips as red as coral: teeth as white as pearl: chin as round and dimpled as a peach: cheeks like a rose: neck like a swan's: arms plump: hands small: fingers tapering: waist about the size of a napkin-ring: and feet so tiny that you can hardly see them.

Fortunately for herself, Jane Doe was no heroine. She was a well educated, well-looking, sweet-tempered girl of nineteen; destitute of affectation; as free from vanity as any young woman needs to be; and, in sober truth, not superior to, nor different from, ten thousand other young women in her social and geographical position. But for all that, perhaps by reason of all that, Alfred Traverse loved her. He loved her dearly. And he had told her so, many a time. And she believed him without asking him to swear to it. *Why* he loved her, is nobody's business. And supposing it were somebody's business? Can anybody tell *why* anybody loves anybody? That indefinable something which love or sympathy seeks for itself and finds for itself, and wishes nobody to point out or describe; which is independent and irrespective of physical beauty; which, reciprocally, grows with one's growth, strengthens with one's strength, and becomes a part of one's very being; and which in fact exists at all only because it *is* secret and exclusive between the two whom it unites in bonds stronger than death—why should any one vainly attempt to explain it?

And Alfred Traverse, whom Jane Doe loved in return quite as dearly as he loved her, and maybe a fraction to spare—who was Alfred Traverse? Had he chestnut curls and remarkable features, figure and feet? · Did his voice resemble a trumpet? Was he a giant in physical strength? Could he handle an unmanageable horse like a kitten? Were dogs afraid of him? After throwing a score of ruffians out of a third-story window, each man of whom was twice his own size, could he out-fence a fencing-master? out-shoot a gallery keeper? out-box a champion? and do ten thousand other things equally indispensable to domestic happiness?

Not at all. He was a young lawyer, attached to his profession and well qualified for it and in it. But there was nothing about him personally, intellectually or morally, to distinguish him from his companions and acquaintances. His age was twenty-five years, more or less: and it is perfectly immaterial whether a little more or a little less. He was a junior partner in the firm of Rebutter, Surrebutter and Co., and his income for the current year was estimated by good judges at three thousand five hundred dollars. The engagement between him and Jane Doe was approved of, and assented to, by the friends on both sides the moment it was proposed to them. The most casual observer will therefore see at a glance that complications, misunderstandings, disappointments, hardhearted fathers, trap-doors, secret passages, locks, bars, bolts, hints, messages, intercepted letters, and all that sort of thing, could not be wrought into and twisted up with the contract between Traverse and Doe, any how you could fix it.

The law firm in which Traverse was a partner had charge of John Doe's law business. Rebutter, Surrebutter and Co. were therefore of counsel for the plaintiff in the celebrated case of John Doe against Richard Roe.

For that reason, among others, Traverse often dropped in at Doe's house of an evening, and sometimes remained there as late as ten o'clock—occasionally later.

"Traverse," said Doe to Alfred, at one of these opportunities, "what are the chances for trial of Doe against Roe at the next term?"

"Very good, I should hope," responded Traverse "Roe has now run through every pretext for delay, known and unknown to the law; always, however, assuring the court and everybody else that he is very impatient for a trial."

"You will be surprised, I suppose, to hear me say," Doe remarked, "that *I* now have a reason for postponing that trial. I think I can find some new evidence which, if not relevant to the issue, will at least be relevant to Roe. Can't you neglect to put the case on the calendar for a term or two?"

"Nothing is easier," replied Traverse; "and no doubt the defendant would chuckle over our seeming negligence, if you really wish for delay. What is the character of the evidence?"

"It is the evidence of a very bad character, if I ever get it," replied Doe, half punning on the words: "but I cannot now give you the particulars, for the very good reason that I don't know them. Still, a mere chance of the game I have in view, is well worth waiting for."

"I don't know about this, John," interposed his sister. "If a new game is to be played in which law is an element and Richard Roe a party, I think I can guess where the chances lie. At any rate, it does seem odd, after all your eagerness to get this case tried, that *you* should propose delay."

"I grant you, Susan, it does seem odd," rejoined Doe: "and you may think me unreasonably reserved in declining a further explanation. Traverse will probably think I might as well have kept to myself what I *have* said. We will imagine I was thinking loud, and so let it pass for the present. Only, Traverse, you will remember to forget the notice?"

"If the case is closed for the present," interposed Jane very demurely—for she, like her aunt, had picked up some of the legal forms of expression from the interminable discussions between Alfred and her uncle on the interminable case of Doe and Roe—"if the case is closed for the present, I suppose I cannot submit *my* point to the consideration of the court."

"We'll reopen it for you, Jane," said her uncle; "what is your point?"

"Only this, if the court please," replied Jane; "the plaintiff has been in a fever of anxiety for months to get this case tried, because, principally, he was afraid some of the witnesses would be absent, sick, or dead. I would like to inquire whether my learned friend has any less cause now, than formerly, for anxiety on that point?"

"The truth is, my dear child," said Doe, not a little amused at Jane's technical sharpness, "the witness I now have in my mind may be worth all the rest, and he is absent already. But I must close the case again, or you will trap me into saying more than I am prepared to tell."

CHAPTER VIII.

IF the trick, by virtue of which Wilson escaped from prison, had been practised on the turnkey, or on any person officially attached to the Tombs, it would have lived exactly nine days in the newspapers and in town-talk. But the high character of Richard Roe gave to Wilson's exploit a prolonged existence of nine additional days: an instance of longevity that has no parallel in the memory of the oldest inhabitant. However, it all came to nothing. .

Wilson had been traced on board of several steamers. One, for California; two, for Liverpool; one, for Havre; and one for Bremen, via Southampton: besides half a dozen for the West Indies. He had been seen in the cars of several railroads. He had made pedestrian tours through several of the United States. He had been upset in a stage-coach, drowned in a canal, lynched for an abolitionist. Many a telegram had notified policemen to come South, North, East, West, and receive the precious rascal. Many a distant constable, without waiting for the telegraph, had brought to New-York this, that, and the other poor devil who, unable to give a good account of himself, and happening to resemble, or not to resemble, the newspaper descriptions of Wilson, had been found somewhere under suspicious circumstances and arrested for the chance of the reward.

But, as aforesaid, it all came to nothing in the way of producing the body of Wilson.

One tolerably good reason for the last mentioned fact, is the other fact that, about four o'clock on the afternoon of the escape, while the rain was pouring pitchforks, and the wind was blowing great guns, Wilson, *in propriâ personâ*, and as wet as a drowned rat, walked into the humble dwelling of a poor widow whom, in his better days, he had made a friend of, by his charities; and who now repaid the obligation by giving shelter to the fugitive and keeping his secret.

The family of Mrs. Pinch consisted of three individuals: herself, her daughter, Phebe, about sixteen years old, who went out to day-service in families as a seamstress; and a son, our sometime acquaintance Tom, about eleven years old, the boy in Mr. Scalpel's shop. There were but two rooms on the ground-floor. That in the rear was occupied by the widow and her daughter as a bedroom; and the front room, which was something larger, was kitchen, laundry and parlor all in one, besides supplying sleeping accommodations for Tom, by means of a sofa bedstead standing against the wall, opposite the cooking-stove.

The widow sat dozing before the stove, where coal and wood were arranged, but not yet lighted for preparing the family supper, when Wilson entered. She started at the sound of his footsteps; then, mistaking him for the landlord, she began to apologize for not hearing his knock; and, presently, becoming broad awake, she exclaimed:

"Gracious me, Mr. Wilson! Is this you?"

"Hush!" said Wilson; "are you alone?"

" Yes," she answered. " Phebe is out at work; and it is not yet time for Tom to be home."

" Then," said Wilson, stepping hastily to the door of the room and bolting it, " if you think yourself under any obligation to me, help me now. I am able to pay you liberally for all you can do. In the course of the night, or to-morrow morning at the latest, the police will be in pursuit of me. If you can hide me here, I shall be safe."

" Mr. Wilson!" she exclaimed, " what have you done?"

" Nothing, now," said he, " but escaped from prison. But, for God's sake, leave explanations till I can make them at leisure and in security. Can you give me a hiding-place?"

" For to-night, I might," answered the poor woman, wringing her hands in the extremity of distress.

" As well not at all," cried Wilson; " to-night I may be safe anywhere. How is this house occupied?"

Above this ground-floor there was but one story and a garret: and, as good luck would have it—so the widow remembered, when the first confusion of her surprise was over—the family of Rabbits who had hitherto occupied the upper part of the house, had been turned out that very morning for not paying rent. A drunken husband, a sickly wife who had seen better days, and a ragged child or two made up the group so removed. It was the old and familiar story, to be heard everywhere. They were miserable enough, but their misfortune was luck to Wilson. The rooms were to let. A bill was to be put up to-morrow, applicants to inquire of Mrs. Pinch on the premises, and she already had the key. A cooking-stove remained there, which belonged to the landlord. There was no other furniture. So far, everything was favorable.

For present security against intruders, the widow and Wilson immediately transferred themselves into these deserted rooms, taking up two chairs and the materials for a fire, that Wilson might dry his clothes.

Mrs. Pinch, in casting about for ulterior arrangements, remembered that she had an uncle, living or dead, in Wisconsin. Wilson might personate this uncle, as the latter had never lived in New York, and thus the relative positions of the fugitive and the widow's family could be easily defined. Furniture could be procured at once, to make the apartments comfortable. Care must be taken to prevent the children from becoming too familiar with their uncle Sam; and to that end, uncle Sam must be an invalid—a part easily played. Mrs. Pinch summed up these details with an overflowing heart. Wilson had, in former days, assisted her in the hour of extreme necessity—had, in her estimation, saved herself and her children from starving: and the opportunity of rendering so substantial a return, was equivalent to receiving an additional benefit.

A fire being now lighted, and a blanket furnished to Wilson, so that he might wrap himself up in it while his clothes were getting dried, the widow withdrew to make preparations for supper. Wilson took a survey of the premises. He put the fastenings of the door to their right use; took off his boots; hung his coat on the back of a chair, spread his vest on the seat of it, enveloped himself in the blanket and sat down in front of the fire. The night being provided for, he must plan for the morrow.

"The old dodge of the first steamer, or the first train," he reflected, "is played out. If a man wants to be snug, let him hold on to quiet quarters in the metropolis. Let me see. My heavy whiskers must come off: that's one important item of disguise. Short hair is fashionable; reducing mine to a close crop will be another item. Add to that, blue spectacles. As for clothes, I have worn plain black for an indefinite time. Change the material to gray, and a sack in place of a frock coat; then clap over all a soft hat, and the devil himself wouldn't recognize me !"

And, with this sagacious conclusion, he fell fast asleep.

Mrs. Pinch resolved not to enlighten her children, that night, about uncle Sam's arrival. They need not know it, perhaps, for a day or two. Phebe was usually absent during the day, and Tom was at home only at his meals and at night. She, therefore, made special provision for Wilson's supper, and left her benefactor to take care of himself according to the circumstances—he having assured her that, as a bed could by no chance be procured until the next day, he could easily for one night make himself comfortable with a blanket on the floor: a better resting-place than he had had for some months, all things considered.

The first thing in order in the morning, after the children were gone, and Wilson had discussed a comfortable breakfast, was to procure a suit of clothes for the fugitive, and the means of removing his hair and whiskers. As there was plenty of money at hand,

Mrs. Pinch had no difficulty in carrying out her uncle's views. Scissors, razors, combs, brushes and ready-made clothes were produced in a fabulously short space of time; and after Wilson had availed himself of the widow's services in reducing his hair to an average length of half an inch all around, he despatched her for certain indispensable articles of furniture. He then reaped off his whiskers, shaved down the stubble, and inaugurated his person into his new apparel. The selections had been well made; and it was obvious that a glance at a looking-glass, which might be expected to arrive soon, would show that Wilson himself could easily mistake himself for almost anybody else.

The new clothes being well on, his next care was to get the old ones well off; for so long as any two square inches of them remained together, recognition, identification, or some other infernal bother would come of it. He felt reluctant to destroy a good suit, for it might be of service to almost any man, having been that day good enough for Richard Roe; but, on the whole, self-preservation is the first law. Accordingly, shears and hands reduced the pantaloons to tatters; the vest disappeared in the same way; and the coat, in turn, yielded to the destroyer—

"What's in that pocket? Papers? Did the old joker leave any private letters to tell tales? By heaven! this beats cock-fighting! Here's my cake and my money, too! I've doubled my capital without knowing it. I've got old Sobersides on the hip yet!"

The furniture came. A small valise came, into which portable valuables might be stowed. Pens, ink and paper came, with contingent articles of stationery; and one of the first things Wilson did, was to make a will, which he sealed up with gum and secured with wax : for he had heard that gum fastening, like all other things in this fast age, would give way to steam power. The particulars of the will did not then transpire. They *will* transpire in due time. But apart from that carefully sealed-up envelope, Wilson had no valuable papers of any sort or description whatever, in his possession.

In the course of the day, the landlord called, and was much gratified to find that he had lost no time in changing tenants. He had little thought for anything beyond money; and, receiving a month's rent in advance, and in gold, too, he troubled himself no further in the premises.

Wilson had made a capital beginning.

CHAPTER IX.

DOCTOR JENKINS's wife was jealous—perhaps the greatest blunder that a physician's wife can commit.

The wife of any other man has a nominal remedy for that disease, because every other man is the slave of time. He is bound to hours. They may be late hours; they may be irregular hours; but, in the sailor's phrase, he fetches up somewhere. And if he doesn't come to time, he can be required to explain. Again, any other man can be watched and followed and spotted. However numerous his friends, however ramifed his business, however scattered the localities where any contingency may call for his presence; these all have a limit, which can be expressed on paper and made to assume the exactitude of a mathematical proposition. So that, a woman can compare the possible limits with the actual practice, and thus detect a false step if it varies but a thousandth part of an inch from perpendicularity. And then, having ascertained the perturbation, she can follow it up to its primary cause with terrible certainty.

But the physician can baffle her skill, generally. He can set at naught her art. He can defy her science. Not intentionally perhaps; not systematically; not even consciously, need this be: but from necessity, and in the nature of the case—always, and

of course, excepting necessary exceptions. Look at
it! Can any human sagacity tell, by conjecture,
where he goes? why he goes? or when he goes?
Do the night watches, or the day watches, clocks,
sundials, or hourglasses find him asleep? Did Ar-
gus ever see his eyes closed, unless when he was
winking? And over and above all other impediments to observation and espionage, doesn't he go
about in a gig with a fast horse, so that all the tricks
of watching, waiting, following and pursuing are, as
by a horse-laugh, laughed to scorn?

Hence, the folly on the part of a physician's wife,
when she sets out to cultivate jealousy. Other women, if they stick to it, may hope to discover something; but the task of a physician's wife is nearly or
quite hopeless from the start. Nevertheless, Mrs.
Jenkins one day said to her husband:

"Doctor, you were a long time at Mrs. McPherson's this morning."

"I was so, indeed," answered the doctor; "but
how did you happen to know it?"

"Mere accident," she rejoined, looking as cool as a
cucumber. "I saw your gig there on my way to
Stewart's; and it was there when I returned."

"The poor lady is quite ill," the doctor remarked
quietly, resolving to give no advantage to the enemy
in a controversy which long experience told him was
at hand. He knew the symptoms, of old.

"Ah, indeed?" continued the lady, perceiving that
the doctor was on his guard, and therefore herself
beginning to look daggers up at the ceiling and around
the room; "it's very odd, though, that Jane McPherson should have told me this morning her mother was
much better."

"Where did you chance to see Jane McPherson this morning?" pursued the doctor; "she has been at Mrs. Barber's, in Brooklyn, for more than a week; although this afternoon she has been sent for, on her mother's account. As a matter of curiosity, I would like to know where you saw her?"

"*At* Mrs. Barber's," answered the lady, puckering up her lips to say something unexpected and which would cost her some effort; "I owed Mrs. Barber a call and I went over there from Stewart's."

"You have 'owed' that call a long time, my dear," said the doctor, with just enough irony in his tone to be offensive. "You quarrelled with Mrs. Barber a year ago; and in a way that I should imagine left very little chance of a reconciliation."

"Oh!" retorted the lady bitterly, "I suppose you are coming around in favor of eternal hatred, as you formerly preached up everlasting friendships."

"By no means, my dear," replied the doctor; "I have little occasion to prompt you in the way of hatreds. But in the way of reconciliations, I must say this one strikes me by its oddity."

"It is the oddest thing in the world, isn't it?" returned the lady, waxing more wroth at each step of the conversation; "the very oddest thing in the world for people to make up their quarrels?"

"Oh, no," said the doctor, "not at all odd in the abstract. I wish there was more of it in the world."

"He! he!" cried the lady, trying to extemporise a laugh; but, for want of due preparation and of the right mental materials, she broke down in it: "he! he! you'd like to reconcile difficulties a little nearer home, wouldn't you, doctor? But I can tell you, sir, the way to reconcile difficulties is for the one who is in the wrong, sir, to put himself in the right, in the first place. Deception, sir, is at the bottom of these things. Leave off deceiving your wife, sir, or rather trying to deceive her; for I give you fair notice, you can't make it out—I'm on your track, sir! Leave off deception, sir! Tell the truth, sir!"—and, by this time she had worked herself up to a point of oppressed and indignant innocence that required something more than words for its adequate utterance. She therefore relieved her overburdened heart by animated gesticulation, and her little fist came so near the doctor's face, that the difference between her action and a blow was really nothing to speak of.

The heart of the doctor, as the saying is, leaped into his throat at the unutterable indignity.

"Madam," said he, resolutely, taking a step back, and assuming an attitude that offered very little encouragement to the lady for a repetition of her gesture, "you this morning went out of your way to watch my gig, knowing from my own voluntary information that I was to call on Mrs. McPherson. You then went over to Brooklyn to call on a lady whom a twelvemonth ago you insulted so outrageously that her whole circle of friends dropped your acquaintance on her account. And *why* do you now put yourself in the power of a lady who then deservedly humiliated you? You do it in order to make a clandestine inquiry about the health of one of your own friends in New-York, in the hope that the daughter of that friend may give you an account of her mother's health that shall differ from and contradict what you expect me to say on the same subject;

you having already decided in your own mind that my calls on Mrs. McPherson are for a purpose other than a discharge of my professional duties. And you now have the hardihood to produce this contradictory statement by way of confirming your jealous suspicions of me. Madam, I will not indulge you so much as to corroborate my statement about Mrs. McPherson's illness. Nor will I for another day endure your treatment of me. You have played *Mrs. Snagsby* on me past the point of endurance. Do you happen to recollect that passage in the twenty-fifth chapter of *Bleak House?* Mrs. Snagsby, madam, like yourself, made nocturnal examinations of her husband's pockets; secretly read his letters; opened and re-sealed letters arriving for him in his absence; privately examined his books, papers, valuables, locked and unlocked; listened behind doors, watched over the stairs, hid herself in closets for further watchings; followed him and paid servants to follow him wherever he went; and made herself not only bone of his bone, but shadow of his shadow; and at last did all this so constantly and so openly that she became the laughing-stock of her servants and her neighborhood. Dickens drew that entire character with a pen of inspiration, and my experience proves its literal truth throughout, even to the minutest particular. I advise you and all jealous wives to read that book, and to recommend it to your friends. And, in the meantime, you may take due notice that from this moment you may suspect what you please, follow me and cause me to be followed where you please, and allow yourself to be influenced by what *friends* you please. And when you think you have discovered something discreditable to me, you may make the most of it. You shall never have another opportunity to abuse my confidence. And, as to your good or ill opinion, your friendship and your hostility, I equally despise and defy them."

The doctor had been repressing his resentment for some years. He had suffered in his practice and even in his private friendships by the meddling, aggressive, rampant jealousy of his wife—he, meantime, aiming at the doctrine of "*conciliation*," which in fact only encouraged Mrs. Jenkins in rebellion, while every one but the doctor saw that his only safe policy was "*coercion*." At last the doctor saw that himself; and he summarily resolved to be captain of his own ship. He had reached that precise point in his own history, when this last provocation was thrust upon him; and he therefore made his demonstration in a speech which, if somewhat long, was also somewhat intelligible.

But the lady had been for a long time accustomed to command on the quarter-deck, and she was not to be driven from her own ground, and with her own weapons, in a hurry. The suddenness, the vehemence, and the extreme perspicacity of the broadside, however, astonished her to such a degree that she paused for a moment ere she returned it. Her air resembled that of a huge lady-mastiff, which, on turning a corner, finds herself waylaid and threatened by a gentleman whiffet.

Before the doctor had fairly made an end of speaking, the lady began to realize the inconceivable fact that after years of passive endurance, the man of powders and pills had roused himself to affirmative resistance. Next came a consciousness that this man had actually commenced an equalization of old accounts, by paying back to herself some of her own coin. He had ventured to return to her, reservedly, what she had unreservedly heaped upon him. In a word, he had rebelled : and the way she would crush him, was a caution !

"*You* despise ! *you* defy !" she shrieked out in a tone that set all the hanging articles of furniture to vibrating.

Just at that moment the street door bell was rung with unwonted emphasis : and as the waiter, over-hearing the accustomed little family altercation, and anticipating some fun, was already listening in the hall, he flew to the door and had it wide open before the clamor of the bell was at an end. Another instant, and he bolted, nothing loth, into the parlor with the painful intelligence that old Mr. Brisket, the butcher, had been run over by an omnibus and was lying in an adjoining apothecary's shop, wait-ing for doctor Jenkins.

This interruption did not for one moment impede the torrent of Madam Jenkins's invective : she did not even seem aware of the interruption ; but although the doctor, with a deep sense of obligation to the omnibus-driver, caught his hat and flew out of the house, the lady went on, apparently uncon-scious that her audience was reduced to the inani-mate furniture of the apartment. Indeed, so great was her abstraction, and so blind her overflowing rage, that her hand happening to alight on a large cut-glass flacon of cologne water simultaneously with her catching a glance of her own striding figure in a pier-glass close at her elbow, she dashed the missile at what she supposed was the doctor's retreating flank, and shivered the mirror as if a cannon-ball had struck it.

The crash and jingle of the broken glass brought the lady to a sudden pause; and the waiter, who was still listening in the hall, again rushed in and asked whether madam had rung, and what was her pleasure.

There was no occasion to inquire whether madam had rung. She *had* rung. And her pleasure was, the carriage. Under such circumstances, Jehu was not long in coming. Nor was he long in driving to the residence of Mrs. Swift, a former schoolfellow of Mrs. Jenkins, and her bosom friend ever since.

"Sophia," said the enraged visitor, to her dearest and best friend, "I have caught that fellow again!"

"You don't say so?—where?" exclaimed the dearest and best friend.

"Mrs. McPherson's," answered the afflicted wife; "two hours and a half in that woman's room, and she no more sick than the queen of Spain."

"Pay him off!" rejoined the dearest and best friend.

"Now, seriously, Sophia, wouldn't you?" inquired the complainant: "would you bear it? would anybody but a slave or a fool bear it?"

"My sweet Louisa," answered her dearest and best friend, "I tell you *no.* I have told you so a hundred times. The brute is incorrigible, and you owe it to society to make an example of him. And Mrs. McPherson, too! A man might be forgiven for some things—but Mrs. McPherson! oh, Lord!"

"Mrs. McPherson, or Mrs. anybody else, it's all one for that," returned the doctor's wife, not quite

appreciating her dearest and best friend's distinction;
" but I intend to separate from him, at once."

" I am rejoiced to hear you say that," replied
the dearest and best friend ; " and the quicker the
better."

" You approve of my doing so, don't you, Sophia ?"
continued the outraged lady ; and, receiving an ap-
proving nod from her dearest and best friend, she
went on to the details of her project. These were
speedily arranged to the satisfaction of both ; and,
with many thanks to her dearest and best friend,
Mrs. Jenkins hastened to seek further counsel and
approval at the hands of dear good Doctor Perkins.

Was Doctor Perkins at home ? Of course he was.
He was always at home to such friends as Mrs.
Jenkins.

When the good Doctor became aware of the nature
of the matter in hand ; to wit, domestic affliction
arising from the conduct of a cruel and unfaithful
husband, he suggested that it might be well to open
the meeting with prayer. But the more practical
lady assured him that this was a case past praying
for, and insisted on proceeding to business.

Apart from topics connected with the "infernal
Institution," the Doctor was a consistent practitioner of the system of all things to all men. He
therefore never remonstrated with his distressed
lambs : he only sympathized with them. And when
they wanted his advice, he always ascertained, first,
what course they had resolved to pursue, and then
he shaped his advice conformably. To him, therefore, the task of spiritual or temporal counsel was the
easiest thing in the world.

" My dear madam," he ventured to say, nevertheless, after he had listened to a tale of horrors that astonished the narrator herself, "you are quite sure that these charges against my friend, the doctor, are correct?" And he paused, somewhat alarmed lest he had said too much in favor of the absent friend. But his extreme freedom of speech had neither offended nor shaken the fair calumniator.

"Correct!" echoed she, with the slightest possible sneer: "if these things are not true, Doctor, why am I here to complain of them?"

To be sure. That was an unanswerable argument. The Doctor had not thought of that, when he made his hasty interrogatory

. "Well, Doctor," the lady continued, "what do you advise me to do?"

"I hardly know," answered the Doctor, quite unprepared for the direct question, but clear as to the policy of not answering it until he could get a clue to the lady's intentions: "I am greatly at a loss— this communication is so unexpected—that—a——"

"But, Doctor," interrupted the lady, "this state of things is intolerable. I am determined not to endure it for another day."

"If you find that the burden cannot be borne, my dear madam," the Doctor suggested: "if you are quite sure that your mind is so unalterably made up that no earthly power or influence can have the slightest effect"—and, he was about to add, "if you have counted the cost of an open rupture," for the truth is, doctor Jenkins was an old friend of Per. i is, and the latter, notwithstanding his habitual cows .dy pliancy, was very near giving way to one gen: ous impulse; but the lady again interrupted him:

"Nothing can shake my determination," she

repeated, resolutely, with a full emphasis on the first word.

"And your children?" the Doctor timidly ventured to say.

"They are already at my mother's in the country," answered the lady, "and my own fortune is ample for them and me."

"You intend, I presume, to take legal advice in this matter?" pursued the Doctor, still unwilling to let everything go by the run.

"Certainly I do," the lady replied, "otherwise I should have that man pursuing me: not because he cares for me," she added, trying to inculcate a whimper for Perkins's benefit, "but only for revenge."

"I am very glad you mean to take legal advice," said the Doctor; "in a step of such importance, it is essential to be sure of your ground."

"To be sure it is," said the lady, rising to go. "I have now had the advantage of your good judgment, my dear Doctor, and I shall ever be grateful to you for it. Good-bye, Doctor."

After Mrs. Jenkins had taken leave, the Doctor flattered himself that he had earned her thanks at a tolerably cheap rate. He was not altogether at his ease about his ready desertion of his absent friend doctor Jenkins; "but," thought he, "my lady will find her course not quite so clear when she comes to talk with a lawyer. Let *him* take the responsibility of real advice. He is paid for it. There is no reason why I should mix myself up with family quarrels."

The Doctor wisely reserved all his powers of interference for the safer crusade against the "infernal Institution."

Strange as it may seem, Mrs. Jenkins derived a

large amount of aid and comfort from the interview with her pastor. She expected to find him strenuously opposed to her project, and she armed herself with arguments to sustain it. But when she found him readily accepting her statements, sympathizing with her wrongs, and at least negatively assenting to her proposed course, she attributed to the strength and equity of her case what was in fact solely attributable to the Doctor's habit of "trimming:" and whereas the Doctor's private judgment utterly discredited her story and disapproved her action; she, nevertheless, with the easy credulity of those who believe what they wish to believe, left the Doctor with an unhesitating conviction that she had his full sanction and approval in what she had so rashly undertaken.

Thus encouraged, therefore, and in a quarter where she least expected encouragement, she addressed herself with great confidence to the firm of Rebutter, Surrebutter and Co.

The senior partners were absent or engaged; but on the whole, the lady did not regret that. Mr. Traverse was a capable and responsible member of the firm, and he had received some civilities from her in society, which her position converted into obligations. Therefore, she preferred to consult with Mr. Traverse.

Her rehearsal of her story to the reverend Doctor, enabled her to repeat it to Traverse with great facility: though she was somewhat surprised, as she went on, that he did not interrupt her with exclamations of astonishment, but sat silent and unmoved through the whole narration, making an occasional note, however, on a paper that lay before him.

Traverse was a rising and popular young lawyer: a man of good address; of an extensive acquaintance in society; and he was by no means unaware of the reputation of Mrs. Jenkins. That lady's demonstrative jealousy, both in town and at watering-places, had long been a favorite topic with the gossips; and, ignorant of the fact as was Mrs. Jenkins herself, her name was discreditably familiar to the scandal mongers of the town. Traverse was consequently able to appreciate the narrative of the lady at its true value, before she began it. And when it was finished, he briefly cross-questioned her by his minutes. In his capacity of counsel, he could easily press this examination without reserve, which he could not so well have done, had he been applied to as a friend.

The result was, that the finely spun story, which ran so smoothly on the lady's direct and uninterrupted recital, became, under the clear and logical investigation of the shrewd lawyer, a disjointed mass of improbabilities, hardly any two of which could be reconciled to each other.

This conclusion became so palpable to the lady herself, that she voluntarily proposed to go no further with the matter at present. She was forced to see that, whatever might be the facts with regard to her husband, she had committed a terrible blunder in presenting her case and revealing her plans to Traverse; and she made a merit of necessity by imploring him to keep sacredly confidential what she had imparted. Traverse readily bound himself to the strictest professional secrecy. But he took full advantage of the opportunity to administer to the lady a lesson of reproof for the past, and solemn warning for the

future. Nor did he altogether spare her the knowledge which she naturally would be the last person to
gain, of the notoriety already attained by her erratic
course. For he justly deemed it essential to the
efficacy of his counsel, that she should be made to
see, and feel the effects, personal to herself, of her
recent conduct; as the mortification of such knowledge would go far toward rendering her obstinate
temper more tractable—an obstinate temper being
of all things the most intractable, to ordinary influences.

"I have thus shown you, madam," he proceeded
to say, "that your accusations and suspicions are un-
doubtedly unjust. But supposing they were otherwise.
Admit all you have suspected to be true. Even then,
your duties to yourself, to your children, and to society, should teach you to forego the pursuit of private
vengeance against your husband, whom, I beg you
to remember, you cannot punish separately. Whatever you inflict on him, will react on yourself immediately, and then on your children. And how would
you, in after years, answer to *them* for injuries totally
irreparable, which you had brought on them, in
seeking to indulge the very worst of passions against
their father?"

In the course of this interview, the unfortunate
lady had gone through the various stages of surprise,
anger, disappointment, and deep humiliation. Yet,
through all this conflict of passion, she could not but
see that true kindness and delicacy had dictated
every word spoken by Traverse. It was this consideration which, at last, completely subdued her. The
power of sympathy in social life is like the power of
faith in religion : it literally removes mountains. In

this instance, the convictions of years gave way to a half hour of gentle and intelligent persuasion; the scales fell from the lady's eyes, as if they had been touched by the finger of Omnipotence: her settled purposes of hostility and revenge yielded to the reviving recollections of former fondness; and the wronged husband rose before the mind of the offending wife in a more attractive form than eveh her early fancy had painted him.

"Believe me, my dear madam," said Traverse, in conclusion, "you have but to take one step. The first word of genuine regret, the first syllable of retraction, the first intimation of a desire for forgiveness—pardon me for suggesting what you must understand better than I can. And now, let me once more assure you that the secret of this interview is safe with me. I will see you to your carriage."

Doctor Jenkins arrived at home just at the moment that his wife did; and he civilly, but silently, handed her from the coach. As the two entered the hall, she gently took one of his hands in hers, led him into the parlor, stopped in front of the broken mirror, pointed to its fragments with her disengaged hand—and sunk down at his feet.

"Husband! my dear husband!" cried she, "will you forgive me?"

CHAPTER X.

In the course of time, the health of Richard Roe was so far reëstablished, that he resumed his accustomed seat in his office in Wall-street. Numerous were the congratulations he received; numerous were the questions he was compelled to answer or evade: for although Richard had his full share of ill-wishers and enemies—as what rich and pious man has not? yet, nevertheless, the fact that he possessed, or had control of, an abundance of money, enabled him, as it enables any man, to command a certain degree of consideration from all classes of people.

A sneer at "the dollar"—"the almighty dollar"— is a popular pastime: a pastime that seems to be as congenial to those who *have* the dollar, as to those who haven't it. There is a surprising uniformity of expression on that subject, whether or not the speakers are equally unanimous in their opinions. The true philosophy of the universal custom is probably this: that whereas the rich man speaks slightingly of wealth, in order to impress his auditors with a sense of his moral and intellectual elevation—always accompanied with a sly consciousness that as the dollar is actually *his*, he can take a liberty with it; on the other hand, the poor man, though nominally taking the same liberty, mentally aims *his* sneer not at the dollar itself, but at its fortunate owner—who, in the poor speaker's judgment, has nothing else to boast of.

Be that as it may, the dollar is, in the popular phrase, " almighty." It rules the roast and carries the day, all the world over. Englishmen, Frenchmen, or any foreigner, may superciliously intimate that the sway of the dollar is limited to those whom they indiscriminately style Yankees. But let the Yankees be content! The dollar is of one weight, everywhere. It is an aristocrat, and an autocrat too, in every land that the sun shines on. Its ring is as loud and as musical at the Court of St. James as in the cabin of St. Jonathan.

But, though Richard Roe enjoyed the benefit of *his* dollar in all that dollars could do, he had his own troubles. His bugbear was not a sham bear. His sword of Damocles was not a sword of lath. Wilson hung over his head by night and by day, suspended by a hair. How long that hair was likely to hold, became a paramount question.

A rope may be examined, and the giving way of a fibre may be detected by a careful investigator. And since a rope breaks by degrees, the condition of danger which is identical with its rupture, can be watched, calculated and guarded against. But a hair, being a single fibre, snaps in a jiffy. In comparison with a hair, a rope is a friendly tissue. It gives warning. And that's the reason why Richard Roe would have preferred that Wilson, just now, was hanging by a rope instead of a hair!

Then, Roe had other troubles. His family matters were ajar. He lost his first wife when his daughter and only child, Margaret, was nineteen. If for no better reason than his well-known devotion to appearances, Roe found a second wife indispensable. And although he may have had good reason for seeking a second wife of a fitting description, none of his friends were able to justify the choice he actually made. True, he gave a reason, as he did for everything that he felt needed a reason: but he seldom gave a true one, and almost never a good one. His explanation of making a new Mrs. Roe of a splendid young woman of twenty, was that his daughter needed a companion instead of a step-mother. Unfortunately for all the parties in interest, the new Mrs. Roe, soon after she became Mrs. Roe, entertained a very different opinion.

Again, the good Roe was subjected to petty annoyances by exacting and unreasonable customers. He had hardly resumed his daily avocations, after his illness, when he compulsorily held a levee of these people. Briggs, a capitalist from Boston, came first.

"Roe, how d'ye do?" he commenced. "I've come on to see about the July interest of those Catawampus bonds. You wouldn't answer my letters, and I'll see, now, whether you'll answer my questions."

"My dear Briggs," replied Roe, "I am very much disappointed about those bonds. I feel much worse about them than you do. I feel"——

"Oh, damn your feelings!" interrupted Briggs. "I want my money."

"My dear Briggs, don't swear!" entreated the banker; "that hurts me worse than the money."

"See here, Roe," continued Briggs, "I have come to talk business; and I beg you'll postpone your hurts and your feelings. I bought those bonds on your very strong representations, without, myself, making any inquiry. I now hear a rumor that the company propose to fund the coupons, and I want to know what course you intend to take with yours."

"Why, the fact is," said Roe, reddening a little in the face, "I have sold out."

"Sold out! and without letting me know!" cried Briggs. "When did you sell?"

"In April," stammered Roe; "I—the fact is"——

"In April!" cried Briggs; "in April, when they were worth 95 per cent., and when you advised me *not* to sell! By G—, sir, do you happen to remember that the sole condition on which I bought these bonds of you was, that if for any reason you changed your mind as to their value and concluded to sell, you would give me full notice?"

"My dear Briggs," replied Roe, "it was owing to an accident. Burns of Albany wrote me in April to sell his bonds and said he would forward them by the next day's express. I made the sale: and as the purchaser insisted on immediate delivery as *his* condition, I gave him my bonds. In the afternoon, I received a telegram from Burns countermanding his order; and there was I, stuck."

"Stuck, indeed!" echoed Briggs; "stuck, by getting out of a concern into which you had wheedled forty people and made thousands of dollars out of every one of them. The short of the matter is, '*my dear*' Roe, that you have cheated me. Even if your Burns story is true—though I don't believe a word of it—you were bound to give me the promised notice of selling out. You are an infernal scoundrel, and I will so proclaim you, through Wall-street."

And, exit Briggs.

Mr. Roe's feelings were deeply wounded, not at Briggs's abuse—that the good man could despise—but at his profanity. Profanity "hurt" Roe worse than anything : and he had not more than half recovered from the wounds produced by that wicked man's swearing, when the reverend Mr. Steele, from the rural districts, came in.

"My dear Mr. Steele," said Roe, "how do you do? How's your wife? and Fred? and Betsey? and all the little ones?"

He huddled his questions on the poor parson, as if he would deprive the man of making any inquiries himself. But that couldn't last long.

"Mr. Roe," replied the clergyman, without taking any notice of Roe's questions, "I have at much inconvenience come down to New-York to get from you in person some information which I have failed to obtain from you by correspondence."

"My dear Mr. Steele," began Roe, reproachfully— But Mr. Steele went on.

"My family are suffering, Mr. Roe," he said, "for want of the July interest on those Balderdash bonds. The coupons were returned to me, and I wish to know what is the matter."

"My dear Mr. Steele," replied Roe, sympathizingly, "that Company has failed."

"Failed!" shrieked the poor clergyman: "why, Mr. Roe, you told me those bonds were as good as wheat."

"My dear Mr. Steele," continued Roe, for he "my deared" everybody whom he victimized, "I thought they were."

"But, sir," persisted Mr. Steele, "what am I to do? You well know that those bonds were purchased partly with my wife's inheritance and the remainder from my own hard earned savings; and that the sum total, ten thousand dollars, is all my living, since ill-health forced me to give up my profession."

"Pray, don't speak of it, my dear Mr. Steele!" said Roe. "I feel much worse about it than you do."

"Mr. Roe," replied the clergyman, with some severity, "I have heard you make that remark to other people, and I would like to know what you mean by it. *You* feel worse than *I* do, when I am in poverty and you are a man of wealth! But this is trifling. Let me know at once what course you propose to take with your own bonds, and I may then judge what to do with mine."

"Why," answered Roe, "the fact is, my dear Mr. Steele, I sold out my bonds in April."

"*You sold out, sir!* and left me to be ruined by holding on!" cried Mr. Steele.

"It was the result of a mistake, my dear Mr. Steele," replied Roe. "Mr. Burns, of Albany, wrote me to sell *his* bonds and promised to send them to me by express. I made the sale, and, to oblige the purchaser, delivered my bonds *ad interim*. The next day he countermanded the order; but my bonds were gone."

"And pray, sir," inquired Mr. Steele, "how could you fail to notify me, and at least give me the option of parting with securities, which your volunteered recommendation induced me to purchase? But at any rate, you must make them good to me. The amount, trifling for you, is to me absolute ruin."

"My dear Mr. Steele!" exclaimed Roe: "you cannot expect me to do that!"

"I ask it, and demand it," said the clergyman reso

lutely. " You knew that I had that money invested in a safe mortgage : you wrote me to sell the mortgage and send you the money, to be more profitably invested. I knew nothing of the bonds you proposed to buy ; I trusted you ; and you have ruined me. And if you refuse to make good to me what is lost, my curse and the curse of my family shall rest on you !"

Mr. Steele withdrew. And Roe took down a dictionary, to ascertain whether the use of the word " curse " could be construed into profane swearing. Next to the sin of slavery, Roe considered swearing the thing unpardonable. And the pain he endured in hearing men swear, was one of his greatest comforts. It was his way of suffering for righteousness' sake. And in this case, if he could but manage to get his feelings hurt by Mr. Steele's profanity, he felt that his feelings would be greatly relieved. He had not, however, got ·beyond CON in his dictionary research for " curse," when Mr. Burton made his appearance.

Mr. Burton was a foreigner. He came to America about a year previously with his family, his worldly goods, and fifteen thousand dollars in gold ; which latter commodity, by virtue of an introductory letter, he had the good luck to deposit with Roe for investment. Roe, with his usual urbanity, undertook to do a good thing for Mr. Burton.. He advanced him a small sum by way of anticipated interest ; and soon after informed him that he, Roe, had managed to reserve for him, Burton, a fat slice of the Tuscarora convertibles, paying ten per cent. per annum interest, at the dog-cheap price of ninety-five on the hundred. This gave Mr. Burton an income of one

thousand five hundred dollars, a funded capital of
fifteen thousand dollars, and a surplus in hand of
seven hundred and fifty dollars. The agreeable intelligence was communicated to Mr. Burton at Roe's
dinner-table, after the ladies had withdrawn. Roe
having thrown in a modicum of significant smiles
and *hems*, unfolded the tale of happiness and magni-
ficently tossed down on the red cloth a cheque for
the seven hundred and fifty dollars, less the small
amount previously advanced to Mr. Burton. He
had not even charged Mr. Burton a commission for
doing the business! Burton was so elated that he
made a straight wake through an extra bottle of
green seal.

In the month of January thence ensuing, Burton
was made glad by another cheque for seven hundred
and fifty dollars, being six months' interest on the
Tuscaroras. But in the following July, there came
a hitch. A delay. A disappointment. Nothing
permanent, of course. Tuscarora would never say
die. Still, it was disagreeable. Days rolled on, as
they always will do, Tuscarora or no Tuscarora.
They became weeks. They strongly resembled
months. And still no funds! A rumor of failure
began to perambulate.

Things were at this pass, when Mr. Burton called
on Mr. Roe, as aforesaid. Mr. Burton had heard the
rumor, and his cheeks were slightly blanched as he
inquired what it meant?

"I really don't know what to think of it," said Roe.
"At any rate, it's only temporary."

"Ah," said Burton, much relieved, "then you can
advance the money on these coupons?"

"That's a thing I never do," replied Roe, magisterially, and as if such a thing were sinful. "Holders must wait."

"It is easy to say that, Mr. Roe," Burton replied: "but this interest is my entire income, and I may wait till my family "—his voice trembled as the consequence rose to his mind—" till my family *want !*"

"My dear Mr. Burton," replied Roe, "don't give way to that sort of thing. I assure you, my dear friend, I feel much worse than you do about it." Roe was a kind-hearted man. He always felt much worse than his swindled customers.

"If you feel so much for my predicament," rejoined Burton, "have the goodness to relieve me by giving me the money for these coupons; or," he added, with a natural suspicion as to the security of the whole transaction, "restore to me my principal and let me dispose of it elsewhere."

"I can do neither of those things, Mr. Burton," said Roe.

"Then, sir," Burton continued in alarm, "make an immediate sale of my bonds and let me know the worst."

"Just at present," Roe answered, "they cannot be sold at any price."

What do you propose, then, to do with your own bonds?" inquired Mr. Burton.

"I should hold them by all means," said Roe ; " that is,—if I had any."

"If you had any!" echoed Mr. Burton. "You told me you had fifty thousand dollars of them."

"I had, at one time, my dear friend," answered Roe: "but I sold out in April."

"Good God, sir!" exclaimed Mr. Burton, striding up to Roe with an air that might easily have been mistaken for a menacing air, "you have sold out, and left me in? Do you tell me that, sir?"

"My dear Mr. Burton," cried Roe, "be calm. Pray be calm! It was the merest accident in the world. Mr. Burns, of Albany, wrote me to sell *his* bonds, and promised to send them by express, the next day. I made the sale; and, to accommodate the purchaser, delivered my own bonds. In the afternoon, I received a telegram countermanding the order to sell: but my bonds were gone."

"Mr. Roe," said Burton, "I came to you in confidence. I trusted you, as I would have trusted a brother. I placed all my property in your hands and left you to manage it, without asking a question. You bought for me bonds which you said were good; *proving* your opinion by an assurance that you held a large amount of them, and *securing* mine, as it were, by promising to sell mine if you ever found occasion to sell yours. You have, nevertheless, deliberately deceived me. Will you, sir, give me ten cents on the dollar for those bonds, namely fifteen hundred dollars for my fifteen thousand?"

Mr. Roe could by no means permit his dear friend Mr. Burton to make such a sacrifice: but he would lend Mr. Burton five hundred dollars on the deposit of the fifteen thousand of bonds as collateral security —conditioned that the bonds should be forfeited to Roe, if the loan was not repaid in twenty days.

There needed but this! Mr. Burton had recently heard that Roe had accumulated a fortune by purchasing large amounts of worthless western bonds, at low prices, and palming them off on confiding friends and customers, at par. He *now* believed the story.

"Mr. Roe," said he, "you are the villain that you

have been represented to be. And may that God whose laws you have outraged bring you to poverty and disgrace, and that right speedily!"

It was a great comfort to Mr. Roe that Mr. Burton had sworn one round oath in the course of this interview. And that wasn't all. He had imprecated vengeance from above on Roe's head. Roe, therefore was doubly comforted.

No sooner was Mr. Burton gone, than Mr. Somebody else came in, on a similar errand; and the number of this class of troublesome, captious, complaining customers exceeded a score before the morning was ended. So great a number, all in one day, forced Richard Roe to remark—"It never rains but it pours."

True: but Roe was equal to the emergency. He didn't break down. He took comfort in persecution. He knew that blessed are the persecuted—or something of that kind. Besides, he had that morning made several capital hits in family prayer, and his fund of grace on hand was unusually large. Moreover, having been persecuted, he was now about to have a chance to persecute in turn. He had suffered some at the hands of Paul and he would avenge himself by paying off Peter.

Mr. Hicks came in, with an embarrassed air. "Mr. Roe," said he, "I received your letter— and——"

"And," interrupted Roe, sternly, "you waited till a quarter past three before you replied to it."

"I am very sorry, sir," Hicks began again——

"Does your sorrow pay that note, sir?" again interrupted Roe, looking as solemn as if he really "asked, for information."

"Mr. Roe, don't be hard on me!" entreated poor Hicks. "I have already made great sacrifices to keep down the interest on that loan. Pray remember, sir, that within six months, I have actually paid you forty-two per cent., all for interest, and you know, Mr. Roe, that the security you hold is ample."

"I know nothing of the kind," retorted Roe, peremptorily.

"Why, Mr. Roe, only consider," said Hicks, who had relapsed into a mental calculation and lost Roe's last remark; "that is at the rate of eighty-four per cent. a year for the use of money; and you, Mr. Roe, a christian man! Why, sir, it is usury, and ruin. The Bible says——"

"Do you come here, sir, to tell me what the Bible says?" interrupted Roe in a voice of thunder; "and to talk to me about usury? Doesn't your Bible tell you to owe no man anything? and don't you owe me ten thousand dollars? Didn't our blessed Saviour cast into outer darkness the man who owed him one talent, because the debtor wouldn't pay him his own with usury? and do you talk to me about usury? Besides, isn't a bargain a bargain? Didn't you come to me for the ten thousand dollars when it and nothing but it, would save you from bankruptcy? and didn't you agree to pay—yes, *offer* to pay *any* rate of interest? and didn't you promise to take up the loan at the end of the month? And do you now come here to talk ' Bible ' to me?"

"But, Mr. Roe," gasped Hicks, perfectly overwhelmed by such a torrent of interrogatories, "I have paid the interest and you hold ample security."

"I tell you again," thundered Roe, "I hold nothing of the sort."

"Why, Mr. Roe!" exclaimed Hicks, "you hold fourteen thousand dollars of those Erie Bonds which were never until just now sold at less than seventy per cent."

"Read my letter again!" replied Roe with a sneer that made Hicks tremble.

Hicks drew the letter from his pocket, and re-marked with a faltering voice "you say here, Mr. Roe, that you will sell those bonds at any price they will bring, if the loan is not paid before three o'clock. But, sir, I was called home by the sudden illness of my wife and I sent you word that I would call very soon after three ; as I have done."

"And you thought, I suppose," continued Roe, "that after I had sent you my solemn promise in writing as to what I would do, that I would delibe-rately break that promise and *not* sell the bonds, just because your wife is sick ? What's your wife to me, sir ! And what business have you with a wife, when you can't pay your debts ?"

"But, Mr. Roe," cried Hicks, regardless of Roe's brutality, "I trust, nevertheless, that you have *not* sold them at their present depressed price ? They have been sold within a day or two as low as sixty-five."

"They have been sold to-day at *fifty*," replied Roe: "at least, I can answer for one sale at that price—a little lot of fourteen bonds that I held as collateral. They produced seven thousand dollars, and I hold you for three thousand dollars, balance due on your note."

Poor Hicks said not one word ; but, dizzy and faint with the shock of such intelligence, he grasped at a chair : and, missing it, he fell heavily to the floor

" Mr. Jackson," said Roe, in the mildest of tones, "I am going home to an early dinner. Will you see to Hicks? I believe he hurt himself against a chair." And Roe hurried home, where he delivered an admirable Grace before Meat.

A disinterested spectator of this morning's incidents might have remarked, " What an unutterable villain that fellow is !"

But the subject of that insinuation would have rejoined—" Sir, I am Richard Roe, banker and church member." And, if that magisterial announcement failed to demolish the caviller, Roe would perhaps have added,

" Sir, don't measure my corn in your bushel. I am not as other men are, extortioners and so forth : no, sir ! nor as these complaining publicans. I fast. I pay tithes. I do many things."

At Roe's request, Mr. Jackson " saw to Mr. Hicks ;" and found him in a state resembling the stupor of apoplexy ; from which, however, the unfortunate man revived under the prompt attention of Jackson.

Jackson was Roe's confidential and head clerk : he was Wilson's immediate successor. He had seen the progress of this affair with Hicks and endeavored to dissuade him from continuing the loan on such terms. But Hicks was a vacillating man, and he kept on from week to week hoping for " a favorable turn " in his business or in the times, until the present disaster overtook him. Jackson had gone through a hardening process in Roe's service, but he had many good qualities that yet survived ; and he could not be aware of the details of the late scene, which he partly overheard, without deep resentment against

Roe : especially, when he considered the facts of the loan to Hicks.

On the day the loan was made, the bonds were worth eighty, in the market, and Roe actually sold them for cash, thus placing himself in funds from Hicks's own property to the amount of more than eleven thousand dollars, and taking the risk of buying the bonds back again when the loan should be returned. Out of this sum, he then *lent* Hicks ten thousand dollars at seven per cent. a month ; and retained in his own hands more than one thousand dollars of Hicks's own money. At the end of the six months, he had received from Hicks no less than four thousand two hundred dollars of usurious interest. Then, by falsely pretending to have sold the bonds at fifty per cent., he brought Hicks three thousand dollars in debt, over and above his loss of the bonds and of the interest he had paid on the loan. As Hicks originally bought the bonds at par, his actual loss exceeded eleven thousand dollars, of which nearly one half was pocketed in cash by Roe.

CHAPTER XI.

A ROD IN PICKLE.

IT was clear to the mind of John Doe, that Wilson's escape from prison had been aided and abetted by Richard Roe. What Roe's motive could be, was another question. And still another and much more important question, was how could the motive be discovered? Perhaps the affair was not John Doe's affair. Perhaps the affair, whosesoever it might be, was not, to John Doe, worth the trouble of investigation. But John Doe, as the brother and representative of Mrs. Elizabeth Peters, had brought against Richard Roe a suit at law for the recovery of a large sum of money, alleged to have been fraudulently appropriated by Roe from the property of Joseph Peters, deceased, formerly a partner of Roe and husband of the aforesaid Elizabeth Peters.

That Roe had in fact largely defrauded the widow of his late partner, was fully believed by the widow herself and by all her relatives. Moreover, a certain amount of proof could be produced, which at least sufficed to justify very grave suspicions of Roe's honesty in the premises; and certain notorious facts in regard to Roe's position went far toward corroborating what was believed and what was suspected. But the facility with which a cunning man can practise frauds on the property of a deceased partner, and afterward, by secreting or destroying the books and papers, obliterate the proof of such fraud, renders the existence of fraud entirely compatible with the inability of a claimant to substantiate it.

Hence, in the action of John Doe against Richard Roe, the absence, hitherto, of conclusive evidence in the plaintiff's favor, by no means established his want of a ground of action, or his inability to recover on it. Indeed, as the case now stood, if a jury could be made to believe what the plaintiff and his friends believed, a verdict in the plaintiff's favor was inevitble. But that *if* was the rub.

In this condition of things, Doe felt himself justified in seeking proof of Roe's rascality outside of his own case; because, however irrelevant to Doe *versus* Roe such facts might be, they would perhaps enable Doe to coerce Roe into a fair exhibit and settlement of the contested accounts, under a threat of exposure in new matter to-be-discovered. That, therefore, was the ground of Doe's interest in Wilson's escape; or rather, in Roe's agency in that escape.

The facts already ascertained by Doe, in that matter, were communicated to Traverse, as one of his counsel; and after a full consultation, the two concluded to employ a detective to ascertain the whereabout of Wilson, if such information were attainable.

Mr. Snap was a prompt, shrewd, indefatigable officer. A man, too, of large experience in the detective branch of police business. He had not previously given much attention to this case. He had read the newspaper accounts; thought too much had been published on the subject; doubted whether a sufficient reward had been offered, and whether much real vigilance had been exercised. Was, nevertheless, surprised that no trace of the man had been found.   And, considering that no such trace had been hit upon, and that nothing which could be relied on had been heard of the fugitive in any direction, he'd be d——(begging the gentleman's pardon ! that was the *style* of so many men that Snap came in contact with !) he'd be hanged if he didn't believe that the fellow had never left the city at all.

"That," said Doe, "would be good news."

"I'm not so sure of that," returned Snap. "I would rather follow a man over half the railroads and steamboats in the country, than through the holes and corners of New-York.   But we'll see.   Is this a matter of public business, Mr. Doe ?"

"Private entirely," answered Doe, "and it must be kept so.   I would prefer that you undertake it exclusively by yourself.   And as for the reward, which you think the authorities offered on a small scale, I will say at once that if you find Wilson and put me in communication with him, you may name your own price for your services."

"That's very liberal, sir," said Snap; "very handsome indeed : but, sir, it's a little uncertain.   We like a fixed sum.   And then, for instance, suppose after a long look and time and expenses lost,—suppose I *don't* find him ?   I don't wish to be unreasonable, sir ; nor sharp at a bargain ; but business is business."

"You are perfectly right, Snap," Doe replied; "and I like you the better for being explicit.   I will pay you two hundred and fifty dollars for the search without the man : two hundred and fifty dollars more *for* the man : and if in your own judgment, at the end, the labor and trouble are worth another two hundred and fifty, you shall have it."

"That's the talk, sir, and 'done' is the word," replied Snap. "If Wilson is anywheres between the two rivers, I'm down on him. But I don't yet know the man. Can you describe him?"

Doe and Traverse both tried a hand at description, but they found it not easy to convey their knowledge intelligibly. Doe, however, thought Wilson could almost certainly be recognized by the peculiarity of his beard. He knew but one other man who wore his whiskers in that style: to wit, Richard Roe.

"Not too fast, sir, if you please," rejoined Snap. "You may bet high that Wilson's hair and whiskers are among the missing. He's not an old hand at dodges, but he's sharp enough for that, anyhow. His clothes, too, won't be like anything you've ever seen him wear."

And Snap went on to say that they had him in the Rogue's Gallery, sure. He could see his likeness there, and could get a copy: and if the man who took it could only play barber by shearing and shaving the picture, he would have him, beautiful.

The fact that Wilson was not an old hand, would insure his not being hid in any of the regular beats. There was so much ground as good as examined, to start with. Then, the man can't keep all the time shut up. He must have his exercise. He will be walking out, evenings: 'specially rainy evenings. This search was to be a matter of umbrellas, most likely. And shoe-leather, anyhow. And eyes.

"As to the Rogue's Gallery, gentlemen," Snap proceeded, for like many other men he was loquacious on points where he was strong, "I have often told them at the office that they should take a back view of a man as well as a front.   Don't you know, sir," turning to Traverse, who seemed to catch this idea more readily than Doe, " you see a friend ahead of you in the street, and you can tell him by his back, sure? Whether it's the shape of his head, or neck, or shoulders; whether it's his walk; or, whatever it is, you always know him, and no mistake?"

" That's very true," said Traverse, " and I have often been struck by it.   But why is a likeness of the back better than a front view?"

" Why, bless you, sir," said Snap, " don't you see, that while a man can always change his face by a wig, by shaving, by whiskers, by spectacles, and so on, he can't disguise his back? That's just the one thing all the time, whatever he does to his face and his riggin."

"Every man to his trade, Snap," interposed Doe: " I shouldn't have thought of that."

" Ah, sir," rejoined Snap, " set your mind to one thing, and get your living according as you learn it, and if you're not a dead flat, sir, you'll get to be a sharp.   This is a trade, as you say, sir, and that's all there is about it."

In due time, Snap possessed himself of a copy of Wilson's likeness.   And after studying it microscopically and every other way, so as to make each feature familiar to his eye, he involuntarily turned it over to see the back: which, unfortunately for his purpose, was wanting.

" Why the devil don't they take the back views, as well?" muttered Snap.

CHAPTER XII.

The propriety, extrinsic and intrinsic, of second marriages, is an inexhaustible subject of discussion. First, because there is no limit to its number of points: and, secondly, because when a thoroughly exhausting argument on any one point has been delivered by A, B and his successors can severally repeat, word for word, what A has said, without in the slightest degree boring, or even fatiguing, any one of an audience. But for this fact, somebody in the course of time would probably reply to somebody that he had a distant recollection of having once heard *that* (whatever the point or argument of the moment) before. As the case stands, it is well known that such a remark was never made. Hence, as everybody thoroughly understands this subject, and loves to talk upon it, and never tires of hearing others talk of it, the subject is, as aforesaid, inexhaustible.

There are cases—well: take the man who has celebrated his silver and his golden wedding, and afterward buried the companion of a long life. That man is, for a time, inconsolable. Everybody expects him to be inconsolable. And he himself, who certainly should know best, announces the fact, officially. His children are all of age; all but one are married and settled and have children of their own. They are indefatigable nevertheless in all the possible attentions to papa, as the next generation are to grandpapa.   There is nothing wanting in this respect. The one unmarried daughter is an invalid, requiring all manner of attention from friends and servants, and herself incapable of rendering attention to her aged father. The father therefore stands desolate in his old home. What is he to do?

Let him obtrude himself on his children and grandchildren a little more than he was accustomed to do; and the old gentleman begins to be troublesome. Let him request a little more than their accustomed attentions to him in his own house; and the old gentleman is getting childish. What is he to do? No doubt, the very best thing he could do is, to die. But Providence sees fit to spare him. That old man has, through all his mature life, been the *first object* of his other self, whom Providence has now called away. He finds it very hard to be *nobody's* first object; but to be, on the contrary, the object of everybody's objections. By and by, and before long, though the old gentleman has an unusual share of health and strength, he finds himself breaking down in both, from sheer loneliness and desolation in those many and tedious hours of every day when no one but a wife could be with him. And, to make a long story short, he meets with a lady against whose age and general fitness not the slightest sound objection can be raised—and marries her. It is not a question of propriety. It is not a question of love. It is briefly a question of life.

Yet—even here—and in what must be admitted to be an extreme case; not a relative, friend, or acquaintance; not a man, woman or child can be found who does not denounce "*the old fool!*" It is needless to add, that any less meritorious or less excusable case of matrimony—any case *not* superlatively extreme—meets with denunciations, in comparison to which, "the old fool" is quite a moderate and inoffensive remark.

Richard Roe was aware of all this. And as he found that he couldn't please everybody in his second marriage he wisely resolved to please nobody—but himself; as has already been intimated. His relations with his daughter, who was about the same age as his new wife, were unfortunate for both father and daughter. He belonged to that class of men, of which specimens may be found everywhere, who look upon children in no other light than as future depositaries of the name and wealth of their parents; and who, therefore, consider the birth of a daughter as a mere calamity: since she cannot establish herself in life without losing her name, and virtually losing her fortune by bestowing—which is the same thing as squandering—it on the son of another man, with whom this class of fathers have nothing in common. From the first, therefore, Roe had never treated Margaret as his child. She ought to have been a son: she *was* a disappointment. He took little notice of her. He left her to her mother and the servants. He never cultivated her affection, and he never *had* it to any considerable extent. A different state of things might have ensued after the death of Margaret's mother, if her father had remained single; or, if he had married suitably and with her concurrence. But the new match was in every particular ill-assorted; and, so far from its having been entered upon with the knowledge of Margaret, she was not even apprised of her father's intentions until after the marriage, the ceremony having been suddenly and almost clandestinely performed while she was absent from town.

Subjects of variance in a family thus constituted, were not, as the phrase runs, far to seek. Indeed, they were so near at hand and so abundant, that they soon took the form of a system, and became a completely inaugurated triangular duel, the explosions of which were as perpetual, if not as frequent, as the ticking of the parlor clock. The order of shooting was the only irregular feature of the war. Sometimes Mr. Roe would pop at his daughter, the daughter at the step-mother, and the step-mother at her husband, because he began it. Again, Margaret would pop at Mrs. Roe, Mrs. Roe out of turn at Margaret, and then at Mr. Roe, because he didn't begin it. And so it went on, pop, pop, pop, from morning to night.

"I wonder," said Mrs. Roe, one morning after breakfast, "whether there is any truth in that scandal about the Jenkinses."

"Such as what?" inquired Roe.

"A separation, I believe; or something of that sort," rejoined the lady.

"That woman," Margaret chimed in, "is enough to drive any man to a separation, whether the story is true or not."

"My daughter," said Roe, meekly, "we ought not to speak ill of our neighbors."

"Perhaps not," Margaret replied; "but in this case, the lady saves us the trouble: she speaks ill of herself. Or, rather, she enacts her ill-conduct so publicly that everybody hears it from her own actions, which speak louder than words."

"These things may be exaggerated," suggested Roe, with a significant look toward his wife: "ill-natured people can make something out of nothing."

Mrs. Roe did not fancy Margaret's interference nor her husband's insinuation; and she intimated to Roe, by way of a preliminary pop, that there was no ill-nature in speaking ill of Mrs. Jenkins, while, however, there might be much in defending her.

"How is that, my dear?" inquired the banker, rather sharply: for while he heard aspersions on others with an ostentatious charity, he considered himself privileged, especially in his own house.

"In the first place," replied Mrs. Roe, "defending Mrs. Jenkins is condemning the doctor; and that certainly is ill-nature, for he is a man above reproach. In the second place, to defend Mrs. Jenkins, is to justify a public display of family differences, for she makes hers public without the slightest compunction. My advice to married women, if they have quarrels with their husbands, is to fight them out at home."

"I should suppose that would be your precept, my dear," Roe rejoined, with great dignity, "since it is your practice."

"And my practice is on a very poor subject," retorted Mrs. Roe. "As for the Jenkinses, the story is true, and Mrs. Swift is my authority."

"And pray, my dear," said Roe, boldly, "who believes a word that Mrs. Swift says?"

"The simple-minded individual '*my dear*,' who has the oppressive honor of being your wife, and the pleasure of being a niece of Mrs. Swift?"

"Oh, I forgot!" lied the conscientious Roe.

"Forgot, indeed!" cried the lady with great disdain : " forgot that Mrs. Swift is my mother's sister. Now, Margaret, what do you say to that ?"

" I say, it's not true, and father knows it," replied the dutiful daughter; for her blood was now well up at the fact of the incessantly recurring altercation.

" Ah," cried the step-mother, " then, probably, you will admit that this time your father began it. I believe that at our last scene you pronounced me the aggressor."

" I really do not remember, Mrs. Roe," answered Margaret, " nor do I think it at all important. If you are not in fault this time, I'll engage you will be the next time.   There's but little to choose when the fox and the goat fall out."

" Margaret," interposed Roe, with magnificent moderation, " you had better leave the room."

" Oh, no ! let her stay," interceded the young wife : " she is so good a judge of who begins, I would be delighted with her judgment who gets the best of it.   By the way, Miss Roe, I *hope* your affair with Mr. Gray is not broken off? I heard some loud talking after I went up stairs last evening, and it occurred to me that he shut the door with peculiar emphasis when he took leave.   To be sure, this might have been all in my imagination; or," she continued, with a superb toss of her head, " it might have been the effect of whiskey.   He was so strong on the respective merits of Bourbon and Monongahela, while I was in the parlor, that I couldn't help thinking he had made free practical experiments on both."

This broad insinuation against her lover, not now for the first time repeated, touched Margaret to the quick.

"I think with you, father," she said, "that I had better leave the room. This interesting young woman is becoming personal. As for Mr. Gray, madam," turning to Mrs. Roe, "I advise you to gratify your curiosity by applying to him. I remember the accidental closing of the door and the loud talking; and, since you heard the sound of the latter, I do wish you had heard the syllables of it! I think you would have verified the proverb. But, madam, though doors are sometimes closed with a noise accidentally, I am not aware of their ever being closed without noise accidentally: and though loud talking may be suspicious, low talking may be much more suspicious. I observed, one evening last week, when *Mr.* Roe was out of town, that your talk with Mr. Jackson was not loud, and that quite late in the evening the door was closed so delicately that I could not help fancying some one inside assisted in the closing. I mention these trifles, because you remind me of them. No doubt, everything between you and Mr. Jackson is proper: yet scandal does whisper that you fancied the man before you fancied the master." And the indignant young lady swept out of the room, leaving her two antagonists something to chew upon.

The withdrawal of Margaret did not mend the family jar. On the contrary, and as was natural, such a revelation left the remaining combatants with a new cause of exasperation. But Roe, though thus enlightened, had the worst of the battle, and retired vanquished and breathless. "My lady Tongue" always got the better of him.

As to Jackson? Pooh! Roe knew better than that!

Perhaps he did!

CHAPTER XIII.

BROWN AT HOME.

WHEN in the course of events doctor Jenkins and his wife came to a perfectly good understanding, which now promised to be permanent; and when they had frankly exchanged opinions as to the state of the outside world in reference to themselves, they concluded, as a matter of policy, to bring that outside world within their own domicile by means of a ball —"ball" being in current parlance the intensification of what was formerly known as "a party."

The reconciled couple thought it better to take the bull of scandal by the horns, and leave gossips to draw their own conclusions as to the past, while they, the gossips, were forced to see that for the future the hatchet was buried. There will always be individuals who regret to see a quarrel ended, even when the welfare of a whole family depends on its reconciliation, and who would, moreover, hope that the reconciliation might be temporary: but such exceptions are incidental to a general rule. The rule is, that sensible and respectable people rejoice when a calamity so common as a family quarrel is brought to an end: the exceptional fools must be suffered to run their own course, with a reasonable prospect of breaking their necks at the end of it.

"My dear Louisa," said the doctor, with all the fondness of old times, "we have secured the main point: never fear but the friends whom we wish to call such, will rally around us."

The next consultation in the premises was held with Brown.

Brown could give them any night they chose, being so early in the season: but, of course, no lady would think of giving an out-and-outer short of three or four weeks' notice. Better four weeks than three. To be sure, "previous engagements" could not interfere; but the dignity of the institution must be maintained.

The cards produced a great excitement. Everybody was taken by surprise. Spontaneous committees of three ladies were improvised in the parlor of every house and at the corner of almost every street. But none of these deliberative assemblies could pass a vote of declining. As nobody would now give a ball on the same evening, "regrets" could not be explained by "previous engagements;" and, therefore, absence would carry the appearance of not being invited. That argument was conclusive. Everybody accepted. Such unanimity never was heard of, before. It was gratifying to the Jenkinses, as indicative of sympathy and approval; yet it had its inconveniences. Invitations in New-York are always issued on the theory of fifty contemplated regrets to every hundred cards, and a houseful hoped for on that basis. This universal acceptance, therefore, foreboded anything but room for the dancers.

The emergency required another consultation with Brown.

"Why, madam," said Brown, "it's a plain case. Your house won't hold 'em, and that's all there is about it."

"Then," replied madam, in despair, "we must recall half the cards and date them for the next evening."

"In which case, madam," interposed Brown, "you may put it down for an empty house on both nights. The illustrious Napoleon Bonaparte, madam, once remarked that 'one bad general is better than two good ones.' Now, madam, if you please, call me the bad general; but let me work it out all alone by myself."

"The idea, Brown, of your being a bad general!" said madam, with an arch smile.

"Can't say, madam! Can't say," retorted Brown. "There might be better, madam; there might be worse. The proof of the pudding, they say, lies in the eating. I mistrusted how this thing was a-going: experience, they say, teaches. And so I worked it out over night. I took notice, madam, that the house next door has a bill on it—To Let, Furnished. That's the talk, says I: and I inquired within. The rooms are furnished very respectable: not to match this, but they'll do for an evening. We can connect the two houses by cutting away the board petition on the rear piazza. And there you have it, madam, just like a knife."

Brown was pronounced to be a genius: a very Napoleon: and things took their course.

Among the unwritten laws of fashionable life, is a statute prohibiting a lady from being the *first* to arrive, or appear, at a ball. No lady must arrive until some other lady is already there. The rule is peremptory, and it is but justice to the ladies to say, that they endeavor to obey it. Yet, if the rule were literally enforced, if nobody was ever first, it is difficult to understand how anybody could manage to go at all. Even the attempt at obedience leads to inconveniences.

The number of hair-dressers is limited. No lady can go to a ball without having her hair dressed. No hair-dresser can be in two places at once. Hence the ladies must submit to rotation, and rotation requires that some be commenced early. When a lady is finished, being unfitted for anything else, she leans against a column, as Lord Byron did, and waits. It is six o'clock. It is seven o'clock. It is eight o'clock. It is nine o'clock. It is ten o'clock.

The husband, or brother, or beau, who has had no trouble about *his* toilette, and did not begin it till half an hour ago, thinks it is about time——

"Oh, dear! not this hour yet!" exclaims the patient lady. "Nobody will be there before eleven, at the very earliest."

"When I was a young man," remonstrates the unhappy escort, "we used to think that half-past eight——"

But it's quite immaterial what Mr. What's-his-name thought when he was a young man. *Wait* is the word.

Somewhere in the vicinity of eleven o'clock, Brown, who has been saving his wind, begins to blow his whistle. And, therefore, two or more carriages are at the door. For nobody need tell Brown that the occupants of the *first* carriage will not move until another carriage comes; hence, to make sure, he reserves his first whistle for the third carriage. That's the rule.

The ice being finally broken, carriages and people are as plenty as blackberries. One would think that all the horses and vehicles in the town had simultaneously started for a common goal : and now, the passengers cannot move fast enough. They seem disposed to avenge themselves for having lost so much time in waiting.

By twelve o'clock, every inch of standing room in the first floor of both houses, and the second floor of one house, is densely covered. Sitting for anybody is simply out of the question. The second floor of the other house is appropriated to the supper, by and by. The third stories are used for cloak and hat rooms. Three musical bands are so placed as to " fill " the rooms occupied by the guests. Their object is to keep time for the dancers, dancing being the chief business of the evening—*Anglice* morning. How people manage to dance where they have barely room to stand still, is no part of their historian's affair. Whoever wants a solution of that mystery, must ask Brown.

After the musicians have poured forth a steady stream of sweet sounds for three mortal hours ; after the dancers have pushed and elbowed and thrust themselves against each other for the same length of time; and after the older inhabitants have jostled and crowded and stared at each other (attempting now and then a compliment or an execration, but never making a syllable audible in the overwhelming din) for the same three hours : the setting in of a human current begins to be perceptible somewhere, and the mass finds itself moving in the direction of a stairway which lands near the supper-rooms.

Here, the scene defies not only the historian's pen,

but the poet's imagination. A solid cordon of "gentlemen" is formed around the tables, each of whom looks out for number one. Each obviously went there for that purpose, and for no other purpose. Each, being there, grabs what he can, and bolts what he grabs. When he has finished or become sated with one plate, as there is no room for it on the table, he pitches it under the table, and tries something else. Each man thus disposes of a share of some eight or ten dishes, gives the same attention to the several varieties of wines, except not throwing the empty glasses under the table, and then—*would* retire, to give somebody else a chance, if he could. What all the ladies and the remainder of the gentlemen do for *their* supper, beyond standing there crowded, squeezed and jostled for another hour, is a problem for the aforesaid poet's imagination.

It is now four o'clock, and Brown is as efficient in helping these good people off, as he was in helping them in.

The ball was a brilliant success. It was more than that. It was the most delightful ball on the one hand, and the most magnificent ball on the other hand, and if there were a *third* " hand " it would have been the most *recherché* ball on that hand, ever given, ever known, ever heard of in America.

Why it was all this : *why* it received such enthusiastic and admiring laudation, is, again, the province of that poet's imagination to discover.

Brown very properly came in for a share of the honors. He had exceeded himself. For that matter, and if such a thing were possible, he had cast himself into the shade. He expanded, elongated, eructated. He received a medal of blue and gold, with innumerable quarterings and three donkeys rampant.

The Does were at this ball. So were the Roes. So were the Swifts, the Perkinses, the McPhersons, the Barbers, the Grays, the Whites, the Greens, the Blacks. Everybody was there. Nobody that is anybody was *not* there. Gossip and scandal were there incarnate, exuberant, ubiquitous; but they could not develop. The roar of the entertainment squelched them for the time being. But time to come did for them what heat did for the trumpet of Munchausen's trumpeter: it brought out the din-suppressed sentiments as fire melted out the frozen music.

Mrs. Swift, who was always to be found on the winning side, thought that family reconciliations were blessed things, especially where dear children were concerned. For her part, she coincided with—— strange! she could never remember the names of authors!—with—with—well, never mind the author! the words are " Blessed are the peace-makers."

Mrs. Roe quietly reminded her aunt Swift that *that* was Macaulay.

Mr. Smith ventured to differ—Byron.

Miss Bloomfield was confident she had heard that at Wallack's.

Young Roberts was sorry to contradict any one, especially a lady: but as that line was in his last German lesson, there could be no dispute about the author—Gaiety.

Mrs. Doctor Perkins was happy to concur in opinion with Mrs. Swift as to peace-making; but she really was under an impression that Mrs. Swift had favored, instead of opposing, the separation of the Jenkinses.

Mrs. Swift, in reply, was willing to undertake almost anything for an old friend; but Mrs. Perkins must excuse Mrs. Swift if Mrs. Swift declined to be responsible for the defects of an old friend's memory.

Louisa Jenkins was a companion of Mrs. Swift from childhood; she was her dearest and best friend: and how she, Mrs. Swift, could do an injury to her dearest and best friend, candor itself must judge.

Other circles of gossips, which had not among them any friends of Mrs. Jenkins from childhood, took a different view of the reconciliation. The ball was a success, certainly. No one could doubt that. And such a ball was conclusive as to public opinion. But these reconciliations between people of a certain age, often had a motive and were not always permanent. This was a patching up of a very old rent. And putting new cloth into old garments was very often only jumping out of the frying-pan into the fire.

Men don't usually trouble themselves much about the smaller grades of scandal; and among them, the Jenkins matter attracted but little attention. Doctor Perkins had occasion to say, now and then, that the least said is the soonest mended: which, as the Jenkinses had recently withdrawn from his church, and connected themselves with a clergyman of a different calibre, was considered quite a moderate comment. Richard Roe had rather more to say, because he felt that it was expected of him. Richard's charity was ever large and demonstrative—when it cost nothing, and when it was not needed by those who had in any sense wronged, offended, or thwarted *him* or *his*. "It is really beautiful," he said, "to see two people who in former days had so often taken sweet counsel together and walked to the house of God in company, returning again, as with harps in their hands, into the sanctuary, and kneeling before the Lord that bought them!" Richard, however, couldn't quite understand why they preferred, of late, the preaching of the reverend Mr. Duncan; who never, to Richard's poor judgment, seemed to have got hold of the root of the matter. But. Mr. Duncan was comparatively young. He might improve. He had a pious mother, whose name was Rachel.

CHAPTER XIV.

WILSON remained for a time in quiet, unobtrusive retirement. By the attention of Mrs. Pinch, he was supplied with all the newspapers, daily and weekly, all the magazines, and all the new novels. These occupied the leisure hours of every day. For a change, he took observations through the blinds of his front windows, and made quite a study of the carts that frequented the vicinity: the milk carts, wood carts, fruit carts and fishermen's carts. He soon knew the drivers and their horses, and could make an approximate estimate of the amounts of their daily sales.

The grocer's shop, directly over the way, was a great resource to him. The grocer, additionally to the usual variety of family articles, kept for sale imported wines and liquors of the very first quality; and probably he sold these by the small quantity, for a large number of laboring men called there daily, each of whom uniformly came out of the shop smacking his lips and wiping his mouth with his hand or his sleeve—or his handkerchief if he had one. The grocer also made a display of vegetables and fruits of the season, which were exhibited around the door. And Wilson came to be familiar with the faces of the customers of these articles; among whom was a ragged urchin about seven years old, who passed by every morning on his way to school and contrived to steal an apple, regularly, for lunch.

These things might have proved very stupid to a spectator who had the ordinary powers of locomotion and the freedom of the city; but to Wilson they furnished substantial recreation and amusement. A certain amount of physical exercise, over and above these mental enjoyments, was however necessary to health; and Wilson attained this by using a pair of dumb-bells in the daytime, and by long walks on dark and rainy evenings. Meantime, he thought over a variety of plans for a journey, or a foreign residence, but without coming to any conclusion.

Mrs. Pinch had occasional interviews with Wilson: and although the aid she received from him as the price of his meals was an important addition to her income, his presence began to give her vague apprehensions of danger; and she thought that whenever he could with security to himself change his quarters, she would be greatly relieved.

The task of managing the children was various. At first they both manifested great curiosity to see their uncle Sam. But as he was kept very much out of their way, was always an invalid and got up a reputation for being more or less ill-tempered, Phebe soon ceased to care about him. But Tom was not so easily disenchanted. An uncle was, to his apprehension, suggestive of odd sixpences, a new penknife, and something for Christmas. Besides, Tom was a dealer in medicine, and his inquiring mind kept him on the lookout for the ailments of those who called for remedies. He soon learned what was good for a cold, for a headache, for a toothache. He began to have some notion of fevers, chills, palpitations; and he learned that general debility was a favorite disease with Mr. Scalpel's customers. In short, he was rapidly getting to be a doctor; and, as his uncle Sam was sick, all he had to do was to find out what ailed him, and he might have the luck to cure him: a feat that, in Tom's judgment, would " pay, splendid."

"Mother," said he, one night, as he was preparing to go to bed, "what's the matter with uncle Sam?"

"Oh, he has a kind of a pain," replied Mrs. Pinch, in a tone intended to discourage further inquiry.

"Pain, eh?" echoed Tom. "Where is it, I wonder?"

"Go to bed, you foolish boy," answered Mrs. Pinch. "What do you know about pain?"

"I guess I know considerable," rejoined Tom stoutly; "and if you'll tell me the simtoms, mother, maybe I can cure him."

The audacity of this suggestion astonished the widow. And the boy's pertinacity rather alarmed her. But finally, reasoning with rapidity back to the cause of his meddling, and catching the ludicrous feature of it, to wit, that Tom had smelt medicine long enough to fancy he could prescribe it professionally, she burst into a fit of laughter.

That so disconcerted poor Tom that, for the time, he gave up his castle in the air and tumbled into bed. But the incident didn't tend toward relieving the widow's apprehensions in the matter of uncle Sam's sojourn.

One cold, blustering night, when the wind and rain were sharply contending with each other and with all substantial objects in their reach; just as the clocks were striking eleven and as Wilson was preparing for bed, he was astonished at hearing a heavy and irregular step creaking up his staircase: and immediately afterward, some one knocked and rattled loudly at his door. He snatched a revolver and a policeman's club from a drawer, and laid them at hand on a table.

"Open the door, G—— d—— you!" cried a voice without.

"Who's there?" demanded Wilson, as firmly as he could.

"If you don't open the door, d—— you," the voice continued, with increasing vehemence of thundering against the inanimate obstacle, "I'll let you know who's there, by G——."

By this time, Wilson became aware that whoever the person might be, he was a man very considerably the worse for liquor. And knowing that a sober and resolute man, six feet high, with arms at command, could stand in no personal danger from any one in a state of intoxication, he unfastened and opened the door.

And, as he had foreseen, he was confronted by a man about half-seas over. The stranger was of medium size, probably forty years of age, ill-dressed, soaked with rain, and exhibiting a countenance brutalized by years of intemperance. And additionally to the coarse ferocity of his drunken features, his face was now inflamed with rage at being refused an entrance into what he seemed to imagine was his own apartment.

"Why the h—— didn't you open the door, you d—— b——?" he exclaimed, as if addressing a woman, though no woman was there. Then, suddenly changing his tone as he found himself face to face with a powerful man with strange surroundings, he added, "who the h—— are you, mister?"

"Somebody who'll put you where you'll stay put, if you don't stop this infernal noise," cried Wilson sternly, grasping the club, and flourishing it around the drunkard's head till it whistled again. Indeed, it was by the hardest that he refrained from dealing the intruder a conclusive blow; for the danger to himself of a row at this late hour, involving a visit from the police and a probable discovery of his indentity, rendered him nearly as much beside himself with wrath as his opponent was with rum.

But a drunken man is not easily intimidated, nor was this fellow quite so far gone with drink as Wilson at first supposed. On the contrary, with a quickness and agility for which Wilson was totally unprepared, the stranger sprang aside from the club, made a rush under Wilson's arm, and laid hold of the pistol which Wilson had just before placed on the table. Retreating to the farther side of the room, he then brought the weapon to bear on Wilson, and stood ready to shoot.

"Now d—— you! who are you, and what are you doing here?" he said in a loud tone, but not quite so boisterous as his previous address.

At this instant Mrs. Pinch rushed into the room, followed by Phebe and Tom: all having been startled out of their beds by the uproar. The new comers saw at a glance that the intruder was Jo. Rabbit,

who with his wife and children had recently occupied
and been ejected from the rooms now held by Wilson. The man had been "out on a spree ;" and, following the instinct of former associations, had in his
drunkenness taken a road "home" that was more
familiar to him than the way to his new locality in
another part of the town.

Mrs. Pinch appreciated the true state of the case
in a moment, and saw the importance of bringing
Rabbit to comprehend it, if in his present state he
could be made to comprehend anything. With a
courage that is peculiar to her sex in emergencies of
extreme peril—for, though most women have a child-ish dread of fire-arms in friendly or careless hands,
they will stand firmly against them when in the
hands of an enemy—with this courage, which seems
to be in woman rather an instinct than a sentiment,
Mrs. Pinch placed herself directly in front of the
pistol and placed her hand on its barrel.

"Rabbit," said she in a perfectly quiet tone, "you
forget. This is not your room. You all moved away
from here—don't you remember ?"

The calm tone and manner of a weak woman who
was braving a danger that few men would care to
encounter, coupled with the fact that Mrs. Pinch and
the Rabbits were old friends, brought the ruffian to a
parley. He withdrew the pistol from her hand, took
a step to the right so as to stand free with regard to
Wilson, and thus held himself in readiness to use the
weapon, while, nevertheless he said to his antagonist
in moderate and conciliatory terms :

"See here, mister ; suppose we ground arms and
take a drink ?"

An angry reply was at the very lips of Wilson ;

but he repressed it. A pistol-shot with whatever result, or a prolongation of the quarrel on whatever terms, could not fail to end in an interference of the police; which above all things was to be dreaded. Wilson, therefore, met the exigency with great coolness and address, resolving on the instant to give this fellow not only "a drink," but so many of them as should effectually wash out any distinct recollection of this night's experiences.

"I agree to that, my boy," he said, in answer to Rabbit's proposition; and, tossing his club into a corner, advanced to receive the pistol from Rabbit, which the latter handed to him without hesitation.

"Mrs. Pinch," Wilson continued, "we will not ask you to join us; and as for the children, they ought to be in bed." Then he added, in a whisper, as she was retiring, "keep all quiet. I'll manage this fellow!"

Wilson cleared the table of papers and brought from the back room a bottle of brandy with two tumblers and a pitcher of water. He filled first for himself, mixing the weaker element in much the larger proportion. Then, taking up the other tumbler, he observed that there was dust in it, and he went again to the back room—to rinse the dust out. He held his left hand well around it when he returned and hastily poured into it a small quantity of the brandy: when, as if recollecting that his visitor might prefer to adjust the proportions for himself, he pushed it toward him, saying:

"You know best how you like it mixed."

Considering that the night was wet and cold, and that Rabbit had not taken a drop since morning, that personage thought it would be prudent to fortify his stomach with an extra charge. He accordingly mixed about three brandies to one water and tossed it off with infinite relish, wishing there might be plenty more where that came from and good luck to the gentleman that owned it.

The brandy in that bottle must have been very strong, or Wilson, in rinsing dust out of the tumbler, must have left something in the tumbler more potent than dust: for in a short time, Rabbit was as fast asleep as a man in health possibly could be. So fast, indeed, that Wilson, after making a preliminary experiment or two, was satisfied that *nothing* in the usual course of events would wake him for several hours.

That being sufficiently ascertained, Wilson exchanged his own boots for slippers, so that he might tread lightly down the stairs. He then grasped Rabbit by the shoulders and dragged him slowly through the door, down the stairway, into the street. He returned for Rabbit's hat: looked up and down for straggling passengers, and for vigilant policemen—for Wilson knew what every one knows; few things are more difficult to be got at, than a policeman when you want him: and few things are more omnipresent than the same individual when you don't want him. In this case, the state of the weather and the elements, which were so uncongenial to Rabbit's stomach, proved equally dangerous to the outward man of the guardians of the peace. In other words, the street was clear and silent, except for the wind and rain.

Wilson therefore, with little trouble and no risk, dragged his man around the first corner and placed him in a half-sitting position on the leeward side of a grocer's shop, against the door, and under the protection of sundry empty boxes and barrels, and an awning overhead. He then crowded the fellow's hat over his head, and made his way home again much faster than he came.

It may be supposed that though the children of Mrs. Pinch went back to their beds and soon forgot the evening's excitement in sleep, their mother, who better understood the dangers of this affair, watched anxiously for its termination. Carefully as Wilson had managed, not a movement escaped her vigilant ear. She *supposed* she understood the dragging down stairs of Rabbit's inanimate body; though, considering the daring character of Wilson and his determination to brave any risk rather than be re-arrested, she could not but feel an intense solicitude until he returned from the street. She met him at the door as he came in, and followed him up to his room.

Wilson could not prudently keep, nor did he desire to keep, the details secret from Mrs. Pinch. He, therefore, stated them, fully: explaining the dusty tumbler by remarking that he put into it a small quantity of morphine; which, without affecting the taste of the brandy, rendered it powerfully narcotic. On the whole, Rabbit was served right. No serious harm could come to him; and the chances of his so far remembering the events of the evening as to be able to give any intelligible or credible account of them, even if when he became sober, he was disposed to do so—were very slight. And when he was sober, and on any ordinary occasion, there was no probability of his repeating his visit.

This really rational view of the case gradually quieted the apprehensions of both parties to the conference, greatly as they had at first been alarmed. They would take more care about keeping the outside door fastened; and would keep a lookout for stray visitors. But on the whole, no cause for any new measures seemed to arise from this startling occurrence.

CHAPTER XV.

THE honest Dutchman who rejoiced in the proprietorship of the shop, at the portal of which Mr. Joseph Rabbit had been deposited for safe keeping, was an early riser. Moreover, his residence was within the same premises as those where he transacted his business: in plainer terms, he lived over the shop. And when he and his boy set about opening the shop, on the morning now in question, they found that the door, which usually stuck a little at the bottom, swung inward without. any pulling, and was incontinently followed by the body of a man with his hat over his eyes; which body, being unable to support itself, and being suddenly deprived of what had for some hours supported it, lazily measured its length on the floor.

Intoxicated men, at proper hours for being intoxicated, are so common about these grocers' groggeries that this incident in the abstract would not have been alarming to the honest Dutchman. But the thing was ill-timed: so far, unusual: and it could not be regarded in the abstract. Taken in the concrete, which was the only way it could be taken, the incident *was* more or less alarming, because the case might be something more than intoxication. Still, as the body was warm, flexible and capable of breathing; capable, also, of a satisfactory grunt as it came to the floor; and as neither wound nor blood was visible, the alarm was short lived.

It was a clear case of liquor; and moreover, a case for which the honest Dutchman fĕlt himself somewhat responsible. For although this rum customer had not been seen on the premises for some weeks until the immediately preceding night, yet, formerly, he had been a frequent participant of the Dutchman's hospitalities, and on the night referred to, had found his way back again to the old haunt. But the Dutchman had seen him depart in pretty good case about eleven o'clock, and he could not imagine how he came to be here now.

But Hans was a practical man. And so soon as he found that he could not find how the drunken man came there, he set about finding out what was much more to his purpose: namely, how to get rid of him ?

It is an old and veritable maxim that there is no friendship in trade: that is to say, in business, every man must look out for himself. Hans understood this. Besides, he was a man of ready wit: and he had, moreover, read in his own native tongue the Arabian nights—as will shortly be obvious. Hans might, indeed, have considered that as Rabbit was an old customer who had put him in the way of taking care of so many pennies that they now amounted to many pounds; and, as turn about is fair play, and a few shillings of old profits expended in sending this poor man home on a cart would hardly be missed: Hans *might* have considered these things, but he didn't.

He looked into the street somewhat as Wilson had done on the preceding night, and for a similar purpose. It was yet early. The morning was dark. Rain was falling. His old competitor in business, whose shop stood obliquely across the way, distant about one hundred and fifty feet, was not yet astir.

"Dietrick," said he to the boy, "catch him by te feet, whiles I grabs him by te shoulters, and haf him ofer to Schmidt's in no time. If tey see us, ten ve are takin him to te police. If not, by tamn! Schmidt vill fint von customer ven he ton't vant him!"

Not much sooner said than done. And Rabbit was deposited at Schmidt's unopened shop door, in a position very nearly as comfortable as he lately occupied at Hans's.

The experiences of Schmidt on opening his shop door were so similar to the experiences of Hans in a like case, that a particular description of the latter cannot be needed. Rabbit's experiences were also substantially the same in both cases : excepting that as the door-sill of Schmidt was raised about six inches above the shop floor, Rabbit's head and shoulders had so much further to fall, and his body lay so much the more uncomfortably by reason of a six inch curve of the back in the wrong direction. This circumstance made it necessary for Schmidt, on the ground of common humanity, to pull the body into a change of position ; and as he had no spare room inside of the shop, he dragged him outwardly and laid him on the front step. This was a task of some difficulty ; because Schmidt's boy had been kept awake all night by cramp in the stomach and over-slept himself this morning, leaving Schmidt, who was a very small man, to do the work without assist-ance.

The calamity of Rabbit—if it can be called such—
was a windfall to the little boys in that neighborhood. Boys delight in the unexpected and the terrible. And here was a case of murder, or something
much like it, at their very doors—as, one after another, the urchins straggled out of their dens to take
the fresh air and whistle up or run down an appetite
for their breakfasts.

A crowd, very respectable as to numbers, whatever
might be the fitting epithet for their social position,
soon gathered around the unfortunate Schmidt's
door. In turn, by and by, this crowd attracted the
attention of a stray policeman, who previously was
making his way home on the sly, by reason of an
over-night's delinquency : but who now saw an unexpected opportunity to make use of his official prerogative, and cover up recent deficiencies by a display
of present vigilance. He solemnly reproved the
crowd for their vain, idle, unfeeling curiosity : he
vociferously impressed a passing cartman into the
public service ; and, having employed some of the
bystanders to place Rabbit on the cart, he mounted
guard over him and triumphantly drove off to the
station house.

The victorious policeman had no desire to over-
estimate his services on the present occasion. If anything, he would prefer to underestimate them. His
manifold perils of life and limb in capturing the
redoubtable Rabbit, might perhaps become any other
narrator better than himself. But unfortunately, as
no witnesses were present, to tell their story or to
confirm his, and as Rabbit was hardly in a condition to contradict either : he, the policeman must
throw himself on the indulgence of the captain

while he delivered a round and entirely unvarnished tale.

The captain considered the story a good one—rather too good to be true. And he sent a recommendation to head-quarters, that the policeman be rewarded by a forfeiture of three days' pay for being absent from roll-call.

Rabbit was not altogether unknown to the department. And this was by no means his first appearance on these boards in his favorite character: though here, as elsewhere, the performance came off at an unusual hour. As he was, however, insensible from intoxication, the committing officer postponed the official questions and reprimand, and summarily ordered Rabbit to his old quarters with a wholesome and necessary bit of advice: namely, to sleep himself sober and be in a hurry about it.

If Wilson had been present in the character of an invisible spectator, he might have had some misgiving as to Rabbit's prolonged pursuit of sleep under difficulties. He might have had a doubt as to the quantity of morphine with which he replaced the dust in that tumbler. Yet, he was familiar with the commodity. He had, years ago, acquired the very bad habit of dosing himself with it; and, since his arrest, he had kept himself provided with it through the agency of friends—that being the only favor he asked of them. He was so habituated to its use, that he could dispense with almost anything else, rather than that. What he now had, was part of a liberal supply procured in reference to the contingency of a sudden journey that he might, at any hour, be called on to take. *Could* he, however, in estimating its strength by his own power of endurance, increased by long use—could he have miscalculated its effect on a man who, probably, had never before swallowed a drop of it?

———

The incidents of the preceding night were not happily adapted to check the spirit of inquiry recently developed in Thomas Pinch. He resumed the subject at breakfast.

"Mother," said he, "does uncle Sam look like my father?"

"Like your father!" echoed the widow in great astonishment: "what do you ask that for?"

"Because," answered Tom, as much abashed at his mother's astonishment as his mother could be amazed at the inquiry, "I suppose people's fathers and uncles always looks alike: and seeing I don't remember how *my* father looked, I only asked."

"My son," rejoined the widow, abashed in turn at her own want of address in maintaining Wilson's assumed relationship, "my uncles are the brothers of *my* father; not yours: and, to be particular, my uncles would be your great uncles."

"Oho!" cried Tom, relieved. "All right. I see. Only, uncle Sam don't look to be old enough for that."

"Tom," pursued the mother, evasively, "what do you want to bother so much about your uncles? They don't bother about you."

"More shame for 'em, if they haven't got little boys of their own," persisted Tom. "Now, I should think uncle Sam would want us up in his room sometimes, and he such a sick man, and nobody to play with. Anyhow, he didn't look much sick last night, standing up against old Rabbit's pistol and he nothing but a club in his hand."

"Why, you know, Tom," interposed Phebe, "they can keep firing all the time with a club, and a pistol don't go off but once or twice."

"Hurrah for you, Phebe," cried Tom, graciously giving his sister full credit for an idea that was not so much out of the way as it might be. "But suppose the feller with the pistol gets a bullet on to you first? What's the club good for then?"

"The man with the club," responded Phebe, nothing daunted, "musn't wait for that. He must rush in."

"Good again!" cried Tom. "But, you see, that's just what uncle Sam couldn't do, and that's what I look at. He was away over here, and Rabbit had the pistol right at him, over there. I guess, if we hadn't come in, there'd a been a muss, though! But I shouldn't think, mother," Tom continued, running from one thing to another seemingly with no better purpose than to relieve his overburdened mind, "I shouldn't think uncle Sam would be taking drinks with that old Rabbit."

"Don't you know, my son," said the widow, "that Rabbit was drunk, and that was the easiest way to get rid of him?"

"I should rather think," rejoined Tom, expanding with the conviction that he was about to utter a moral reflection, "that *that* was the easiest way to hold on to him."

Tom uttered this significant apothegm gravely and without the faintest notion that there was anything funny in it. But his mother and sister caught the ludicrous effect of the play on the words, and began to laugh.

A person older than Tom and withal better versed in repartee, would have accepted this laugh as a tribute. But Tom understood it in no other light than as an affront to his dignity. However, as two upon one are long odds in an argument, and as a laugh is the hardest thing in the world to argue against, Tom wisely concluded to pocket the offence, lest by going further, he should fare worse. Besides, the expiration of the time allowed him for breakfast, furnished an admirable pretext for a retreat, which he accomplished without being pursued by the enemy.

From the moment of Wilson's arrival, one of the most perplexing problems was, how to keep the curiosity of these children in a quiescent state? How to gratify it, without increasing it? And, above all, how to prevent the arrangement with uncle Sam from being so interesting to them, that they should make it a subject of comment to third persons? This was a knotty point for mother and uncle. They had much solicitous consultation upon it. And at length they decided that the simplest course was the safest: namely, that the uncle was in town on a little private business, and his being there must not be mentioned to any one outside of the house.

CHAPTER XVI.

The officer's intimation to Rabbit that he had better sleep himself sober, was given in a friendly spirit. Yet the good counsel slept in a foolish ear: at least, an unconscious ear. But that was not the fault of the officer. Was it for him to find ears, brains, or apprehension for his prisoners? Yet, nevertheless,—and the fact deserves honorable mention, as an exception to the general rule of gratuitous advice—although Rabbit was unconscious of the admonition, he gave heed to it: he followed the offered advice: at least, he slept away with all his might; and if sleep didn't bring sobriety, it wasn't for want of hard snoring.

Meantime, Rabbit's accommodations were of the most substantial character. Oak and iron, with the exception of straw and woollen, were the frailest materials on the premises. No doubt, therefore, they would last his time. But his time was of the longest. The apartment he occupied was arranged for the accommodation of perhaps twelve persons; and whenever the room was full, the occupants, if not strictly bedfellows, were terribly near it. In this instance, absentees had become the companions of Rabbit, and again become absentees, while he slept on.

The rule of confinement applicable to parties found

intoxicated in the streets, is a shut-up in the Tombs for ten days ; or, a fine of ten dollars : at the prisoner's option.   But the " time " of a common drunkard is never worth a dollar a day to anybody but the man who sells him liquor : hence, he usually finds it advantageous, in a pecuniary point of view, to serve his time out, for the authorities will not permit him to starve while he is " in."

At length, without knowing where he was, or what o'clock it was, Rabbit—in the dead waste and middle of the night—returned to a semi-consciousness of being somewhere.   He probably had been dreaming of some dear friend, for he thrust out his right hand with some force, saying,

" Damn it, I tell you no !"

Whatever were the merits of the question thus summarily voted upon, the *noes* decidedly had it. For the clinched hand of the toper came into rude contact with the nose of a very near neighbor, who had been deposited by the side of Rabbit about two hours previously.

As it chanced, this neighbor, though ostensibly committed for drunkenness, had in reality been playing old soger for a night's lodging at the city's expense, and rations for ten days thereafter : his reason being the same as is given by a bank when they protest a note—" no funds."   He was therefore easily waked ; and had, in fact, already opened his eyes at the first two words of Rabbit's exclamation, herein-above quoted.   He saw nothing when he opened his eyes, because the gas lights were turned down to a small point.   But the moment he shut them again, which he did at the broad hint of Rabbit's fist, he saw stars innumerable.   There is something very curious in this faculty of seeing stars with one's eyes shut. Probably, electricity is at the bottom of it.

Whether owing to the general darkness of the place, or to the obfuscation incident to a sudden blow between the eyes, the individual thus emphatically assailed, as he half rose in his couch for vengeance on the rude disturber of his pillow, pitched into his immediate neighbor on the right—which, however, was the wrong, because Rabbit lay on his left. This new customer had been brought in, comfortably tipsy, early in the evening, and was now in prime condition to be roused up for a fight. The aggressor had the best chance in the contest, by virtue of having taken the initiative and put in the first blow; but his assault was so ill-directed, owing to his confusion and impetuosity, that he failed to gain the full advantage of that movement and really accomplished nothing beyond waking his antagonist. In both senses he waked up the wrong passenger.

The contest was exceedingly animated, for the men were well matched. Their position at the outset rendered the usual formality of knocking each other down, inconvenient and unnecessary, as both were down already: so, it was literally rough and tumble. Their tumbling soon brought them into contact with other strange bedfellows—for, if the platform on which they all lay was in any sense composed of movable parts, they were placed so closely together as to be practically but one—and, in an inappreciable space of material time, some eight or ten men became involved in the *mêlée:* each hitting and being hit, cursing and being cursed, as rapidly as the fists and tongues of the several belligerents could fly.

The tongues had this advantage, that the want of light offered no obstacle to their free exercise.

When rowdies are entertaining themselves with a fight in the street, the mere appearance of a police-man has a sedative effect on some of the combatants, while the strong arm of arrest brings the more per-severing to terms. But when the same men are arrested and locked up, the mere appearance of policemen has very little effect upon them: arrest and lock up having already done their worst. Conse-quently, neither the sudden lighting up of the arena, nor the entrance of a squad of city-guardians who rushed in to ascertain the cause of the disturbance, had any beneficial effect on the present war. Nor did the threats and warnings of the officers produce any better result: for the reason, perhaps, that not a syllable of threat or warning could be heard. The noise of those who fought, exceeded that of those who sought to quell the fight, in the proportion of two to one.

Fortunately for the prisoners, the officer in com-mand had some compassion for the drunken fools under his charge; and instead of directing the sum-mary process of an attack with clubs, he ordered one of his subordinates to unwind the coil of hose attached to the Croton water cock for security against fire, and to bring him the pipe. This was the work of a moment. The officer then brought the pipe to aim on a group where the heads were thickest, turned the stop, and let fly. The effect was terrific! Water flies from a hose-pipe at the rate of about two hundred feet in a second: and, allowing the muzzle to be a quarter of an inch in diameter, you will easily see what an amount of the fluid, at that stunning rate of speed, must have dashed remorselessly into the eyes, ears and mouths of the inebriates, and how utterly they must have been overwhelmed by it. Of course, the fight was at an end.

"Now," said the officer, "stow yourselves away in your bunks. And the first man who speaks one word, good, bad or indifferent, shall have a broken head for his trouble. You may thank your stars that your heads are not all broken as it is."

The prisoners were still in a state of perplexity, as to how they became involved in this predicament. But they had sense enough to see that, however they became so, the officer was in earnest, and that their better part of valor was—submission. Accordingly, before many minutes had elapsed, they all were, or appeared to be, fast asleep.

Doctor Perkins may be as magnificent as he pleases on the "infernal Institution." He may delight his gaping hearers with the details of its degrading effect on " our colored brethren," till they all honestly believe that slavery is the only sin now existing in this glorious republic. Yet, here is a sin at Doctor Perkins's very elbow, which reduces men below the slave, below anything that bears the form of humanity. Which makes them unreasoning brutes, lying about the streets, to be carted thence into " pens " where they necessarily receive the treatment of brutes. Which alternately makes them monsters and slaves—monsters, at their own hovels, where they inflict on their wives and children worse treatment than the driver can inflict on the negro :

slaves, when imprisoned for drunkenness and requiring treatment more degrading than the chain and the lash.   And this view of intemperance involves results only to the individual subject and his belongings : whereas, almost every offence in the calendar of crime is directly traceable to the same source : which, therefore, becomes the heaviest curse of our social organization.

The " apostle of temperance " may here raise his head majestically, and say " have I not labored to subdue this curse, and spent my time and my strength for its overthrow ? and warned you, oh ye people, what would come of it, if ye would not join hands with me in this holy crusade ?"

Unfortunately, Messrs. Apostles, that is all true ! If you, and such as you, had *not* attached yourselves and your ultraism to a cause that was a " holy crusade " at the outset ; if you, and such as you, had not sacrilegiously repudiated the practice of our Saviour by sanctimoniously attempting to transform wine into water ; and if you, and such as you, had let alone and stood aloof from an enterprise that was doing *better than well* when you obtruded your officious tinkering into its conduct, and finally by your zeal without knowledge brought it down to be a hissing, a scorn, a byword for all people : *then* the spirits of the great originators of that enterprise would not have reason to look down from their high places and " curse " *you* for preventing the extermination of the curse.

The intemperance of the rabid " Temperance Reformers " has put back the progress of rational " temperance " for half a century.

CHAPTER XVII.

THE task undertaken by Snap proved to be no sinecure. His project was based on the theory that Wilson had not left the city, and that theory he saw no occasion to abandon. On the contrary, the continued absence of intelligence of the fugitive from any quarter, confirmed him more and more in his original belief. But, though this conviction was essential to the search, it by itself was of little practical value. To be even *certain* that Wilson was in New-York, was only a short step toward finding him.

Snap had remarked to Mr. Doe that this search was to be a matter of shoe-leather, umbrellas and eyes. And his remark was quite correct. Shoe-leather had suffered. Umbrellas had suffered. And if eyes had not suffered, their exemption could be attributed to nothing but the superiority of their materials. They certainly had been kept well at work.

Snap's want of success could be no matter of reasonable surprise. The man had very little to go upon. A daguerreotype likeness of the bust of a person with whom he had no previous acquaintance: which person would keep snug by daylight, would never venture out of doors except in darkness and in some one of a hundred possible disguises, and

would be in the streets only at intervals and never
at any given point in the area of a large city for
more than a second of time—this was the sum total
of the case: and this presented rather an aggrega-
tion of discouragements than a ground of hope for
success.

Snap held occasional interviews with Messrs. Doe
and Traverse, and the three strained their mental vision to the utmost, to penetrate the mystery; but it
remained a mystery still.

"One thing in this business," said Snap to his employers, "puzzles me more than all the rest. And
that is, where the fellow gets money from."

"Money!"said Doe and Traverse, both in a breath.

"Money," repeated Snap, quietly and positively.
"He has to live and to pay somebody for helping
him to keep hid so close. Now, you see, where does
the money come from?"

On this hint, Doe and Traverse exchanged glances.
And, money being mentioned, it occurred to Doe to
hand over to Snap a second (or third) instalment of
the promised two hundred and fifty dollars. Mr.
Doe said that he and Traverse would study up the
money question, and meantime, Snap must continue
his task.

"There," said Doe to Traverse, after Snap withdrew, "there is the finger of Richard Roe again."

"No doubt of it," replied Traverse. "Our inquiries have led us to *know* that Wilson has no
friends able to supply him with money. There certainly is some dark complication between those two
men; and if we could but get a clue to it, we
would make short work of 'John Doe against Richard Roe.'"

"That's very true," said Doe. "Oh, if we could but get that clue! By the way, wouldn't it be a good joke if Tom could help us out of this money mystery? He did wonders on the chloroform."

"Tom happens to deal in chloroform," answered Traverse: "which makes all the difference. Money matters, I imagine, are rather out of his line."

The conversation was interrupted by the entrance of Miss Doe and her niece, accompanied by the reverend Mr. Duncan, all just returned from a walk.

Mutual salutations and explanations being disposed of, Mr. Duncan was invited to remain for tea. His relation with the Does—pastor and parishioners—rendered him always a welcome guest: and as he was a widower without children, who therefore disappointed no one by absence from his own house, he often availed himself of the welcome. It is proper to remark that Mr. Duncan had attained the age when many clergymen attain the D.D.; but he had more than once *refused* that proffered distinction.

"We have just been speaking of the Jenkinses," said Miss Doe to her brother. "They left their own church and came to ours so suddenly, they must have had good reasons for the movement."

"I should think," replied Doe, "that their having endured Doctor Perkins's monomania for seven years furnishes at least seven good reasons for the change. If *I* were to work out the problem, I should multiply the seven by fifty-two."

Mr. Duncan, wishing to lead the conversation away from the merits of a brother clergyman, remarked that the Jenkins children were very interesting and attractive.

Jane thought little Fred Jenkins was one of the sweetest boys she ever saw. Traverse thought that little Mary was entitled to the preference. And Miss Doe altogether preferred Robert, who was the head of the group in age, size and deportment. The Jenkinses had evidently made a lodgment in the regard of the Does.

"I never knew much of the differences between the doctor and his wife," said Miss Doe, " although when a matter is so much talked of as that has been, one must hear something. But I am glad to find among our friends a disposition to forget what the parties themselves have reconciled. The peace of families is of as much importance as the peace of nations."

"Much more so," said Mr. Duncan, "to the individuals immediately concerned. I think there must have been busy meddlers and bad advisers in that affair."

"Of whom, in the latter category," said Doe, " I'll answer for it, Doctor Perkins was one."

"I have no knowledge of that," replied Mr. Duncan, "and I had no such thought when I made my remark. I should hope that if he had anything to do with it, he fearlessly performed his duty."

"Unfortunately," returned Doe, " that's just what he never did on any occasion. He never committed himself to anything but the wrong side of the nigger-question—wrong, I mean, in his way of treating it."

"My good friend," interposed Mr. Duncan, " let me keep the discussion within the limits I contemplated. Speaking generally, family troubles are always aggravated by outside 'friends,' as they call themselves. To be forced into confidences of this nature, is one of the incidents of my profession: and I have seldom known an instance where the difficulties have not been rendered almost hopeless by the interference of third parties. Indeed, third parties often create the difficulty in the first place. I have many a time thought that if I could persuade the people of my congregation to mind their own business, as St. Paul wished the Thessalonians to do, I should have rendered them the greatest temporal service in the power of a clergyman. Again, it is a fatal error for a wife to carry her supposed grievances to indiscreet friends. When that step is taken, the evil is well nigh past remedy."

"Is it only ' a wife ' who falls into that error, Mr. Duncan ?" inquired Miss Doe, sufficiently alive to the "rights of women."

"I am quite sure," replied the clergyman, "that you, Miss Doe, will not suspect me of injustice or discourtesy to your sex, if I remark, that wives are much more prone to jealousy than their husbands. In my capacity of a professional and confidential referee, I certainly have found it so."

"Perhaps," Miss Doe intimated, "they more frequently have cause for being jealous."

"Still again," persisted Mr. Duncan, "I must say I think not. Of all the complaints of that sort that my position has compelled me to hear, I have found few that had any real foundation; and even when there was some ground—— "

"And even when there was some ground," interrupted Doe, as Mr. Duncan hesitated how to characterize the exceptions, "I'll answer for it, if the wives had some wrong, the husbands had much provocation."

A smile which showed itself, on the pleasant features of Mr. Duncan, in spite of his efforts to repress it, betrayed the probable accuracy of Doe's conjecture.

"Pshaw, John!" exclaimed Miss Doe, "you are an unbeliever in everything, but the superiority of your own sex. But, Mr. Duncan," she continued, turning to the clergyman, "since you are so well aware of the delinquencies of our sex, I think you should propose a remedy."

"I assure you, my dear Miss Doe," he replied, "that when I find myself in the unpleasant predicament of listening to a complaining wife, I use my utmost endeavors to persuade her to seek a remedy for herself. I advise her, first, to take nothing against her husband for granted; secondly, to shut her ears against the information or advice of volunteer friends; and thirdly, to seal her own lips as to all third persons. If, on calm reflection, she believes she has good reason to suspect her husband of indifference or wrong toward herself, I advise her to set about wooing him back to his allegiance. In that task, she will succeed, and success will be happiness. But the more common effort to *quarrel* a husband back to his allegiance—to bully him into affection—ends in hopeless estrangement, at the least. The remedy, therefore, that I propose, is the conciliatory course. But for a simple and universal preventive, which is better than any remedy, I would advise a total revolution in female education. I would have girls taught at school what in after life they will be called on to practise: not metaphysics; not recondite science; not a confusion of tongues; but something which, in the domestic relation, they are TO DO.

Nothing abstract, but concrete training for what are to them life's professions : namely, the offices of a wife, a mother and a mistress of the Home Department. Young men are trained to *their* professions and vocations : why should young women waste *their* spring-time in learning practical frivolities, so that when they come to the real business of life, they find themselves totally incapable of discharging its duties? Pray, excuse my vehemence : but, on my word, when I now-a-days read a prospectus of a young ladies' school and see what a parade is made of 'branches' which the girls can never more than touch with the tips of their fingers, and which if, by miracle, one of them *should* grasp, would crumble to dust in her hands: and when I see, year after year, these printed lists of 'branches' ostentatiously increased and each competing principal claiming a superiority over her rivals by reason of, and in proportion to, the greater length of *her* list—as, 'Miss Smith teaches only seventy-two branches, and I teach seventy-nine '—I am tempted to wish the whole institution abolished, and that no *book* but Murray's grammar should be used in female education. This may be ultraism, but at least it is ultraism in the cause of common-sense. And now, in conclusion, the moral of all this is on the surface. If women are trained to the practical duties of life and made to become attached to them by the fact of understanding them and appreciating their importance, they will devote themselves to their own households, each for her own self: and then they will have no time to look after the affairs of their neighbors. They will, in short—to complete the quotation from St. Paul—'study to be quiet, to do their own business, and to work with their own hands' in whatever 'work,' properly belongs to their station."

"For my part," said Doe, at length breaking the pause that followed the clergyman's speech, "I am much obliged to you for your homily. You have expressed my sentiments to a T."

"Which," added Miss Doe, "is as much as to say that Mr. Duncan is as great a heretic as yourself. However, to be very candid, I do not think Mr. Duncan is altogether wrong in his views. I have often wondered what answer could be given by the promoters of this method of female education, to the question—*why* do you teach, or rather attempt to teach, all these things to young ladies? Is it for *their* benefit, or your own?"

"I would like to inquire," said Jane, with all fitting humility, "what is to become of me? I have been finished on this proscribed system, and I don't fancy beginning again."

"Indeed, my dear child," replied her aunt, "you are *not* finished on the present system at all. I flatter myself that, whatever risks you may have run in the embellishing process, you have concurrently gained at home as much solid practical knowledge as any of your ancestry had—and that's saying a great deal, though I say it who shouldn't say it."

"Which," interposed Traverse, "is as much as to say, that if a young lady of the present day is taught at home all she ought to know, her going to a modern school will not ruin her."

"That's it, precisely," said Mr. Duncan; "and that's the best that can be said for the present system of female education, speaking generally. There is one honorable exception to this, in a case where the proprietor is an old friend of mine, and whose name I suppress for obvious reasons."

Upon which, Peter, who hadn't had a bad turn for several weeks, summoned the family party to tea.

"Mr. Duncan," said Traverse, when they were seated at the tea-table, " we were speaking not long since of the great ingenuity of the men of our day, as developed in mechanical inventions; and you held this condition of things to be one of the evidences of the increasing intelligence of the age."

"Yes, certainly;' such was my inference," said Mr. Duncan.

"Would you not, then, hold the invention of amusements, though of less practical value, to be nevertheless equal evidence of intelligence?" pursued Traverse.

"Of course, I would," replied Mr. Duncan, "if the thing invented addressed itself to the *mind* of educated people: indeed, in that case, the result would imply, so to speak, a more intellectual intelligence than other inventions."

"Then," continued Traverse, "how do you rate the intelligence of a people, some of them dating back many centuries, who produced the great social games that have come down to us—draughts, backgammon, whist and chess? Games marvellously adapted to all classes of mind: games, two at least of which the highest minds have never thoroughly mastered; which have amused, solaced, occupied mankind for many generations; and which no modern ingenuity has been able to supersede, nor even in the slightest degree to improve—games, in a word, and in the fullest and most absolute sense of the word, that are *perfect ?*"

"There can be but one answer to your question, Mr. Traverse," the clergyman replied; "and that you have virtually supplied by your own commentary. Clearly, the intelligence that invented those games was of the very highest order : and, in their marvellous adaptation to the taste and capacity of all classes of people, we find not only the inspiration of genius, but a creative power almost beyond the prerogative of genius. The perfection of those games, and the vast superiority attained by the old masters over all their imitators in the arts of painting, sculpture and architecture, may well admonish the wisest of our day to speak with becoming reverence of 'the wisdom of the ancients.' That phrase involves much more than is popularly attributed to it."

CHAPTER XVIII.

A VALENTINE.

Mrs. Swift could not quite forgive her dearest and
best friend, Mrs. Jenkins, for changing her mind
about the separation so distinctly agreed on between
the two ladies ; and especially for not giving her,
Mrs. Swift, official notice of the change. She did not
like it, to have been put to the expense of so much
good advice, all for nothing. And she did not like to
be held responsible by some of her " dear five hundred" for mysteriously and confidentially whispering
a secret in advance of the fact, which proved to be a
false report.

To be sure, her giving currency to such a report
was a violation of confidence as toward her dearest
and best friend; but she had been very cautious
about telling the story : she had never even hinted at
it to any other than very discreet people, nor had she
repeated it otherwise than under the most solemn
pledges of secrecy—which pledges were kept as well
as such pledges are wont to be. She was therefore
clearly of opinion that her dear Louisa had no business to make up her quarrel with her husband, privately ; and leave her, Mrs. Swift, in the lurch. She
had been "in" at the starting of the secret, and she
felt entitled to have been in at its death.

The question of the doctor's complication in the
matters charged by his wife, was not the sort of thing

to interest Mrs. Swift. Her object was to swim in other people's troubled waters, without caring how they became troubled. She had nothing to do with the mere facts of such a case. Facts are stubborn things; and, of all things, she disliked stubbornness. It is a quality which, from the very bottom of her heart, she despised. As the case was presented to her, her dearest and best friend was in trouble; that was "fact" enough for Mrs. Swift. And the duty of Mrs. Swift was simply to get her friend out—or, help her further in—as luck would have it. In view of all this, Mrs. Swift, as aforesaid, was aggrieved.

To be sure, the Jenkinses, in their new position of unity, justified the proverb: they "stood," and stood strong, in society. They were of the FF's; they were rich; they were associated with all the best people. They were therefore to be cultivated by all means and more than ever. Hence, Mrs. Swift could not afford to be otherwise than on the best terms with her dearest and best friend—if she could help herself.

But, while she was thus reasoning up the case, as if her continued intimacy with her dear Louisa was quite at her own option, she had a faint suspicion of a coolness on the part of that lady. She began to catch the inkling of an idea that the disregard of her ready advice might be accompanied by a disapproval of its utterance: for, when people have escaped from danger, and begin to reflect on the counsel that would have plunged them into it if followed, their *thanks* for such counsel are very apt to be proportioned to the value of the counsel—even if the counsel was of their own seeking. And that goes to show the danger of giving advice to a friend under any circumstances whatever. If the advice is followed and proves to have been good, the party benefited will not readily forgive your superior sagacity: and, whether followed or not, if it proves to have been bad, you may count on being held responsible for all the actual or possible evil that did or could come of it.

In the present case, when Mrs. Jenkins fairly came to herself, and was able coolly to estimate the services of Mrs. Swift, she could not repress a mental execration on that lady's mischievous heartlessness; although she was candid enough to confess to herself that she *sought* what she found—thus forming an exception to a general rule, which other Mrs. Swifts had better not presume upon!

When, therefore, Mrs. Swift called on Mrs. Jenkins—which she did soon after the ball—with a view to ascertain how the land lay, her dear Louisa received her in the usual way. There might have been a slight hesitancy and embarrassment on both sides; for that is often the fact, when people meet, with a mutual consciousness that something has been, or may have been, amiss: but to a third person, nothing of the kind would have been perceptible.

After the first greetings were over, and a sufficiency of compliments and disclaimers about the ball, had been exchanged, the conversation became somewhat disconnected: which, again, was an indication of restraint—as if each lady, having in her mind something to be avoided, was forced to let her tongue run one way while her thoughts were running another way. When people find themselves so situated, they have a common dread of a pause: and, rather than pause, they will repeat a thing two or three times; or, start off on something so far from the track, that the association of ideas becomes unwontedly mysterious.

"I was *so* much amused at the Herald's account of the ball!" said Mrs. Swift just in time to save a pause, although she had made that very remark no less than three times before.

"I did not see it," rejoined Mrs. Jenkins; "I was so much occupied with getting over the ball, that I had no leisure to read what the newspapers said of it;" being the third time she had made that identical reply.

"So, you have left our church, Louisa?" said Mrs. Swift, abruptly saving another pause, and flattering herself that the church was safe ground.

It happened, however, that when the mutual explanations of doctor Jenkins and his wife brought to the doctor's knowledge their pastor's disreputable style of advice to his parishioner, the disgusted couple resolved to quit his church and drop his acquaintance. Mrs. Swift's essay on the church, therefore, was not happy.

Mrs. Jenkins replied that she had become rather tired of Doctor Perkins. He seemed to be a man of one idea. And her husband was so often prevented from going to church by his professional duties—though, to be sure, that would occur in any church: still, she liked Mr. Duncan much better, both as a preacher and as a man.

Mrs. Swift conceded the general principle that there is no accounting for tastes. She did not think Mr. Duncan's voice was good. She thought the full, round, sonorous utterance of *her* "dear good Doctor" was best adapted to the church service. And then, Mr. Duncan went so little into society!

. "However," she added, brightening up as that fact suggested a safe topic and a peep into other people's affairs, "I hear he goes often enough to the Does."

"Not, I presume, as a rival to Mr. Traverse?" said Mrs. Jenkins, inquiringly: for Mrs. Swift's manner indicated something gossippy, though her friend was at a loss to understand its particular reference.

"No, indeed!" replied Mrs. Swift; "as nobody's rival, but as somebody's admirer. Rivals are somewhat beyond Susan Doe's mark, I imagine. One suitor at a time is as much as she could hope for; if, indeed, she ever had one before."

"Susan Doe!" echoed Mrs. Jenkins, gradually apprehending what Mrs. Swift would be at. "I never had the slightest idea of such a thing! But, on my word, now you mention it, I think that will do very well. Susan Doe may not suit your fancy, Sophia; but I consider her one of the finest and most lovable women I ever knew."

"Why, Louisa, she's forty years old, if she's a minute," responded the dismayed Mrs. Swift.

"True," said Mrs. Jenkins, "and Mr. Duncan is not much less than fifty. And what then? I presume you will not contend that real attachments are limited to people who are under five-and-twenty—or to any age at all, for that matter?"

"No; certainly not," answered Mrs. Swift; for the question was put in a way that almost extorted the answer; although, in fact, she *would* have contended that very point, if she had her own way about it; "but," she added, "to think of an old widower and an old maid setting up a new establishment!"

"What would you have?" inquired Mrs. Jenkins. "Surely, you would not approve of Mr. Duncan's taking a young wife?"

"For that," replied Mrs. Swift, "if my judgment were called for, I should decide for his taking *no* wife. Some people seem to think that marrying again is a necessity, instead of a caprice. I don't regard it so. My husband died ten years ago, and I never had an idea of replacing him."

Mrs. Jenkins thought to herself, that a lady who could speak of "replacing" a husband as she would speak of replacing a broken soup-tureen, was not likely to appreciate any further discussion on that point, and she dismissed it by inquiring whether the rumor about Mr. Duncan was probably well founded?

Mrs. Swift was not prepared to say, positively. That sort of thing about people at that time of life was not likely to be ill-founded. Mr. Duncan did certainly call often at Mr. Doe's to see somebody, and Mrs. Swift would like to know who it could be, but Susan Doe? As to the fact of the calling, her coachman, Stephen, was intimate with Mr. Doe's waiter, Peter; and Mrs. Swift had it from Stephen direct through her maid, Bridget, who had it at first hands from the cook.

Such a mass of concurrent testimony was not to be disregarded; and Mrs. Jenkins admitted the calls. Their object might easily be what Mrs. Swift conjectured, and that object met Mrs. Jenkins's entire approbation.

At this juncture, Mrs. Swift, having exhausted her budget of safe topics, and still fearing a pause, bade good morning to her dearest and best friend, with a conviction that some screw was loose in their friendly relations.

———

By one of those remarkable coincidences, so brilliant in history, it happened that, concurrently with the foregoing interchanges, a similar subject was under the consideration of Traverse and Jane Doe.

Jane had spoken of Mr. Duncan's conversational power and of his varied information, apart from his profession : and concluded by saying that, altogether, Mr. Duncan was "her admiration" for a clergyman.

"According to the best of my judgment, Jane," said Traverse, " Mr. Duncan is 'the admiration' of others in your family, both as a clergyman and as a friend."

"I believe he is," returned Jane, in a matter-of-fact way; " my uncle thinks"——then, perceiving by Traverse's looks that something more was intended, she interrupted herself and added,

" Oh, you mean that my aunt thinks so, I suppose ?"

"I do confess," returned Traverse, with a theatrical flourish, " that there *is* some such stuff in my thoughts."

"Then," said Jane, "perhaps by way of completing the quotation you would add that the man delights not *you ?*"

" By no means," answered Traverse; "I admire him quite as much as your uncle does, or as you do: only, I think your aunt out-herods us all."

"I shouldn't be surprised," said Jane; leaving those four words to do the work of eight, as is customary in colloquial parlance, "if it were so" being understood. "Yet, I assure you, I have heard nothing of it."

"Which is very strange!" rejoined Traverse, solemnly. "But I hope the arrangement has your approbation, even if you have not been consulted?"

"Why, Alfred," remonstrated Jane, "you are getting on rapidly with this affair! rather more so, I imagine, than the principals. You call it an arrangement!"

"I presume there is at least an understanding," replied Traverse; "at any rate, if there is not, there soon will be. I wish," he added, half interrogatively, "I wish it would do to quiz them a little."

"That might be dangerous," Jane replied; "and I wouldn't offend my aunt for the world—although, once on a time, she did carry her jokes rather far with me. By the way, how would a valentine do?"

"The day is too far off," said Traverse. "The secret will be out of itself before that time."

"But what's the need of waiting?" inquired Jane. "Those embossed sheets with sharp darts and bleeding hearts are valentines, independently of days. Let us put our heads together——not quite so close, thank you!" as Traverse was taking the suggestion literally; "let us study out a verse or two, and hear how they will sound."

———

One of the subjects of this conspiracy, to wit, Miss Susan Doe, was a constant attendant on the services of the church, both on Sundays and at the Wednesday evening lecture. She was usually accompanied by her brother and niece, and often of late by Traverse. But it sometimes happened that the engagements of those gentlemen deprived her of their escort on her return from the Wednesday evening lecture: and as Mr. Doe's pew was directly in front of the pulpit, Mr. Duncan could always see when she was thus unprotected. ·Nothing was more natural, under such circumstances, than that, what between Miss Doe's taking her time, and Mr. Duncan's making the most of *his* time, after the service was concluded—the two should chance to meet in the vestibule, and the pastor should see to it that the parishioner had no difficulty about getting home.

These antecedent facts may be of little importance in the abstract; but they led to another coincidence, which should be recorded as a counterpart to the coincidence recently herein-above related.

On the very Wednesday evening when Mrs. Jenkins and Mrs. Swift by themselves, and Traverse and Jane Doe by themselves, had indulged severally in the little matter of gossip already recited, Miss Doe was seated alone in her pew and Mr. Duncan was particularly happy in expounding 2 John, i. 5. The good man was touchingly earnest in his discourse. Every word seemed to come from his heart. And, when that is the case, a congregation will always be attentive. They were so, on the present occasion. Miss Doe was wholly absorbed; so much so, that she was an unusually long time about getting out of the church; and almost the first remark she made, after being assured by Mr. Duncan, in the vestibule, that "it was no sort of trouble—he was quite at leisure"—was an assurance that she had seldom been so much gratified—and—all that sort of thing.

On this hint, Mr. Duncan made up his mind to speak. Exactly what he said, can be only conjec-

tured by third persons : because, a succession of omni-
buses was just then passing, which made it necessary
for the two interlocutors to say what they had to say,
in each other's ears.

But, however inaudible to outsiders and listeners
were the spoken words, their effect seemed to be—a
clear understanding between the parties uttering
them.

Young people sometimes bungle and boggle this little necessity at a terrible rate : but if you wish to see
the thing done up in a hurry, and well done, just you
look out for a fancying couple of a certain age !

Why, my dear sir, Doe's house is not a hundred
yards from the church !

———

While Traverse and Jane were still sitting in the
parlor, tagging doggerel lines on a sheet of paper,
preparatory to the contemplated valentine, Miss Doe
returned from the lecture and entered the parlor with
the reverend Mr. Duncan.

And it was exceedingly funny, the way these four
people deported themselves !   Here were individuals
who knew more, much more than they would unfold :
people who had designs and suspicions which nothing
could induce them to reveal : people looking wise in
one direction and foolish in another direction : people
simpering, and people repressing a laugh : people
who had some things in common, and other things
in particular : people who could, an if they would :
but nobody in all the crowd who was just then prepared to " let on."

———

A few evenings later in the autumn, the Doe tea-table was thus occupied: Miss Doe, at the tea and coffee urns; Miss Jane Doe; Mr. John Doe; the reverend Mr. Duncan; Alfred Traverse. It was Miss Doe's waffle-party; the first of the season. And if Miss Doe, in the housekeeping category, was strong on anything, she was strong on waffles.

The party was a merry party, independently of waffles. No secrets had yet transpired: and few things tend to make people on better terms with themselves, than the consciousness of possessing a secret, on the one hand, and the consciousness of "smoking" it, on the other.

Presently, Peter, having absented himself to answer the bell, walked in with a very large letter for Miss Doe. A letter nearly as broad as it was long.

Miss Doe eyed the missive with much curiosity; but nothing whatever could be gained by outside inspection. She hesitated a moment. Nobody was present but intimate friends, and they would excuse her? Certainly. Of course.

The letter was by no means a long letter. On the contrary, it was a short letter. It appeared to contain poetry. Two verses of poetry. Miss Doe made short work of the reading; and then, with a blush that had in it more of scarlet than of pink, she summarily crammed both letter and envelope into her pocket, remarking with great presence of mind, and with a self-possession that showed how little this communication had disturbed her equanimity,

"Mr. Duncan—will you take a little more chocolate in your—tea—I beg your pardon!—waffles?"

If the very life of Jane Doe had depended on her keeping a long face, that young lady would have been done for, at this crisis. She thrust her face, as far it would go, into her coffee-cup. She used superhuman efforts of restraint. But it was no go. Or, rather, it was all go. A burst—a peal—an explosive shout of laughter, such as seldom rings from the throat of a well-bred woman, came tumultuously forth into her coffee, forcing the cup from her face and scattering the fragrant beverage all about the table.

Probably, that was the best thing Jane Doe could have done. For nothing is more contagious than genuine laughter; and, as everybody immediately joined in, it all passed off as the result of Miss Doe's unintelligible jargon of waffles, chocolate and tea.

CHAPTER XIX.

THE superintending care of Providence over the lives of physicians while engaged in their professional duties, is a subject of frequent comment. They go from one sick chamber to another, at all hours of the day and night; and in all conditions of bodily health, many of which conditions render men unusually susceptible to disease; yet, though they are thus more exposed to contagion than other men, they very rarely suffer from it. But this impunity does not extend to the subordinates and accessories of the medical profession : for example, to the apothecaries' boys who carry potions about to the patients. And it chanced, from this cause, or some other cause, that Thomas Pinch was taken ill with what proved to be the varioloid.

The news of his illness came to Mr. Doe through Phebe, Tom's sister, who was employed two or three days in each week by Miss Doe in miscellaneous duties about the house, and in needle-work; with a promise of a sewing-machine of her own some of these days, when she should have learned how to use it: by means of which she would be able, with her mother's coöperation, to set herself up in business.

Mr. Doe was well aware of the danger incurred by patients from the treatment of inexperienced and half educated medical practitioners—whom, however,

8*

many people consider to be "good enough for the poor"—and he engaged doctor Jenkins, who was his own family-physician, to look after Tom's case. As a matter of precaution, it was deemed advisable that Phebe should remain at home while her brother was ill. She might, otherwise, carry the disease into families where she worked; and, besides, she would be wanted to nurse Tom. And, meantime, Mr. Doe would see that there was no want of money for the comfort of the invalid and his attendants.

To people who can be well taken care of, and who have the advantage of an experienced physician's services, the varioloid is not much to be dreaded, beyond those considerations which belong to personal appearance. But in this regard, the Does hoped that Phebe might escape the disease, for she was a very comely lass. Both she and her mother, however, must now take their chance of that, as both had undergone the danger of exposure before they were aware of it. Doctor Jenkins took the precaution of vaccinating them; and, at their request, the same precaution was extended to their uncle Samuel.

The result was, that Tom came off bravely from his encounter with the enemy: Phebe and her mother escaped the disease entirely; and uncle Sam had it "the worst way;" coming out of it, indeed, with life and health, but so disfigured that niece, great niece and great nephew would never have recognized him again by his face.

Wilson, for a time, was not aware of the great change in his personal appearance; for doctor Jenkins advised a removal of the looking-glass from his room until Wilson became prepared for the discovery It was not missed for some time, for Wilson's eyes were weak from the disease, and his room was kept dark. When, at length, he called for it, Mrs. Pinch explained its absence by remarking that the hook by which it was suspended became loose, and during uncle Sam's illness, she would not annoy him with the noise of driving it fast. She would now, in a day or two, borrow a hammer, and fasten the hook.

When Wilson was so far recovered as to be permitted to get up and dress himself, he unsuspiciously made his way to this revealer of plain truth, and—he was very near dashing it to pieces!

That! What! Him! Good heavens! what had Mrs. Pinch been doing to that looking-glass? The thing was *impossible!*

But by and by Mrs. Pinch stood by his side, in front of the glass, and the faithful mirror gave back *her* image in its integrity. The fault, then, was not in the glass.

Wilson was greatly discouraged at first. But he was a philosopher, and made the best of it. He was no longer in the way of making or desiring female conquests; and, if his beauty was spoiled, his future identification by the emissaries of the law, was placed well out of the range of probability. Besides, he had plenty of money for present use, and a screw on old Roe for future supplies. Meantime, he was in good quarters. Hail Columbia! The world hasn't come to an end yet!

Wilson could now resume his old recreation of looking out of a window, without taking pains to prevent himself from being seen.

It seemed a very long time since he had looked into the street. And he was surprised to find that so little change had taken place in the external world since he last-looked out upon it. There was the old gray bob-tailed nag at the head of the fish cart; and the milkman's cart with its footboard split in the middle: and the baker wearing a white hat for the same reason that a miller does, namely, to keep his head warm. There, too, was the grocer's array of vegetables and fruit, and his succession of customers smacking their lips as they withdrew from his hospitality, and even the ragged schoolboy stealing an apple, which, by this time, had probably become an article not of luxury but of necessity. Wilson hoped that the lad would be more circumspect, however; for other eyes than his might happen to detect the pilfering. This idea, once afoot, grew upon Wilson to such an extent that he began to watch the boy's daily approach with a nervous solicitude that, at last, took away his appetite for breakfast, and disturbed even his dreams with visions of discovery and arrest. This was partly owing to his weak state of body and mind, and partly to his circumstances of restraint and confinement: causes that deprived him of any regular occupation for his thoughts, and forced them to dwell on trifles too unsubstantial to feed them. Those trifles were about as nourishing to the mind, as a diet of soap-bubbles would be to the body.

The result of this mental disturbance, was a determination on the part of Wilson to give the boy warning of his danger. He accordingly sat by his open window one morning until the object of his solicitude approached the grocer's premises; and then, by a *hem* and a whistle, he attracted the lad's attention, beckoning the little fellow at the same time to cross over the street. The young chap was taken by surprise, and did not readily obey the call; but on Wilson's repeating it, and saying, in a conciliatory tone that he wished to speak to him, the boy ventured to come beneath the window.

This near approach to such a face as Wilson's by no means improved its attractiveness in the eyes of the lad, and did very little in the way of encouraging him to make the acquaintance. However, he inquired what the strange-looking man wanted.

"I want to tell you something," said Wilson, showing a bright, new "quarter" between his thumb and finger: "come in. I'll open the door for you, my lad."

The beauty of the new quarter, fresh from the mint, had such a modifying effect on the speaker's ugly face, that the urchin assented, and Wilson hurried down stairs to admit him. As soon as the boy stood in the hall, Wilson said to him, at the same time imparting the specie,

"See here, my boy; you've been stealing that man's apples for a long time. I want just to tell you, that the old fellow is on the look out. Now, mind you let his apples alone, eh?" And he reopened the door and dismissed the astonished boy into the street.

"I rather guess he won't come that dodge again in a hurry!" said Wilson, complacently, as he fastened the door, and walked up to his room.

A man must be pretty thoroughly demoralized, when the consciousness of having done a good thing fails temporarily to raise him in his own esteem. Wilson felt like a new man after this exploit; and, thereupon, he set about some plans for the future with renewed confidence.

He had been advised by doctor Jenkins to take exercise in the open air as much as possible. *That* he could now do with great comparative safety, thanks to that ugly physiognomy, which he could not yet bring himself to contemplate steadily in a looking-glass. It would be better, though, to have an entirely different suit of clothes. Those hitherto worn might have become familiar to some prying chap, without Wilson's knowing it. He would have a shawl, too. He had never worn one of the d— things; he couldn't imagine why any man should thus make an old granny of himself, by daylight, at any rate. But just now the shawl would aid his disguise.

As to remaining in New-York? Let him see. Some other place would be safer: nobody out of New-York would, now, ever have the remotest notion of his identity. As to funds? Hum. The exchequer was in a healthy condition: average of specie far beyond liabilities. Yet, it would never do to go elsewhere until the strong-box was replenished. By the by, it was every way a blunder in Roe to betray his estimate of the value of those papers and *yet* allow them to slip through his fingers. A thousand dollars! Why, a man who would undertake and carry out what Roe undertook and carried out for the possession of those papers, would pay ten thousand dollars to recover them *without* undergoing such a terrible ordeal. Ten thousand dollars? Let him see. How would he open trenches on the old fellow? Might begin, say, with an anonymous letter. Stir him up with a long pole, or a sharp stick. Let him see. Ticklish business, these anonymous letters! But there was time to consider. As to conscience in plucking Roe, the infernal old swindler! He had cheated fifty men out of more than that, by letting 'em in on bottom principles to schemes that had *no* bottom; he taking good care to get out before the bottom did, if there was one. Conscience, indeed! He thought he saw himself letting up Richard Roe "for conscience' sake!"

In the course of that day, Wilson was provided with new clothes and a shawl, as per programme: and after he had tried them on and taken the shine off by a long walk in the evening, he went to bed and dreamed of ten thousand dollars, bottom principles, and Richard Roe's conscience.

The next morning he watched the effect of his moral lecture on apples. At the usual hour, the boy appeared and passed along; but he took no more notice of the apples, than a cat takes of a bowl of cream when she knows somebody is watching her. He bestowed the compliment of a passing salute on Wilson, nevertheless. He cocked his eye at him, to begin with. Then, he clapped the end of his left thumb to the tip of his nose, gyrated his fingers to and fro as a man does when he plays the fife, and marched by, as erect as a drummer at the head of his regiment—in Broadway.

Wilson was rather inclined to think that that boy's conscience had not been much touched, nor his morals much improved, by the lesson he had received. But then, to be sure, Wilson had not bargained for cultivating anything in the boy except the sentiment of self-preservation. He flattered himself that he had hit *that* nail squarely on the head.

"Now," said Wilson, complacently, "one good turn deserves another. Here goes for an anonymous letter to Roe.   For, after all, supposing there is time enough? This sort of thing *takes* time. And the first step need be only a feeler.   Let me see.—Sir! No: make it, Dear Sir. (I mean that it shall be 'dear,' before it is over.)   A friend of W*****, who escaped in a *vial of chloroform* and crossed the North River on an iron bar, wishes to say that W. has certain papers which were left by mistake in the side pocket. These papers are valuable to any one who knows their value, and are perhaps valuable to the owner. They are for sale, for cash. If the owner would like to buy, he can name his terms by advertisement in the Herald."

That will do.   Sign it Sly: and by and by drop it into a lamp-post letter-box. Then, look out for an advertisement.

Wilson then lit a segar, took up the last number of "Harper's Magazine," and made himself comfortable.

CHAPTER XX.

THE condition on which Jo. Rabbit could be honorably discharged from confinement on the morning after his unconscious travels from pillar to post—to wit, the payment into somebody's treasury of the sum of ten dollars, lawful money of the realm—not having been complied with, the aforesaid Jo. was ignominiously transferred to the Tombs, and there deposited for the full term of ten calendar days, Sundays included.

Being in the Tombs, he was provided with bed and board—more accurately speaking, *board* and board, for the bed and a plank were very much the same thing—and a companion, who was detained for some other cause and whose acquaintance proved not to be an advantage to Rabbit. He was a burglar and thief by profession. No locks had been found complicated enough to keep him out when he wished to be in; nor had any fastenings been strong enough to keep him in, when he wished to be out. Moreover he had always done up his professional duties so artistically, that proof against himself had never been perfected. He had something of Richard Roe's adroitness in getting his friends into trouble, yet keeping his own neck free. He appropriated the chief share of all partnership plunder to himself, while his associate did the chief share of the work, and in

the sequel did the state more or less service at Sing
Sing.

A man of this stamp was constantly in want of
assistants ; as he would never practise without a colleague, and his colleague for the time being was
tolerably certain of being caught and used up, as the
end of each successful exploit.   Hence, when a new
enterprise was on foot, a new recruit was to be sought
to fill vacancies.   The name of the personage with
whom Rabbit was now domiciled and to whose careful training he was about to be subjected, was Jack
Spring.

Rabbit was in the happiest frame of mind for the
ministrations of Spring.   He was so wearied with
disasters and so tugged with fortune, that he stood
ready to set his individuality on any chance that
would mend it, or mar it.   When sober, he was a
cool, brave man ; and, in the judgment of Spring,
who had made men a study, he was a marvellous
proper person to be initiated into some of the outer
and inner mysteries of his art.

Men who know the value of time can accomplish
a great deal in ten days.   Messrs. Spring and Rabbit,
therefore, previously to their respective periods for
honorable discharge, had come to a perfect understanding of what they jointly wished to do, while
Rabbit had acquired a very pretty notion of the way
to do it.   He went from freshman to junior almost
per saltum, with a fair promise for a degree at the
first "commencement."

When the two friends got out of bounds, the
superior artist put his novice through a few safe,
practical paces, that he might get his hand in, and
acquire that confidence which is indispensable in the

field. For it is one thing to practise plunder in the abstract, and quite another to apply it to real chattels in the face or fear of antagonistic flesh and bood.

Rabbit was an apt scholar. He proved himself up to everything that was undertaken on a small scale; so much so, that while he obtained only moderate percentages of the profits, he made a very good living out of his dexterity. Among other things, he gained a good suit of clothes, in which his appearance enabled him to undertake the gentlemanly branch of the profession. This suit was kept at Spring's lodgings, and was there assumed and relinquished as occasion required, but was never used except on professional business. His wife, therefore, knew nothing of what was going on. She saw less of him than formerly; but she observed that he had temporarily abandoned rum and seemed to have the means of living without any visible means of obtaining them. This would have been a happy change for the hitherto wretched family, if kind treatment on the part of Rabbit had accompanied it; but another part of the new order of things was that Rabbit had become more abusive than formerly of his wife and children.

In due time, Spring projected an enterprise well suited to his genius and ambition. He proposed to make one fell swoop of jewels that should place him in easy circumstances for life, giving Rabbit the usual chance of a reasonable share of plunder with a large proportion of the risk.

By way of getting familiar with the intended scene of action, the two gentlemen—now well dressed— called at one of those large establishments in Broadway where gems and precious stones seem literally to

grow, to purchase a plain gold ring; to wit, a wedding-ring. Rabbit took the lead in the application
and was very particular about the size and weight.
And when at length he had suited himself in those
respects, he gave minute directions for the engraving
of names and date; promising, in conclusion, to call
for the ring on the next evening.

While Rabbit was thus occupied, Spring, with the
most innocent listlessness, was peering around among
the glass cases; informing himself very accurately,
however, where the large diamonds and other precious
stones lay thickest; and making a speculative guess
how many of them he could grab in a hurry if the
intervening obstacle of a horizontal plate-glass were
removed.

By the time he had completed his survey and
thoroughly mastered its details, so that when time
and tide served, he could improve his seconds to the
uttermost, Rabbit on his part, and at a distance of
some thirty feet further up the floor, had made an
end of his bargain for the wedding-ring, and the two
took their departure. There was nothing in the
transaction, hitherto, likely to attract attention or
remark of the employés of the establishment. It was,
thus far, an every-day occurrence, such as the clerks
would hardly have been able to recall or describe the
next day.

As the two friends were passing along Broadway,
Spring, who had been on the look out for such an
article, directed Rabbit to step into a shop near by,
and purchase a dozen of large fire-crackers that were
hanging in the window: which Rabbit did, while
Spring waited on the outside. Those large crackers
are a great improvement on the old-fashioned pipe-

stem size, once valued so highly by the boys for fourth-of-July purposes. They cost more money by the piece, to be sure; but, estimated by their noise and their explosive power, they are much cheaper in the grand result. They go off like a pistol or a gun; and if you venture to hold one in your hand as it explodes, you will find occasion for an amanuensis the next time you write to your friends.

Spring next sent his friend into a plumber's shop for a few feet of lead-pipe, to take into the country. Size not very important; but, as one must choose, even when one is indifferent, say three-quarter inch size. And in the same way as to length; say, ten feet. Rabbit, again, did as directed, but with very little idea of what Spring would be at.

One more shopping place supplied Spring's wants. This was a stationer's shop, where Rabbit bought a ball of twine and several sheets of stout wrapping-paper.

The friends then proceeded to Spring's quarters, where Rabbit as usual resumed his old clothes, while Spring with a hatchet amused himself by cutting his lead pipe into lengths of about six inches. He then made a ground tier, on a table, of four crackers, four on them, and again four to conclude; and in that shape he made them fast with twine. He next piled the pieces of lead-pipe making a double ground tier, placed the crackers on that, and piled up a covering on each side and on the top, with the pipe; and again made all fast with twine. In conclusion, he baled the whole with sundry thicknesses of brown paper, taking care to bring the fuses of the crackers in a neat twist through a small hole in the paper and projecting from it about one inch.

"Now," said he to the admiring Rabbit, "when you touch a lighted segar to this coil of fuses, the crackers will take care of themselves in about two seconds. Then, supposing the parcel to be lying on the top of somebody's glass case, the weight of the lead, acting with the concussion of the fire, would crack the glass plate and fall through it into the case. Then don't you see, the crackers will be going off one after another like the volley of an awkward squad of militia, raising the very devil with the finery of the glass case."

"I can understand that," said Rabbit, who had listened carefully to every word of the explanation, "but I don't see what we are to make out of it."

"You *will* see in due time," replied Spring, with great composure. "You had better believe that I haven't been studying this out for nothing. You come here to-morrow afternoon and we will go for your wedding-ring."

And the meeting was thereupon adjourned. Spring, who remained upon the premises, began to pack up and arrange his movables, as if he contemplated a change of quarters.

Rabbit was punctually at his post; and after putting himself into his new clothes, he sat down for final instructions. These were rehearsed, and re-rehearsed, until there was no such word as fail. The party then set forth on their travels, duly provided with segars.

Spring carried in his hand, but concealed in his sleeve, a piece of lead pipe about a foot long, one end of which was bent over into a heavy knob. Rabbit took charge of the fire-crackers. The parcel was neatly done up, and for all that appeared, it might be something just purchased at a hardware-shop.

The adventurers made their way to the jeweller's palace, and walked in as they had done previously, Spring carelessly stopping opposite his diamonds, and Rabbit proceeding some thirty feet beyond him to the clerk who had charge of the ring. Rabbit put his parcel on the glass case, and waited while the clerk looked in a drawer for the ring. The ring was soon produced, pronounced satisfactory, and placed in a neat little box. Rabbit handed the clerk a ten dollar bill, and the young man went back to the desk for change.

At this critical instant Rabbit, who had his handkerchief ready for the purpose, let it drop over the parcel to prevent the preliminary *fizz* and smoke from being perceived, and with the other hand touched the combustible material with his segar. Then, stooping to the floor, as if he had let something fall and was pursuing it, he made a short run out of reach of the explosion.

No man can tell with certainty what he will do when unexpectedly alarmed; and the reason is, that alarm and surprise work together to take away his self-possession: leaving him for the moment incapable of taking good care of himself, or of looking out for anybody else. And in that fleeting moment of helplessness, on his part, and on the part of a dozen men together in the same circumstances, a great deal may be done by a resolute man who is fully prepared for the exact condition of things and knows that these astonished people cannot interfere with him. Therefore, while every man in the establishment was entirely absorbed by a series of explosions that seemed to come spontaneously from the very centre of one of the glass cases, filling the apartment with noise, smoke and flying particles of glass—Spring, without any observable motion and without making any noise distinguishable from the din around him, had, with his lead-pipe club, shattered the glass that stood between him and his hopes, and with several hasty snatches with both hands, had transferred to loose pockets in his coat a very large amount of valuable gems.

The only thing that remained for him and his associate to do, was simply to walk out at the door, into which a mass of people from the street were now beginning to throng. In the confusion of the moment, no effort was made to prevent their egress, for at the moment their depredation could not be known.

They took different routes toward Spring's lodgings, where Rabbit changed his clothes and where a hasty division of the spoil was made.

The percentage allotted to Rabbit was not large; yet what Spring gave him was, to a man in his circumstances, a fortune, provided he could contrive to "realize" on it to advantage. The parties separated on the best of terms.

It was, now, "every man for himself." Rabbit, having nowhere else to go, went home. But Spring, who had provided for the emergency, took himself off to parts unknown.

CHAPTER XXI.

Margaret Roe's lines had not fallen in pleasant places. The indifference or aversion of her father had, indeed, thrown the young woman more entirely into the charge and the heart of her mother, than would otherwise have been the case; and therefore, as was natural, the mutual devotion of the mother and daughter became extreme. For many years they had been all-in-all to each other; and each had found in the other a compensation for the delinquencies of the head of the family—to wit, Richard Roe. But the death of Mrs. Roe, when Margaret was about nineteen, was a terrible blow to the poor girl, who thenceforward would have found herself alone in the world but for sympathizing friends outside of the domestic circle; and but for an affair of the heart, already referred to, which might, and might not, promote her happiness.

Subsequently to the loss of her mother, when Margaret of necessity became mistress of her father's household; when intense grief was gradually yielding to time and friendships and the cares of the domestic establishment; and when the negative comforts of a quiet home were asserting their influence on her wounded spirit, the ridiculous marriage of her father almost drove her to despair. The new-comer was not only an uncongenial and unfitting

associate of both father and daughter; she was also
a discordant element, whose entrance into the family
drove peace out of it.

During the lifetime of her mother, Margaret had
become attached to Sam. Gray, a young man about
town, whose father some people supposed to be rich,
and of whom, more anon. Margaret's mother had
negatively encouraged this attachment: not as one
that she would have preferred, but from the seemingly
good character of the young man, and from the
general fact, that a true affection, thus early commenced, if otherwise fortunate in its result, was
likely to prove a resource and an escape for her
daughter from what the mother easily foresaw would
never be a happy home. Her chief objection to
young Gray, was his want of any regular pursuit;
he had been brought up as *a gentleman*—a vocation
very liable to terminate in bad habits, though
nothing of that kind had betrayed itself while she
was alive to watch for it.

What, however, her sagacity had foreboded, began
now to be developed. Gray showed evidences of a
fondness for strong drink, which of course were observed by everybody else sooner than by Margaret.
Some of her mother's friends, and here and there one
of her own intimate companions, had endeavored to
present this thing to Margaret in its proper light.
But here was brought out one of those perversities
of female nature, so incomprehensible to the mental
analyst.

A young woman will often jilt a young man,
without assigning or having any reason at all. Yet,
when it happens that there is abundant cause for a
lover's dismissal, and all the friends of the lady see

it, and exert themselves to the utmost to make *her* see it; she will set her face like a flint, and adhere to her lover with a desperate infatuation that defies all interference, and which seems even to increase in proportion to the efforts made to overcome it.

Unfortunately, Margaret's instance was no exception to this inconceivable rule. She persisted in interpreting friendly and earnest opposition into cruel persecution of both Gray and herself; she now felt deserted by every one : and with a fatuity that finds a parallel only in mental aberration, she founded her chief hope of happiness on the constancy of Gray—which, in the opinion of her friends, was her greatest curse.

Things were at this pass, when the scene took place, as related in chapter twelve of this history. That scene was not unusual in its tone; but its details somewhat transcended former experience. Mrs. Roe's taunting reference to Gray's infirmity was, to Margaret, utterly unendurable. Margaret had borne much from her own friends on this topic—friends who were, in some sense, authorized to speak. But Mrs. Roe, whom Margaret detested as an intruder, and despised for her weaknesses of character, and who moreover lived in a glass house—for *her* to interfere, and assume an air of superiority and read Margaret a lecture in her own house and home ! it was a thing not to be borne. It was, even, a thing to provoke retaliation ; and if Margaret's imputations, in reply, were well founded, retaliation might be very easily attained. In fact, she had made quite a perceptible approach toward retaliation by her startling disclosure about Mr. Jackson. And when, subsequently, she came to observe the altered manner of

Mrs. Roe; with what an involuntary deference that lady seemed all of a sudden to regard her; how the bold and defiant look was exchanged for timid and furtive glances: neither Margaret's unsuspecting nature nor hèr general simplicity of character could prevent her from being aware that she had, however unwittingly, lighted on a secret of first rate proportions.

Roe took a different view of Margaret's discovery. He attached no importance to it. He considered the story to be extemporised for the occasion, and as a medium of venting an angry woman's spite. The thing was cleverly got up. Well thrown in. He had repeatedly laughed over it, as an instance of Margaret's adroitness. In the matter of fence, his daughter was clearly an overmatch for his wife. Richard could judge of that, because he was an unconcerned spectator. An unconcerned looker-on in Vienna has that great advantage: he can impartially estimate the skill of the combatants; he can appreciate the good hits because they don't hit *him*. As for the truth of Margaret's imputations, that was all in my eye. He not only knew Jackson, but he knew himself. He had his own mental and physical weight and measure calculated to a hair. He would like to see the man who could get ahead of Richard Roe! He had "done" every man who came in contact with him, either as a borrower or lender, for twenty years past.

Notwithstanding all that, there is something so luminously absurd in underrating that certain—or rather, that uncertain—kind of enemy, Richard thought he might as well keep a lookout. Mrs. Roe, with much less circumlocution of reasoning, had resolved to keep a lookout. And it is needless to add that Margaret had resolved that *she* would keep.a lookout. Thus, the triangular duel was maintained, but the weapons were changed.

While the three are occupied in their silent warfare of eyes, a brief introduction may be conceded to the sole surviving parent of Margaret's persecuted lover.

The elder Gray, to wit Isaac Gray, the happy father of the youth who was so strong on the whiskey question, belonged to a class of people who never die out in a large city: or, at any rate, in New-York.

The individuals of this class do a large business on a small capital. Without possessing any visible ways and means, they live in fine houses, entertain expensively, and have a snug box on the banks of the Hudson. Their names are always to be found on committees of invitation to some public man, and among the officers of public meetings, complimentary benefits, anniversary balls, and so on. Their persons may be seen in Wall-street making the round of banks and insurance companies. They have offices in the Exchange, or somewhere, and they "spread themselves," generally. Isaac Gray was not elaborately conspicuous among these people; but, he was " one of 'em."

Every man has his weak point, and most men are strong on something. Isaac was strong on entertaining: that is, he was master of the art of getting up an agreeable party.

The proof of a dinner, or a supper, may lie in the eating; but the faculty of happily selecting guests, is not among the gifts of every one who is in the habit of inviting them. Isaac, in his day, had been caught at parties where no two of the guests had ever met before or had anything in common; and the paralytic dulness of those experiences taught him a lesson. He made the thing a study. And he finally learned that no party should consist of more people than can be seated: and that either they should be, for the most part, mutually acquainted, or, by pursuits, habits, and tastes, they should have so much in common that technical acquaintance is superseded by congeniality—the latter quality being the really indispensable condition. A party thus made up is a scene of enjoyment. No one is glad when it is over. The people make the party: the table is only an adjunct. But if the table becomes an absorbing feature, your party, so far forth, is a failure. A feast is a commonplace thing in which no one can fail: and feasting is a selfish, not a social, enjoyment. Lady Macbeth had the right view of that matter when, in reference to this very point, she remarked that mere feasting, or feeding, were best done at home.

It is tolerably clear, that a man whose wealth was as dubious as Gray's, even if that personage did understand the philosophy of entertaining at somebody's expense, could not well have a son who, in a pecuniary sense, was a desirable match for a young lady. Nevertheless, many people supposed Gray to be rich. He must be rich, or he couldn't spend so much money. Gray was a widower and Sam was his only heir.

Meantime, the triangular duel of eyes had proceeded among the Roes without any particular result.

But one day, Philip, having been despatched by Mrs. Roe with a parcel of notes to station W, of the United States Post Office department, encountered Margaret in the hall, with his hand full of the aforesaid missives: and, by mere chance, Margaret caught sight of one note among the rest, addressed in a strange hand, the chirography not being striking in itself, but conspicuous from the single circumstance of being unfamiliar. Wishing to see more of this note, Margaret inquired of Philip if, among those notes, there was an answer for Mrs. McPherson?

Philip, not having explored the mysteries of reading and writing, was unable to inform the young lady, but the young lady could see for herself, as he submitted his budget to her inspection.

When one person is looking for something, a by-stander will always *help* him by looking too. Thus Philip, though wholly unable to read, very assiduously helped Margaret to look for a note addressed to Mrs. McPherson.

The first glance of Margaret at the note in a strange hand, showed her that it was addressed to Mr. Jackson in a disguised character, and could have emanated from no one but Mrs. Roe. Her resolution was taken on the instant, but Philip's officiousness in helping her look was an impediment.

" Philip," said she, examining the furniture in the hall, " have you dusted those chairs to-day?"

Philip was as ready to help Miss Margaret look for dust as for notes; and he inspected the chairs, replying triumphantly that they *had* been dusted that morning.

Margaret seemed to be satisfied with the answer, and Philip departed for station W. In the course of the same day, Margaret had occasion to pass station W; and, seeing nobody there, she went in and deposited in the letter-box an envelope addressed to Richard Roe, Esq., number so-and-so, Wall-street. On the outside of the envelope, was a very neat blue stamp; and inside of it was an unopened envelope addressed in a disguised hand to Mr. Jackson.

Jackson was well acquainted with the several members of Mrs. Roe's family, as also with Mrs. Roe herself, previously to her marriage; and as the acquaintance had been subsequently maintained, and Jackson often met Mrs. Roe in society, and frequently called on her at Roe's house, one might inquire—why this formality, and perhaps risk, in communicating with Jackson by note, when in the ordinary course of events the lady could and would meet him on common and familiar ground and could say verbally what was here written?

The answer is, that some people have a fancy for doing things mysteriously. Besides, since the recent bitter and enlightening altercation between the three Roes, and the mutual espionage that followed it, Mrs. Roe came to the conclusion that for the present Jackson had better discontinue his visits; and she had already so informed that gentleman by a note addressed similarly to the one now despatched, but not similarly interrupted in its journey.

And now, when the lady chanced to have something special to communicate, she took this method of sending it.

CHAPTER XXII.

Subsequently to the Jenkins ball, the Does had made a point of being civil and attentive to the reconciled family. The old friendship, for a time interfered with by the eccentricities of the doctor's wife, was now renewed in its original force; and the careful avoidance, by either family, of all references to the past, showed that both parties to the revival tacitly united in a desire to make the new order of things permanent. Frequent interchanges of visits—not of cards—were among the results: and whenever the visit for the time being took place at the Does, the Jenkins children were brought in to wake the echoes of a playroom specially set apart for their use, and to assist at the demolition of sweat-meats and waffles at a tea-table provided in the same apartment. A visit to the Does was a holiday of holidays to the young Jenkinses, Jane Doe being the tutelary genius of the hour, while Phebe Pinch, as titulary maid of honor, became responsible for a share of the entertainment.

During one of these reunions, and while the children were despatching their after-tea frolic, preparatory to going home, the affairs of the Pinch family were discussed in the parlor.

Doctor Jenkins and Mr. Doe continued the subject in a corner by themselves, after the two ladies had branched off on some other topic; and the doctor commented on the fortunate escape of Phebe and her mother from the varioloid, while Tom, though he had gone through the various stages of the disease, was unharmed by it, even in appearance. "Their uncle," he added, "took all the suffering to himself: he is terribly disfigured, and seems to have been the scape-goat of the family."

Doe remarked that he had never heard of their having such a relative.

"As a scape-goat?" inquired the doctor.

"As an uncle," answered Doe.

Doctor Jenkins said that the man resided, or professed to reside, in Madison, Wisconsin; and was temporarily here on some private business. But there were circumstances about it that puzzled him.

"Such as what?" said Doe.

"Why the truth is," said the doctor, "I may attach a factitious importance to this thing by the mere act of mentioning it. One evening, when the man was quite ill and somewhat flighty, he muttered something about 'papers;' and then, addressing himself to an imaginary auditor, exclaimed 'you *for*-got 'em, eh? well, I've *got* 'em, and that makes all the odds.' He also said something about chloroform, though I couldn't make out what. At the time, I could get no reply to a counter question or two that I put to him. But one day when he was convalescent, I repeated what he had said, and he was so much embarrassed that I changed the subject out of sheer compassion and never afterward alluded to it. There is one thing more, by the way. He professed to hail from Madison, and I one day made some inquiries about the place; but he seemed to know so little of it, that I doubt whether he has ever been there. That's all," added the doctor; "and, on repeating it now, I must confess I don't think there's much in it."

"People of that class," said Doe, musingly, and thinking more than he said, "don't half the time know what they are talking about."

The children now came trooping into the parlor, accompanied by Jane and followed by Phebe.

"What!" said Mrs. Jenkins, rising as she saw that her little folks were muffled up for departure, "is it time to go?"

It appeared that it was time to go; the clock having struck half-past eight. Which, indeed, is a time for all young people to be in bed; whereas, the Jenkinses, big and little, have a walk before them previously to any one's going to bed. Adieus are therefore despatched and the visitors set out for home, a united and happy family—thanks to Alfred Traverse.

No one knows that, however, except Traverse himself and the two parties principally interested. They know—they appreciate—they feel the value of a reconciliation which was the alternative of disruption, disgrace and ruin. No volume is large enough to contain all the consequences of wantonly breaking up family ties, especially when the welfare of children is involved.

As the Jenkinses withdrew, Tom arrived with a budget of restoratives for aunt Smith. Mr. Doe wished to see him. And Tom came into the parlor.

Mr. Doe went over the routine of questions about the shop, and the health of Mrs. Pinch; and then remarked that in the opinion of doctor Jenkins,

Tom's uncle had been very ill. The remark was so far interrogatory in its tone, that Tom felt himself compelled to make some response : but, being greatly confused at finding that the family secret had in some way leaked out, he hesitatingly answered—

" Ye—yes, sir."

" I don't think, Tom," continued Mr. Doe carelessly, " that you ever mentioned to me the fact of your uncle's being in town ?"

" N—no, sir," rejoined Tom, with persevering brevity, and with a devout hope that a gun would go off, somewhere near at hand, so that the sound might change the subject.

But there was no occasion to change the subject, because Mr. Doe had no wish to pursue it. He had gained all he sought : namely, the fact that Tom was under injunction of secrecy as to the simple incident of his uncle's being in town. That fact was inconsistent with the theory that matters were all right at the Pinch establishment : and it sufficed to incite Doe to a further investigation in another quarter. He was so entirely familiar with the history of the Pinches, that he knew nothing could be amiss in their family, unless it was extraneous to their own proper affairs—and *that* was just the point of coincidence in Doe's cogitations.

Tom was hardly dismissed, when Traverse came in with Snap. Traverse, impatient at Snap's want of success, and curious to see a little of Snap's tactics, had been out with Snap to take a practical lesson in the nice art of detecting. The lesson proved to be about as instructive as a lesson in angling when the fish won't bite. Traverse gained nothing by his experiment but a conviction that if Wilson's detection depended on Snap's detective powers-in-the-particu-lar-instance, the case looked squally. But how often, in real life, "it is darkest just before day!"

"I am glad you have come in," said Doe, without waiting to inquire whether the couple had hunted to purpose. "No doubt, you have had a pleasant walk; but I, by remaining at home, have found the mare's nest."

"Where's the colt then?" Traverse inquired.

Doe said it might not turn out to be a colt: it might happen to be a long horse which proverbially is *not* short in the currying. However, he went over the ground, such as it was, at the rate of two-forty.

The trio considered.

If for any reason and by any means, Mrs. Pinch could have been coaxed or bribed into harboring a fugitive from justice, her house was just the place for such a hiding and Wilson was just the man who needed it. Moreover, Snap intimated that since, at last, a tangible landing-point was in sight, he was just the man to plunge in for it, sink or swim.

Early the next morning, Snap went to market. He had a busy day before him, and he wanted his marketing out of the way. Besides, he thought Mrs. Sage had overcharged him on turnips, and he would inquire the prices of the Dutch grocers who sell their stuff at smaller profits. There was a very thriving man in this business directly opposite the residence of Mrs. Pinch. Snap would try him. The Dutchman's theory of profits was found to be rational, and his wares were satisfactory in quality on the whole, though the potatoes were rather small. Snap was pleased. He was in want of nothing to-day, for he just then bethought himself that yesterday he had marketed for two days. But, he would call again.

While Snap had an eye to the grocer's merchandise, he had two eyes for the residence of Mrs. Pinch, especially the second story of the house. And, in one of the windows he saw the bust of a man whose face, in the deliberate judgment of Snap, bore a much stronger resemblance to Beelzebub than to Wilson. From the nature of the case, Snap saw that the comely individual over there could be no other than the uncle from Wisconsin. And he took up his line of march for Doe's house, gazing at the miniature copy of Wilson's face as obtained at the Rogue's Gallery, and muttering to himself that 'twas no use to look " on *that* picture and on this."

Snap had not taken the varioloid into account.

On the previous evening, when Snap had parted from Doe and Traverse, with instructions to make the reconnoissance just described, Doe became aware that he had gone too fast in thus employing Snap.

So long as Wilson was at large and inaccessible to lay-hunting, the agency of Snap was indispensable: and Doe had to take his chance what to do and how to do, in case Wilson was found by Snap. But private bargaining with escaped criminals is rather hazardous, especially if it ends in furnishing facility for further escape: and when things came to that pass, if they ever did come to it, the fewer the persons who were engaged in the matter, the safer would it be for them.

In the excitement of what Doe reasonably thought would prove to be a full discovery of the whereabout of Wilson, by the unconscious revelation of doctor Jenkins, Doe had heedlessly stated to both Traverse and Snap what he might more wisely have reserved for Traverse's ear alone. Hence, on the morning now in question, and after Doe and Traverse had fully considered the matter, when Snap made the discouraging report that the Wisconsin " uncle " was no more like Wilson than chalk is like cheese, Doe coolly accepted the information as a final disappointment, and allowed Snap to consider the chase as good as given up. For Doe now saw that he could gain access to Wilson without Snap's intervention, and could carry out the affair much more safely to himself without Snap's aid or cognizance.

The immediate business of the interview being closed, Snap might have withdrawn ; but he had another iron in the fire, more particularly, as he found the chance for his *second* two hundred and fifty dollars disappearing. He therefore submitted the following facts to Doe's consideration.

In the first place, Snap had become aware of the fact that John Doe had a suit at law against Richard Roe ; and he entertained an opinion that when one man has an important law-suit against another, the one man, comparatively speaking, likes nothing better than to get hold of private information damaging to the other man, whether or not the information has any relevancy to the matters legally at issue.

That was Snap's " first place ;" and, after some consideration, Doe admitted its truth—" without prejudice," however.

In the second place, Snap in his peregrinations about the doubtful and not doubtful quarters of the metropolis, angling and bobbing and trolling for the person of Wilson, had unexpectedly hooked other game. He had not caught the dolphin, but he had by the gills what might prove a valuable substitute to his employer.

Snap paused in his oracular allegory, to see how it took. But it did not take at all. Mr. Doe failed to see what all this rigmarole had to do with Richard Roe.

Snap flattered himself that it had much to do with Richard Roe; and, to drop the allegory or the rigmarole, which Snap supposed to be convertible terms, he would say in plain English that he had several times seen Richard Roe make an evening call at a house, number so-and-so, where a man of Roe's position and professions had no right to go; and where by possibility he could not go with either a good or justifitable motive.

"Well, Snap," said Doe, after a little reflection, "this is so far so good—or so bad, rather. But what can you make of it?"

Snap rather thought he could make considerable of it, if such was Mr. Doe's pleasure. Just let Mr. Doe and Mr. Traverse think it up, and see if they didn't think so, too? Let them consider that he could *prove* the visits already made, and no doubt could prove others to be made.

"What is the character of the house?" demanded Traverse.

"I can't say, positive, sir; that is, particular," said Snap.

"Then," rejoined Traverse, "what can you make of Roe's going there?"

"Oh, sir," replied Snap, "I know the neighborhood just like a knife, and you may bet high there's nobody lives thereabout who is in Mr. Roe's line—that is," he added, "no line that he would own to."

"Snap," said Doe, "I don't much fancy this thing, and I am by no means sure how we shall come out of it, if we once get in. My controversy with Roe is for the benefit of others, and although the suit is a righteous one, it may fail for want of evidence. As you have proceeded in this without my sanction hitherto, you may as well carry it through to your proofs in the same manner. If when you place the proof before us, we can make anything out of it to further the suit, I will certainly account with you for it in proportion to its value. But I can make no further promise, now. If I did not *know* Richard Roe to be a hypocrite and a scoundrel, I would not listen to your proposal."

"All right for you, sir," said Snap, as he finally took leave.

"Can we make anything of this, Traverse?" said Doe.

"In a supposable contingency," Traverse replied, "I think we may make a *screw* of it."

CHAPTER XXIII.

An apothecary's shop having any claims to repectability, must be thus organized, namely : one principal, one assistant, one boy. More than this may be desirable ; less than this, is inadmissible. Mr. Scalpel had more than this. He had two assistants, each of whom was nearly as expert as himself in compounding drugs ; he had Tom, who was equivalent to two boys, as boys run ; and he had a supernumerary porter who swept the shop, made the fires, dusted the counters and trundled about heavy casks and boxes.

As among men generally, Mr. Scalpel was nothing particular. He was respectable in his vocation, prosperous in business, and well provided in the matters of family and friends. But as the head of this establishment, he was Tom's special admiration and reverence.

Every habit or peculiarity of Mr. Scalpel was, to Tom, a perfection. And as it is one of the general rules that has *no* exception, that whatever one admires one will imitate, Tom " took after " his employer in everything where imitation was possible. For example, the dignified walk of Mr. Scalpel from the front-door to the rear of the shop, was a little beyond Tom's mark ; but the solemn, stately squeaking of Mr. Scalpel's boots at every step of that walk seemed to be attainable, if Tom could get his own

shoemaker to supply himself with the right material
for soles. And, early in his apprenticeship, he called
on Mr. Crispin for squeaking leather. But that honest
mechanic gravely informed Tom that the squeaking
of sole leather was a mystery and an accident; and
that Tom would do better to wait for it till he came
of age.

Again, Mr. Scalpel had that magnificent trumpet-
tone style of blowing his nose, which some men
attain and other men hold to be a mystery or an
accident. This caught Tom's ear at once, and the
aspiring youth gave chase to it. But here, too, he
was destined to disappointment. He tried it squarely.
He tried it obliquely. He tried it sitting, stooping,
leaning backward. He stood up on a chair to try it.
But all he accomplished was a chronic nose-bleed,
which his mother finally got under by tying a string
of red sewing silk about his neck.

The elder of Mr. Scalpel's two assistants, Frederick
Jones by name, was a young man not quite one-and-
twenty, whose tact and efficiency in the business had
for some time led Mr. Scalpel to see both the advantage and the necessity of making him permanent in
the establishment, by offering him a partnership.
This offer had not yet been made, but it soon would
be.

It was one of the propitious items in Tom's history
that, from the first, Jones had taken an interest in
the boy, and not only smoothed away many of the
asperities of his initiation; but, by hints, reminders
and instructions, helped him to avoid mistakes, to do
everything well, and to make much actual progress
in what belonged to the higher departments of the
business.

Thus, he mastered the mysterious mechanism of the soda-water fountain, in the first week of his apprenticeship; and he showed such readiness in manipulating the syrup-decanters and in graduating the force of the effervescent stream into the tumblers, that the services of the second assistant were soon superseded at this station.

Again, he rapidly caught the art of making up and tying up those neat paper-parcels, in which exercise apothecaries are unrivalled. He then learned the prices of all the nice little things in the glass cases, such as soap, combs, brushes, perfumery and a long catalogue of etcæteras. And at intervals of leisure, and in evenings and rainy days, Jones taught him first to read and then to copy from the Pharmacopœia the names of medicines with their abbreviations and the signs designating quantity. And he gradually interpreted to him those cabalistic combinations of vowels and consonants which, in black letters or blue letters on a golden ground, make such a magnificent display on the swelling fronts of huge bottles, covering both sides of the shop like a wall from the ceiling down to invisibility.

Tom was, therefore, through the kind offices of Mr. Doe, in the first instance, aided by the intelligent kindness of Jones, and his own good qualities, on the high road to fortune.

The wants of Mrs. Pinch, in the apothecary-line, were small; yet, now and then she needed a trifle, and her patronage was very properly bestowed on Tom's shop. On these occasions, Phebe often acted as her mother's messenger. Phebe was a very pretty girl, and her contact with the Does and other good families where she was employed, combined with a natural grace of figure and deportment, gave her a lady-like manner beyond her actual station. It was, therefore, the most natural thing in the world that Jones should have been taken by her appearance, and should have desired to become acquainted with her. For Jones had himself sprung from the ranks, as Tom did. He had commenced his business-life with Mr. Scalpel, as Tom did, though not under so many favorable auspices. He had worked his way up from a poor boy, to a well-to-do man ; and he had not forgotten his origin, nor the ideas properly appertaining to it.

In view of these precedent facts, it may easily be believed that Jones found no insurmountable difficulty in obtaining from Tom, with his mother's concurrence, an invitation to tea on a Sunday evening ; Sunday being the only evening of the week when the two could take a turn of absence from the shop.

Tom was much elated, and not a little delighted at having so important an accession to his mother's tea-table: and after Jones's departure, he expatiated much beyond his wont on the good qualities and efficient kindness to himself, of his superior officer. In fact, Jones had laid himself out to be agreeable ; he was a pleasant young man, both in appearance and manners, and Mrs. Pinch was quite as much gratified as Tom. It is needless to say that Jones, also, was much gratified ; and hence, his visit was a success ; and he was pressingly invited to repeat it.

Phebe seemed to be abstracted, or preoccupied, after Jones took leave. She made no remark about him whatever: a fact that Tom and her mother would hardly have overlooked, if they had not been so busy in making their own remarks. Phebe might have acquired a new idea, or a new sensation: or, she might have been anxious about uncle Sam's health. At any rate, she listened and said nothing.

"The art of our necessities is strange," says the world's great dramatist: and the axiom covers a multitude of common experiences. It may be variously paraphrased, according to the various specialities in which an art grows out of a necessity; or, perhaps, more strictly speaking, the necessity creates the art. Thus, people in this world *do* what they *must* do. Things difficult when they are unnecessary, become easy whenever they become indispensable.

For example, the children of poor people develop their physical and mental capacities much more rapidly than children who are luxuriously cared for. The former will learn to walk, talk and help themselves at one year old, as well as the latter do at two. That is a single illustration among hundreds: and it is all the stronger, from the fact that the little actors who do so much from necessity, are not themselves aware of the necessity.

Another illustration may be found in the history of courtships, as conducted by people in different situations of life.

Take the country bumpkin who has plenty of long winter evenings at his disposal, and has, therefore, no occasion to be in haste. He will make a call on Polly Bissell, just at the moment when the tea-things are washed up and put away, which will be long enough before six o'clock: and he will then post himself in one corner of the huge old-fashioned fire-place, while Polly occupies the other; and there he will sit, looking at the fire—looking around the room—occasionally catching Polly's eye, and dodging quickly away from it—until ten o'clock, P.M., without opening his lips. Perhaps at the next visit, perhaps not till the second or third after the next, he screws up his courage to *hold* Polly's eye when he catches it: and after a time he ventures to grin; and perhaps Polly grins back. After six months, or twelve months of these silent sittings, Polly will remark abruptly, at half-past ten o'clock—"Eh?—did you speak?"

"No," replies Jacob, delighted at an opportunity, at last, to make a remark which is not embarrassing.

"Well," rejoins Polly, "it's time you did!"

On the other hand, take the man of little leisure. Take an apothecary's assistant, who has as nearly no leisure at all as any man in the realm. Can *he* afford to waste months of evenings in one chimney-corner while Polly sits silent in the other? No, sir! He makes short work of his courtship because he *must*. That's the argument. His necessities, in the matter of time, enable him to do in a week, or a month, what Jacob Bumpkin boggles at for a year or two. In other words, the art of his necessity helps him out.

It is highly probable, considering the age of the young woman and some other circumstances, that Jones may have commenced his negotiations with Mrs. Pinch as Mediatrix Plenipotentiary, being thereto encouraged by the very silence of Phebe. But, whoever spoke first, and whoever was spoken to, and whatever was said, certain it is that Jones, of late, seldom takes tea of a Sunday evening elsewhere than at Mrs. Pinch's; and probable it is, that the new idea acquired by Phebe on Jones's first visit, has taken a definite shape.

At any rate, Phebe is no longer reserved in Jones's presence : but she is as cheerful and loquacious and happy when that gentleman is in her company as when he is absent. Rather more so, indeed.

CHAPTER XXIV.

CONSIDERING the various good things that the friends of Richard Roe have in pickle for him, the probabilities do seem to be, that, despite his piety, his bold complacency and his dollars, the good man may be coming to grief.

He has, indeed, in times past, and many times too, slipped his neck out of halters that would have choked anybody else: and his constant escapes appear to have impressed on him a conviction not only that he bears a charmed life, but that acts which nobody—and least of all, Richard Roe—would endure in others, become even meritorious by becoming his. His fund of grace is so large, that it flavors and sanctifies crime itself, when he commits it.

Can this state of impunity, nevertheless, continue?

Richard had hitherto suffered very little from compunction; nothing beyond slight and evanescent twinges of conscience, by reason of transactions which he well knew were unmitigated swindling— except in the affair with Wilson. His dread of the reappearance of the papers in that man's possession still haunted him: for, if they should, by any chance, come to light in adverse hands, neither his impudence nor his complacency, neither his grace nor his dollars, could save him from an open shame. Wilson had, however, been a long time absent. He had, so far, successfully evaded pursuit. Detection became, now, every day less and less probable. Improbabilities were fast approaching the domains of impossibilities. In short, Reason cried "peace," while Fear whispered, "there is no peace."

Richard was wading through the mazes of this ratiocination, one day, in his private office, when two letters were given to him, each of them addressed in an unknown hand. One of them would seem to be a lady's hand, and Richard gave precedence to that by opening it first.

All that he found in the envelope was another envelope, sealed, and addressed to Jackson. That was odd. On reflection, it was very odd.

"Mr. Jackson!" he began, calling to him in the adjoining office; but in a moment he caught a second thought.

"Did you call, sir?" said Jackson, poking his head through the door-way, as he opened the door.

No. Mr. Roe did not call. He merely—a—he wouldn't interrupt Mr. Jackson. He had nothing to say. And Jackson resumed his occupation as unsuspiciously as Roe had interrupted it.

The rascalities of Roe were, for the most part, graduated on a large scale. The natural course of his business lay somewhat out of the track of sneaking villainy; and, from force of habit, not from any impulse of principle, he had avoided that. For instance, his line of practice had not led him into such peccadilloes as opening other people's letters: and when an opportunity for that sort of thing thus suddenly presented itself, he did not go about it as promptly and unhesitatingly as an expert might have done.

Yet here was a letter for another man; and that man, Jackson; the very man concerning whom he, Roe, had some vague suspicions, and whose secrets therefore it was desirable for Roe to be cognizant of, by way of retaliation. And this communication from a lady—eh? could it be—no! no! not quite so bad as that! He scrutinized the writing, though, as if his eyes had been microscopes! No!—This communication from a lady was the most opportune little incident in the world. Besides, the fact of its being enclosed to Roe, showed that some one had taken that method for the very purpose of exposing Jackson.

This course of reasoning took the matter out of the category of improprieties, and placed it among the duties that Richard Roe owed to society, both as a banker and a church-member. Richard would on no account open Mr. Jackson's letters, or Mr. Anybody's letters, under ordinary circumstances. But this case was different. "Different" was a favorite word with Roe. Whenever any one took the trouble to show him that his acts or words of to-day flatly contradicted his acts or words of yesterday, Roe invariably ended the discussion before it began by the conclusive remark, that "*that* is different."

The repetition now, to himself, of the familiar phrase which had settled so many disputed points, necessarily settled *this* point on the spot, and Roe examined the sealing of the letter.

The sealing had been carefully performed. The triangular leaf, or fold, adhered neatly to the envelope along its entire edge up to the very corners, on both sides. Indeed, the edges were so closely pasted, that they seemed to be incorporated with the main body.

This was anything but encouraging on the theory that Richard had intuitively adopted : namely, that he had better reserve the option of forwarding the letter, seemingly in its integrity, to its destination *after* he had mastered its contents. Besides, suppose the letter revealed nothing and exposed nothing ; but was a proper communication sent under cover to Roe, in good faith, from a responsible party and for greater certainty of being safely delivered—in which case, the writer might happen to make troublesome inquiries some day, if the letter did not go properly to hand !

These arguments covered the entire ground : expediency, propriety, safety, conscience and all.

"There is a way," said Roe, trying to recollect something a little out of reach ; " is it steaming the letter till the gum softens ? But if that is it, I have no such facilities here. Let me see," holding the letter to the light : " the note is narrower than the envelope. If the lower edge is nicely cut, it may be carefully gummed up again."

And, suiting the action to the word, Richard applied the point of a pen-knife to a corner of the lower edge of the envelope and ran it along the crease of the paper in a perfectly straight line. So far, so good. The letter was open.

"DEAR J,—It is important that I should see you. Be at the Dusseldorf on Thursday at half-past four.   Z."

"So, so, Mr. Jackson ! are you there with your bears ?" muttered Roe.

He made a note of the Dusseldorf Gallery, Thursday, four and a half ; and hastened to restore the letter to its original condition. The task was not difficult. By taking some pains in adjusting the brush of the gum-bottle, he contrived to paint a narrow stripe of the mucilage just within the edge and between the two sides of the envelope where he had cut it; and then, by an easy and uniform pressure, he brought them to adhere so perfectly that no one who was not looking for such a thing would have observed it. And, as Richard said, " who thinks of examining the lower edge of an envelope ?"

" Thursday !" thought Roe, as he pocketed the letter, and resolved to dispose of it by dropping it into the Post-Office as he went past: " all right. Thursday at half-past four for *you:* Thursday at three-quarters past four for *me.* I will just drop in and see who is Mr. Jackson's anonymous correspondent."

Now for the other letter. This must be from some man, known or unknown.

And with an overflowing amount of good humor and complacency at the way he had " done " Mr. Jackson, he opened the second missive. He opened it mechanically, however. He opened it without looking at it. He was grinning, and chuckling, and laughing in his sleeve over the prospective discomfiture of " poor Jackson " next Thursday, at four-and-three-quarters, when his eye caught the italicized words, " *a vial of chloroform.*" A more comprehensive and appreciative glance apprised Richard Roe that, good as the joke was on Jackson, this last letter was no joke at all. He therefore retracted his laugh at Jackson by laughing out of the other corner of his mouth.

" Fire and fury !" he exclaimed with an impetuosity as natural as it was unbecoming; "am I to be the victim of that scoundrel, after all!   What an ass have I been to put myself in his power!—'For sale for cash!' 'Valuable to the owner!'" he continued, re-examining Wilson's letter: "damn him! it is like the sneer of a tiger.   Let a man pass one point in such an issue as this, and what remains but a whole life under suspense and extortion? By heaven, I will not submit to it!   He would know my terms, would he? and by advertisement?   He shall have my terms; but not through a newspaper!   He shall have them from the muzzle of a pistol, or the point of a bowie-knife.   I will treat him just like a snake: just like a snake!"

But how to meet him, was a question.   How to secure an interview?   The appointment of time and place by advertisement was out of the question, for that would put other people on watch.   He could call for an appointment through the newspaper; and Wilson, knowing Roe's address, could fix time and place for a preliminary meeting by private note. That would do.   And when Roe could once see Wilson and appoint his own rendezvous, Roe would make such an end of the business as would leave no further contrivances necessary!

He hastily prepared an advertisement to the effect that the application of "SLY" would receive proper attention, whenever he would, by note, fix a suitable time and place for an interview.   He then left his office and made the requisite disposition of the note for Jackson and of the newspaper notice.

When Roe reached home, he found the ladies preparing to dine at Gray's; an engagement which he had forgotten in the excitement of the morning: and he set about his own preparations, very reluctantly. He was in no mood for mingling with society, and would much rather have remained at home. But an accepted invitation to dine may not be repudiated at the eleventh hour. Hence, the worthy banker forced himself to go.

Richard had a standing and conscientious objection to dinner parties, apart from his disinclination on this particular day, arising from the impediments to Grace before Meat that are incident to the very nature of the entertainment. From time immemorial, he had inflexibly performed that service at his own family table; not only because it was customary and right and enjoined by the clergy; and was moreover a proper example, an edifying ceremony and a fitting acknowledgment of bounties received; but also because he found it improved his digestion. To be sure, the last consideration might be a mere fancy; Richard might deceive himself by such a belief; but he had little fear of those self-deceptions that were on the religious side of a question. "If one must err," he said, "better err on the safe side." The safe side was his favorite side, all the world over. Richard therefore objected to dinner parties on the joint ground of conscience and digestion.

Nevertheless, as the dinner party had become a social necessity, and frequently in Roe's case was made use of to promote his business interests, Richard philosophically gave way to it both in his own house and elsewhere. But not recklessly—not heedlessly—not unprovided with an antidote to the pernicious entertainment, did the good man rush to the festive board. As on other occasions, so on the present occasion, he "asked the blessing" in advance, before he left his dressing-room; which was equivalent, in Roe's professional parlance, to asking it "on time," taking the dinner on trust, *ad interim*. By this means, he not only saved his conscience and his digestion; but he gained great credit with the people of the world; because, for all that they could see to the contrary, he sat down to meat just like any ordinary sinner, while everybody at the table knew at how cruel a sacrifice he dispensed with his accustomed privilege of Grace. Thus, among other ways, did the good Richard make his light shine before men.

Roe and Gray had a great respect for each other. They were in fact a mutual admiration society, composed of two members. Gray looked up to Roe, for his wealth; Roe, in turn, looked up to Gray for the myterious charm of his dinner parties—he got them up so much better than Roe could, and Roe had never been able to learn the reason. The reason is, that Gray had the tact to let his guests—properly selected, in the first place—shine and display *themselves;* whereas, the conceit and thick-headedness of Roe never suffered him to play the "*humble* host," as Macbeth has it: (another proof, be it parenthetically observed, that the Macbeths were well-bred people:) consequently, Roe never gave his own guests a fair chance. He never left them to make their own demonstrations in their own way. He elaborately "spread" *himself*, in the first instance; and then patronizingly brought out his guests, according to what he considered their best paces.

The present party at Gray's was made up chiefly of common friends; but the Honorable Augustus Snob, Minister Plenipotentiary, Envoy Extraordinary and Ambassador in Particular, to the coast of Morocco, had arrived in town with his wife and sister, from the Far West, *via* the capital: they were about to sail for the sphere of their diplomatic usefulness in a day or two: and Gray, with his usual luck, had caught them as a feature of his dinner. Gray necessarily appropriated the wife of the minister as his right and *on* his right: and Roe, being his chief gentleman-guest, next to the strangers, was gratified by having that lady's sister assigned to him.

It is superfluous to remark that even the sister of a man who has been selected by government as its representative at a foreign court, was a highly educated and thoroughly accomplished woman. But Miss Snob, nevertheless, had an infirmity that, to a certain extent, embarrassed her social intercourse: she was slightly deaf. Perhaps she would have declined this invitation, had she been fully aware of the extent of her deafness. But deaf people seldom attain that point of self-knowledge. They are conscious of losing a word, here and there; but they attribute that to the indistinctness of other people's articulation, rather than to their own want of ears to hear.

Roe had not perceived the lady's imperfection during the preliminaries of presentation, and so forth; and it was only after they were seated at the table, and he had once or twice found himself at cross purposes with Miss Snob, that the true state of the case burst upon him. And deafness wasn't quite the worst of it. The lady was free of speech, as well as hard of hearing; and her inconceivable replies to some of the questions or remarks spoken by Roe in a tone

more audible to the other guests than to the lady
herself, soon brought the banker into a condition very
much resembling a butt. For the company generally
had not discovered the lady's infirmity, and they
could, at the moment, draw no other conclusion than
that the spinster was deliberately making fun of
him : and that, too, in certain conventional terms of
western longitude that exaggerated the drollery of
the thing, excessively. Roe was so much mystified
by the lady's slang, that he did not at first perceive
the effect of his conversation on others. The lady's
terms were new to him. If they had proceeded from
an obscure person, he would have considered them
vulgar : but coming from the sister of a government-
foreign-Minister-abroad, the banker was probably
himself at fault. These terms, thought he, may be
Anglo-Saxon. He had heard much in praise of that
language, as being very intelligible and very strong ;
and certainly, Miss Snob's remarks came fully up to
the latter of those two conditions. Richard Roe is
not the only man who hears or talks about Anglo-
Saxon, without having one definite idea as to what
Anglo-Saxon really is.

Meantime, the minister himself was admirably diplomatic. Gray and others at his end of the table
were naturally anxious to know the prospective policy
of the government touching the ivory question. But
the Honorable Augustus Snob was as firm as a rock.
He couldn't reveal his instructions. The wheels of
government would soon creak on their axle-trees if its
confidential agents were to let on, over their champagne. In fact, it must be obvious to gentlemen that
the very object of making instructions secret, was to

prevent their leaking out. In the judgment of Mr. Snob, though he frankly admitted that his diplomatic experience was limited, blowing government secrets was tantamount to imprisoning treason. For his own part, he didn't vally ivory : ivory was well enough in its place : useful for factory purposes and sich : but not important enough of itself to make him disappint gentlemen's curiosity as to the intentions of government. But he reckoned that, whatever might be the vally of ivory, the vally of his appintment to office wouldn't be tantamount to a chor of tobaccer, if he should go to letting on.

Mrs. Snob had once "been to" somebody's boarding school. She fully approved this luminous exposition of the duties and etiqwets of a diplomatic foreign minister abroad. Speaking of ministers, hows'ever, she did hope that the folks over in Afriky would understand that *minister* had two meanings in the English language, and that "husband" was not a minister of the Gospel.

Mrs. Swift was clearly of opinion that Mr. Snob would not be mistaken for a clergyman, especially if he always wore that embroidered coat; which, by the way, was one of the most magnificent coats that she, Mrs. Swift, had ever seen.

This tribute to "husband's" eminent diplomatic qualifications quite took by storm the heart of Mrs. Snob; and she promised, on the spot, to send Mrs. Swift an ivy toothprick from the mountains of Sarah.

In one sense, Gray had committed a blunder by going out of his usual safe track and inviting this western "feature" to dine. But Gray's luck was in

the ascendant.   Gray and his guests expected an intellectual treat: they experienced a ludicrous one.
For months afterward, that dinner party was a stand·
ing joke in society.   " Equal," some thought, " to
Burton's."

" It is not much to tell of," the guests all agreed :
" but if you had only been there !"

CHAPTER XXV.

Not to speak it profanely, nor even too positively, it is altogether probable that if Tom had reported to his mother the alarming interrogatories of Mr. Doe touching uncle Sam, Mrs. Pinch would have communicated the same to Wilson, and Wilson might have taken summary measures for a change of quarters; albeit he was not prepared to change, and had not determined where he could, would, or should go, when he did change.

But Tom had his own sufficient reasons for *not* making a report of his interview with Mr. Doe. His experience was, indeed, limited. He had seen comparatively little of the shifts and tricks and diplomacy of this tortuous world. Yet the art of *his* necessities had taught him a certain amount of prudence, that would popularly be called "beyond his years"— meaning, beyond the years of those who had not been so early trained to self-dependence. So far as Tom's experience went, he never knew any good to come of "telling on" himself: to wit, communicating the fact that he had—no matter by what irresistible combination of unexpected events—been led, or induced, or surprised, into telling what he had been forbidden to tell. He knew that it was much easier to keep to himself the whole interview, than to explain his share of it in such a way as to escape "fits" at the hands of his mother: fits being Tom's pet antipathy.

Instead, therefore, of going into the particulars of his brief interview with Mr. Doe, Tom on his return home, that evening, gave his mother and sister a "thrilling account" of a poor woman who came into the shop just at the close of the day, to buy laudanum for a toothache.

Mr. Jones had undertaken the customer; and, suspecting from her appearance and manner that she wanted the laudanum rather for the heartache than the toothache, he asked her to let him see the tooth; for he knew a thing or two about teeth, and might recommend a better remedy. The sufferer couldn't well refuse; and, on opening her mouth, she exhibited such a handsome and perfect set of ivory, that Jones saw the disease was not in the teeth. The woman attempted to point out *the* tooth, selecting one as far back and as much out of sight as might be; but Jones was not to be deceived.

When the poor woman failed to convince his experience, she began to complain that the gentleman doubted her word, and would allow her to suffer just because he couldn't see the pain away back in her mouth. Jones, however, assured her that he had seldom in his life seen so perfect a set of teeth, and that there could be no disease, or pain, where there was no sign of it. But at any rate, if the pain was there, he would give her something, without charge, much safer than laudanum. This proposal did not meet the wishes of the applicant, and she was going away disappointed, when Jones assumed a different tone.

It was plain, he said, that she wanted the laudanum for some bad purpose, and that his duty was to prevent the execution of that purpose. Probably her intention was to destroy herself, and *that* she should not be permitted to do. Jones pressed her so hard with questions on the one hand and kind words on the other, that she finally broke down, and confessed that poverty and suffering had rendered life insupportable; and that she had resolved to make way with herself and her baby, which she carried in her arms. Her husband was a confirmed drunkard; he had repeatedly beaten her and threatened her life; he had actually, though unintentionally, caused the death of an older child, some weeks ago, by pushing it against the heated stove; and she was now reduced to utter despair, having been that very afternoon driven out of the house by him, he pursuing her with a hatchet in his hand and swearing he would kill her.

The end of Tom's story was that Mr. Jones had gone home with the poor woman, handed her husband over to the police, and engaged employment and protection for her from a benevolent society recently organized in that quarter of the town.

There was nothing in this story to excite much surprise. But its main point of interest for the Pinches, lay in the fact that the poor woman was no other than their former fellow-lodger, the wife namely of Rabbit, who had so unceremoniously intruded upon uncle Sam some time ago.

Mrs. Pinch was doubly glad at the conclusion of the story. Glad that Mrs. Rabbit was in a way of being cared for; and that that old drunken ruffian, her husband, was in the hands of the police. She did hope that he would swing for it.

Wilson was in a state of comfortable unconscious-
ness of the story that Tom did *not* tell his mother:
to wit, the discovery by Mr. Doe that uncle Sam was
in town. He therefore slept well, and dreamed better. He had got old Roe under his thumb; and
the morning's newspaper, in reply to his anonymous
letter, would *herald* "something to his advantage."
What better prospects could a man have?

He dreamed of thick piles of bank-notes, with a
narrow strip of paper around the middle: of rows of
bright yellow coin, all of a size and so uniformly laid
together that it would do any man's heart good to
look at them: of boxes of cigars, and baskets of
champagne: of—of—in short, anything you please,
and plenty of money to pay for it, and no law to
take anything away. This was making a good night
of it. Wilson's young remembrance could not parallel a fellow to it.

The first thing in the morning, was the newspaper.
It was had, and held to the fire to dry before even
the lark was stirring—a fact which (one may mention parenthetically, and while the steam of the wet
paper is rising in loose masses and floating around
the room) is chiefly attributable to another fact that
the larks have gone South, or somewhere, to spend
the winter. Who can tell what becomes of the old
larks? and, for that matter, of other old birds? They
travel off in the autumn, we know; they return in
the spring, we know; and they cannot be caught
with chaff, we know. Moreover, we know that each
pair of birds becomes responsible for two or three
more pairs of birds; so that the yearly census should
show a uniform increase of four hundred per cent.
True, snipe, woodcock, plover, ducks, brant, geese,

and other birds of passage are shot by sportsmen, and *their* increase is kept down by mortality : but no such obstacle to increase exists in the case of larks, swallows, sparrows and so on. Why, then, do their numbers remain substantially the same from year to year? In other words, what becomes of the old birds?

Answer the question who may; it is nothing to Wilson. His newspaper is now dry, and he is looking out for another sort of bird—a bird on whose tail he yesterday sprinkled a little fresh salt.

"Ah!" cried he, drawing a long breath as he caught sight of an advertisement responding to "SLY," "ah—hum : he wants an interview, does he? Good for you, old Truepenny! That looks like coming up to the mark. The old fellow surrenders at discretion, and makes no palaver about it. Hum. *I* am to appoint time and place by means of another note through the post. Good again! Nothing could be more proper. Where shall it be? The Battery? Too far down. Central Park? Too far up. Union Square? Too public. Madison Square? Not respectable. Egad! why not at the man's own house? *He* will take good care to make that safe. And I shall not take the papers with me, to place temptation in his way. He must trust *me*, this time! I'll send him the note and tell him—tell him—what will I tell him? Tell him 'a friend' will call at his house at eight o'clock this evening. And—for fear he should lay some plan for taking me at advantage, I will tell him in the note that my friend will not take the papers; he goes only to negotiate. And by the way, it may chance that he will recognize me as little as other people. I'll be somebody else, to begin with."

———

What Wilson had lost in good looks by means of the varioloid, he gained in general health; and an increased rotundity of person, consequent on his recovery, coöperating with the disfigurement of his face, went far toward rendering his recognition a matter of impossibility.

When, therefore, he presented himself to Roe in a style of clothing entirely different from anything Roe had ever seen him wear, also without whiskers and his hair cropped short, Roe had not the faintest notion who he was. True, Wilson's note informed him that he would be called on by "a friend;" but Roe considered that as a ruse, not intended to deceive *him*. He *expected* to see Wilson; and he was both embarrassed and alarmed at the substitution of a stranger, and was quite at a loss how to address him.

But Wilson did not keep him in doubt on that point; for, seeing the hitch and appreciating it, he commenced the conversation.

."Mr. Roe, I presume?" said he, taking a chair without waiting to be asked: and as he had taken the precaution to follow the hint of Demosthenes by putting under his tongue a moderate sized filbert, his voice did not betray his identity.

"Yes," answered Roe, with a look of blank disappointment which he could not conceal; "I thought you were—a——"

"Mr. Coon," interrupted Wilson, coolly; "I sent my name by the servant. I hope I am not intruding?"

"To an entire stranger," said Roe, "I must remark that *that* depends on circumstances: the nature of your business, for example."

"I have called," returned Wilson, "at the request of a friend, and in conformity to a note addressed to yourself, which note was elicited by an advertisement in the Herald addressed to 'SLY.'"

"To prevent any misapprehension," Roe continued, "let me inquire what is the precise matter on which you came to speak?"

"The purchase of certain papers," replied Wilson, explicitly and peremptorily, for he saw that Roe was disposed to evade the issue: "certain papers which were mislaid by accident, found by accident, and supposed to be valuable to the owner."

"Do you happen to have those papers with you?" demanded Roe.

"Certainly not," answered Wilson. "You were informed by a note—which I presume you received —that they are in safe hands and are the subject of a negotiation."

"I don't see," said Roe, who seemed to have an invincible repugnance to committing himself with a stranger, and who was considerably nettled, besides, that a stranger should be there at all, "I don't see that I can deal with an unknown person on a subject that is itself quite unintelligible. How do you mean, by saying that these papers, or whatever they may be, are the subject of a negotiation?"

"Negotiation as to *price*," said Wilson, drily.

"Oh," replied Roe, with an air of surprised innocence; "the commodity, then, is for sale?"

"It is for sale, and for cash," Wilson continued, in a tone intended to bring this sparring to a conclusion : " it is for sale, as the auctioneers say, at *private* sale, just now : but if not disposed of very soon, it will be offered at public sale to the highest bidder."

." And pray," said Roe, trying to maintain an air of indifference at this alarming collocation of words, " what may be the price at private sale ?"

" Ten thousand dollars," said Wilson, quietly.

" Ten thousand devils !" was at Roe's tongue's end; but the words were not spoken. Instead of that, he said, with a sneer, " Ah, indeed ? and for how long a time does that very reasonable offer remain open ?"

" At the longest, forty-eight hours," replied Wilson.

" Do I understand that to be your friend's lowest price ?" inquired Roe, in the same tone.

" The very lowest penny," Wilson said.

" Very good," returned Roe. " The gentleman whose interest in this matter I may possibly be supposed to represent—though I have nothing to do with it—is out of town. I will see him in the morning. You may say to the man who sent you here that if he chooses to be himself, in person and not by deputy, at the Staten Island ferry-house to-morrow evening at nine o'clock, with the papers in his possession, the gentleman supposed to be interested in them will meet him there and make an end of the business. By the by," he continued, moving toward the door, as if to terminate the interview, " the understanding about the price had better be distinct: I understand you, that under no circumstances will less than ten thousand dollars be accepted ?"

" Nothing less than ten thousand dollars will be accepted under any possible circumstances," repeated Wilson, rising to go.

"One thing I forgot," said Roe, pausing, as a new thought struck him : "let your principal write me a note requesting my friend to give him the meeting at that place and hour. The request should come in that form—do you understand ?"

"I think I do," replied Wilson, in a very equivocal tone; for a new thought also struck *him*. "I think I understand you perfectly : and," in a muttering tone, not very audible, "you will understand the note when you get it !"

So saying, Wilson made his way through the hall, followed by Roe. Wilson put on his hat as he reached the door, and was about to open it, when the light of the chandelier, falling full on his back, revealed to the astonished Roe a familiar figure.

"Stop !" cried he, rushing forward to arrest his retiring visitor; "are you——"

Wilson, startled at the peremptory tone, turned short on his pursuer and presented to Roe the same impossible face:

"Am I *what ?*" said he.

Roe was completely staggered by the instantaneous transition from the familiar to the unknown.

"I—I beg your pardon," said he, fairly frightened into a civility with which he had not hitherto treated his guest; "I mistook you for—a—what's his name ? No matter." And he opened the door for Wilson, remarking, as people are wont to do, whatever may be the actual state of the weather,

"Fine evening."

"Very !" replied Wilson, "very fine indeed ; and would be even finer, if the wind didn't blow a gale and the rain didn't come down by the barrelful."

"What the devil did the old fellow mean ?" Wil

son continued, as he hurried along, trying to keep his umbrella over his head, which the wind seemed in no humor to permit. "What could he mean by singing out in that style, as if he recognized me after all? But your Staten Island ferry-house is no go, my old boy! The rascal is desperate. I saw it in his eye."

And he tramped on through the rain and the gale, very little heeding either; for he was studying out Roe's purpose, in wanting that appointment for the ferry-house to come from Wilson himself, in his own hand.

"He's as deep as he is desperate," Wilson muttered. "He means to go there, armed: and, presuming on our relative positions, he purposes to shoot or stab me, and swear he did it in self-defence, he having been decoyed there for the purpose of being attacked by me—as witness the note that he wishes me to write. It's well contrived, my old cock! But it's no go."

Roe, on returning to his fireside, considered the matter from *his* point of view.

"I think," said he, "I've done that matter up! The fellow is a mere brigand. He would rob me of my reputation without the slightest scruple; and my character is of more moment to me than *his* life is. I'll go there armed: and if he gets my blood up—and the circumstances favor——"

It's very well to talk about shooting a man when one's blood is up, as Roe says. But when you come to think it over, and the opportunity seems to throw itself in your way—why, then, as Roe says, "*that's* different."

CHAPTER XXVI.

WILSON was not quite so successful in dreams on the night following, as on the night preceding, his interview with Richard Roe. There was in his latter visions more of iron, steel and lead; and less of piled coin and bundles of bank notes with a narrow strip of paper around the middle. And for the reason, probably, that Roe's ready assent to an interview and his assent to the demand for ten thousand dollars did not prove to be one and the same thing. The banker was not so much frightened as he should have been. The problem, how to get ten thousand dollars? was not yet solved.

If Wilson stood on different ground: if he could but meet the enemy on equal terms: if he had, strictly speaking, a fair chance at Roe: he might make short work of it. For there was no manner of doubt that Roe would rather pay the amount demanded, than suffer those papers to see the light. The embarrassment of the case in Wilson's behalf, arose from his inability to protect his own flank, while he was pitching into Roe's front. Roe might turn Wilson's position by the aid of the police. Wilson did not hold that to be honorable: but what would Roe care for Wilson's private opinion.

If, now, Wilson could but *assign* this opportunity for levying black mail to some responsible friend!

Meantime, other agencies, other interests, other influences were at work. The cauldron was by no means quiescent.

Doe and Traverse had cogitated over the new aspect of their affairs, and had come to a decision. *They* were not in fear of flank movements; but they preferred to hunt in couples. They, therefore, set out together for a call on Mrs. Pinch. Traverse, by arrangement, remained off and on in front of the house, while Doe made his visit to the widow.

The widow was at home, at leisure, in very good health, and very glad to see Mr. Doe, to whom she owed so much respect and gratitude. Gratitude is a common debt in this world. Thousands of people honestly owe it. But to find one who honestly pays it, is, as the poet says, to find one man picked out of *ten* thousand. Mrs. Pinch was one of the exceptional instances.

The customary inquiries and replies continued. Phebe was very well, and very happy, and making great progress toward the sewing-machine. (No reference, as yet, to Mr. Jones.) Tom was growing fast in stature and in the favor of his employer. His fortune was as good as made—all *it* wanted was time to grow. How could she ever thank Mr. Doe enough, and be grateful enough, Mrs. Pinch had not been able to discover.

Mr. Doe, in turn, was glad to have been instrumental in relieving so much want and in conferring so much substantial benefit. It is easy to help people; but not always easy to find people worthy of being helped, and who would afterward help themselves so effectually as the Pinches had done.

And by the way, Mr. Doe would mention another

thing before he forgot it. Doctor Jenkins had remarked that Mrs. Pinch's uncle had such a hard time with the varioloid. He, Mr. Doe, took quite an interest in the uncle, owing to what doctor Jenkins had said of him. He would like to see him. In fact, he had called for that purpose.

This was the first time that any outside person had made reference to uncle Sam; and Mrs. Pinch was overwhelmed with terror at such a totally unexpected application. She was painfully at a loss what to do, or say. Denial was hopeless when the fact was stated so simply, clearly, and on such indisputable authority.

Eh—she did not know—a—whether he had stepped out; or was busy; or what. She would see. But Doe saw that her attempting to "see," or her having any communication with her uncle in her present embarrassed state, would defeat Doe's plan, at any rate. He, therefore, stopped her short in her periphrasis, by saying,

"Mrs. Pinch, you need not fear that I shall do an injury to the man. I wish only to get from him information about another man. Let me see him without a word of announcement or preparation; and, you may take my word for it, you shall have no occasion to reproach yourself, and no fear of his reproach."

This, spoken decidedly, and coming from one who so entirely commanded the respect and confidence of Mrs. Pinch, admitted of no evasion, and the widow, therefore, led the way up stairs, cautioning Mr. Doe to "go easy" on the steps, as otherwise her uncle might take alarm at his approach. Consequently, while Wilson was sitting at his table with his face toward the window, writing his rejoinder to Roe's advertisement, Mrs. Pinch softly opened the door, admitted Mr. Doe, and closed it again, before Wilson was conscious that any one had entered the room. As he then turned his head carelessly over his shoulder, without any definite motive, his eye caught the erect figure of Doe; and he sprang to his feet, ready for attack, defence, or flight, according to circumstances.

But Doe, with a cautionary movement of his forefinger and a peremptory "hush! no noise!" brought Wilson to a stand-still, while Doe continued,

"Be quiet. I know you. Make no disturbance, or you will fare the worse."

"What do you want with me?" demanded Wilson, in a gruff yet tremulous tone.

"Information," replied Doe, briefly. "Sit down and hear what I have to say. It is your safest course."

And, as Doe seated himself with an air of quiet dermination, Wilson almost involuntarily followed the example.

"You are of course aware who I am," Doe continued; "and I know perfectly well who you are. But, if you prove tractable, I shall not be your enemy. I want information about Richard Roe which I know you possess, and which would be of service to me as the representative of my sister, Mrs. Peters."

Wilson, in the course of his travels through life, had acquired a faculty of rapid thinking; and, withal, a facility in the rapid solution of knotty points.

In the first place, then, this application of Mr. Doe was exceedingly well-timed. Wilson had just been thinking how much stronger his hold on Roe would be, if he could get another man's hand on the rope. In the second place, here *was* another man, who had an unexpected hold on him, Wilson, by the possession of his secret; and over this new-comer he could have no control or advantage, except as he could make terms with him. Here were fortune and misfortune in pretty nearly equal proportions: but while the expediencies of the emergency were doubtful, one thing was certain; namely, that half a loaf is better than no bread.

All this ran through the mind of Wilson with great velocity, so that only a brief space of material time had elapsed when he said, in reply to Doe's suggestion:

"The papers referred to Mrs. Peters's affairs; but the proof could be had only in Roe's books and in his, Wilson's, remembrance of the transactions."

Doe had not spoken of "papers," and knew nothing of them. But he had in mind what doctor Jenkins had quoted from Wilson on that subject, and he, therefore, rejoined at a hazard:

"You mean the papers that were *forgotten?*" emphasizing the word in a way to make Wilson suppose he knew all about them.

"Yes, in his coat pocket," replied Wilson, beginning to laugh at the joke: "but," he added, checking his laugh at the thought that he was unnecessarily betraying what could be known only to Roe and himself, "what do you know of the papers?"

"If," said Doe, "I know that he *forg*ot them and you *got* them, I probably know enough."

Wilson, after a moment's reflection, was very much startled at this amount of knowledge on the part of

Doe; and he was greatly embarrassed by not knowing just how far Doe's knowledge extended. If he
but knew *that*, he could play his hand accordingly!
But he had no time to deliberate. By telling Mr.
Doe the truth, and the whole truth, he would avoid
quicksands, place himself on safe ground, and secure
the best bargain for himself that the circumstances
permitted. In short, he must make a merit of
necessity.

Meantime, Doe, unaware of the favorable turn that
Wilson's deliberations were taking, and apprehensive
that if he gave his man too much space for thinking,
new obstacles might arise—put in a supplementary
interrogatory:

"Have you the papers here?" said he.

Wilson was afraid to say "no," because he had
just made up his mind to plunge into the direct
negotiation and make the most of it. Therefore he
said, "yes."

"Then," replied Doe, settling himself in his chair
and preparing for an exposition which, if it proved to
be long, would also be final, "I will come to the
point with you. I have not called here to offer you
money and the means of escape, in exchange for those
papers. I will not so far compromise myself. But
don't be alarmed! If I can obtain from you what I
seek, I will endeavor to save you from the consequences of your crime. That forgery was a deliberate
and completed felony; but its actual result to the
parties you defrauded was rendered insignificant by
your prompt detection and your restoration of the
money. And, so far as I know, that was your first
crime. You are a capable business man, and I want
just such a man in my branch office in New Orleans,

where you would be safe from recognition. If you choose to take the chief book-keeper's desk in that office, and honestly devote yourself to my interests there, you shall receive a liberal salary and be in the way of redeeming your future life. One thing, however, on that point must be explicitly understood: that if you are guilty there of the slightest variation from a direct and honest course, I will exert myself to place you in the hands of the officers of the law, and leave you to suffer its full penalty. My object is to secure to myself the advantages of those papers, and to give you one opportunity to reform. If you wish time to consider this proposition, I will wait here for fifteen minutes, and no longer."

" Sir," said Wilson, rising with great respect, and so nearly overcome by feelings of grateful surprise, that he could hardly articulate the words of his reply, " I accept your proposal at once, fully and unreservedly. And if I do not now enlarge on my deep sense of your kindness, it is only because I prefer to let my future conduct speak in more convincing terms. The opportunity you give me, is equally unexpected and undeserved. May God bless you, sir !"

" I presume," said Doe, not wishing to prolong the interview, " that you can make arrangements to leave New-York to-morrow ?"

Wilson assented.

" Then," continued Doe, " come to my house this evening and finish what remains between us. You may as well give me those papers, now."

And Doe withdrew with the mysterious and weighty documents in his pocket.

When Wilson was left to himself, he looked about

the room, as if to prepare for taking leave of the inanimate objects to which he had become attached. Presently, his eye rested on the letter to Roe that he had finished just as Doe came in.

"In my present mood," said he, reading over the missive, "I would not write exactly such a letter as that: but as it is written, it shall go—with a postscript, however;" which he added, in these words:

"*The bird has flown. Look out for his successor!*"

He next called up Mrs. Pinch, who had suffered the most intense anxiety during his interview with Mr. Doe.

She was greatly relieved to learn that no harm was done, and not a little surprised that Wilson was about to take a final departure from his lodgings on the following day. Nevertheless, since the change was considered by Wilson to be not only safe, but very propitious, she cheerfully prepared to speed the parting guest.

CHAPTER XXVII.

MATTERS and things, down town, had gone well with Richard Roe, at the very time when his interests were prospering so indifferently in other localities. He had sold out, *videlicet* bought in, sundry collateral securities at half market-price, which securities had been pledged on loans, after the manner of the loan to Mr. Hicks. Again, he had gone over his old ground of selling bonds belonging to himself, but which were likely to become worthless —" sparing" them at about ninety per cent. to some of his best friends, who, strange to say, after having been " bit" by him half a dozen times in precisely the same way, were still on the lookout for something nice and snug on bottom principles, to make up for former losses. This was like the old sheep's going to the wolf to get her back scratched.

Consequently, although the impendent interview with Wilson, with all its hazards and chances, was pressing on the mind of Roe, he found himself, about three o'clock in the afternoon, in very good case and humor.

He would by and by think about the ferry-house and the Battery. The future must take care of itself. Sufficient unto the hour, was the good or evil. He wasn't quite certain about that pistol: yet, he would have it ready. Was it to be endured that he, with this flowing tide of prosperity about him, (profits that day, some thousands,) should be held in terror, in hourly dread of a felon, who was outside of the state-prison only by reason of Roe's forbearance?

Just at that moment, in came Wilson's letter.

Roe turned pale as he read it. What! a tone of banter, defiance, threatening? and insisting on a meeting not at the ferry-house, but at Roe's own house! and the hard cash ready on the nail, *or not*—just as Roe d——. pleased! And, finally, a post-script more alarming than all the rest.

This was an appalling condition of things. Instead of Wilson's being under Roe's control, Roe was at Wilson's mercy. Could it be true about a "successor?" Had Wilson really put himself out of Roe's reach, and left those infernal papers in the hands of a third party, perhaps as great a rascal and a more capable villain? Roe's large profits for the day, which had so recently been chuckled over, offered but a small consolatory offset to that cursed letter.

Roe went home in a bad humor with himself and everybody else, notwithstanding his large profits for the day. He dined morosely, drank freely, and was as agreeable as could be expected.

Early in the evening, he went out to a church lecture: not at Doctor Perkins's church, for it wasn't his night. Had it been his night, no consideration or temptation could have swerved the feet of Richard Roe elsewhere. No. The lecture was over, down, roundabout, somewhere. And somewhere it proved to be. For instead of going to Doctor White's, or Doctor Anybody's lecture, he lost his way. He missed the turn of the street; went left when he should have gone right; and was at last observed by Snap to call at a certain house where Snap had seen him call several times previously. This time, Snap had his cue: and after waiting awhile, he followed Roe's footsteps into the same house.

He found the parlors vacant as to persons, but comfortably furnished. He sat awhile, waiting for some one to appear. Nobody came. He inspected the rooms with some care. He found an overcoat and hat lying on a sofa, which two articles were indubitably the property of Richard Roe. He examined the hat, found it to be one of Beebee's, nearly new, with R. R. written with a pen on the leather—probably in Roe's own handwriting. He made some mental resolution about compensating Roe for the loss of his hat, and took his departure, carrying the hat in his hand.

The parlor clock at Roe's house was out of order. It had run down. And that is the reason why Philip couldn't take his corporal oath what was the precise hour and minute when Mr. Roe returned home, that evening. Philip, however, *would* qualify to one thing: namely, that when his master came home, he had no hat on his head, but a handkerchief tied over it, to keep off the cold.

The reason for a thing so unusual, was that Mr. Roe, while crossing Broadway, was caught in a gust of wind that blew his hat off, and whisked it into the middle of the street. Before he could recover it, an omnibus, preceded by a pair of horses, had travelled slap over it, trampling it into the mud, crushing it out of shape, and rendering it so totally unavailable for the further use and behoof of Richard Roe, that he made a present of it to the boy who picked it up, and gave him sixpence besides to compensate the lad for his hard bargain.   It was a ridiculous affair and five dollars' worth of pities; but Roe had gained large profits in regular business, that day; and what was five dollars?   All trades must live.   So much the better for Beebee.

____

Several things took place on the same evening.

Wilson called on Mr. Doe; and received a new name and his despatches, with the best wishes of his new patron.   He moreover left with Mr. Doe a memorandum of certain things done by Roe in the matter of Peters's accounts; accompanied by references to Roe's books, which books, if they could be found, would show altered and transposed entries and all sorts of suspicious and equivocal records.   In short, not to particularize items that would be unintelligible in the absence of the documents, Wilson and Doe did a large amount of business up town, as Roe had done down town; although the realized and pocketed profit of the former was much less than that of the latter, for the time being.   Perhaps in the long run, the proportions of gain would be reversed, by the change of a cipher or two on the right side of the decimal.

One thing yet remained between Doe and Wilson: a clearing up, namely, of the chloroform mystery. That is to say, a full account of Wilson's escape from the Tombs, and of Roe's agency in it.

Wilson went over the story minutely, and Doe was thunderstruck.   He lacked words to express his astonishment at Roe's audacity.   The risk the man had taken of being discovered, exposed, disgraced for originating and completing such a bold violation of the law, was, to Doe's apprehension, inconceivable. But he kept these sentiments to himself.

No sooner had Wilson made an end of his business and departed, than Snap came into Doe's parlor with a hat in each hand. Doe did not know what any man wanted, or could do, with two hats : but Snap asked him to examine one of the two which he held out. Doe saw nothing remarkable about the hat. It was one of Beebee's, nearly new, and seemed to have initials—R. R.

" Why, Snap," said Doe, " this must be Roe's hat. How came you by it ? What does this mean ?"

In Snap's humble opinion, it meant mischief. That hat, not long ago, was lying on a sofa in a house, number so and so, whence Snap had just now brought it away ; and, as he intended, within a day or two, to enclose a five dollar bill to Mr. Roe, anonymously, through the Post-Office, he supposed the tort would not be actionable. But what Richard Roe had to do in that house and on such terms of intimacy as to leave his hat and overcoat in the parlor without being there himself to look after them, perhaps Mr. Doe could judge as well as this deponent.

" Snap," said Doe, " it was my intention to advise the abandonment of that chase, but you have been too quick for me. Since you have made the discovery, however, I will consider how far to use it."

Doe then informed Snap that he might discontinue his professional services for the present : and in view of all that had been accomplished, he would pay Snap the second two hundred and fifty dollars. Whereupon Snap departed well satisfied. Snap had in fact accomplished more than he was aware of: but

Doe saw no necessity for telling him so; payment for it, was a sufficing acknowledgment.

"Traverse," said Doe to his young legal friend, who had come in during the interview with Snap, "to-morrow morning Roe will go to Beebee's for a new hat. I propose that one of us shall call there early to-morrow, on any pretext, and wait for Roe to make his appearance. It will be worth all the time lost, to hear from himself the explanation of the loss of his hat."

The next morning, Traverse walked into Beebee's establishment, and took a seat with his back toward the door, to read some letters just obtained at the Post-Office. He was waiting, he said, for a gentleman.

He had not to wait long. Roe came down town ahead of time, for reasons best known to himself.

"Good mor—ning, Mr. Beebee," said Roe, striding bareheaded into the place with unwonted formality, making a low bow, and speaking with the drawl and the flourish which he always assumed, when he felt either very fine or very flat: "I would take off my hat to you, Sir; but the fact is, the wind took it off for me, last evening."

"Ah, indeed!" replied the hat-merchant with his well-known urbanity, and smiling at Roe's joke on trust, for he had not yet seen the force of it: "how's that, Mr. Roe?"

"Well," answered Roe, "it isn't much of a story, and I suppose such a thing may happen to any man when the wind blows. I was going home last night from Doctor White's lecture; and while crossing

Broadway, I was caught in a gust of wind that blew my hat off and whisked it into the middle of the street. Before I could make a movement, an omnibus and horses had travelled slap over it, crushing it out of shape and rendering it so totally unavailable for my further use, that I gave it to the boy who picked it up ; and, as he had a hard bargain at that, I gave him sixpence to boot."

"Ha ! ha ! ha !" said Beebee.

"Ha ! ha ! ha !" said Roe.

"Ha ! ha ! ha !" said the partners and clerks, who had crowded around to hear the story.

"Ha ! ha ! ha !" said Traverse—only Traverse said it in his sleeve.

While the hatter was seeking a substitute for Roe's loss, Roe couldn't "let well alone." He kept on talking.

"Did you ever hear one of Doctor White's lectures, Mr. Beebee ?" he inquired.

Mr. Beebee had not heard the Doctor.

"He is worth hearing, I assure you," Roe continued. "Not, of course, equal to Doctor Perkins ; and then, he is not orthodox on the ' infernal Institution.' But a man of great power ; great power ; very great power."

"Do you speak of Doctor White of Saint Dominick's, Mr. Roe ?" inquired one of the bystanders.

"Of Doctor White, of Saint Dominick's," Roe repeated, sententiously and pompously.

"And of his lecture last evening ?" pursued his interrogator.

"Of his lecture last evening," was Roe's echoing response. "Were you there ?"

"I was there," the shopman replied, " but Doctor

White was *not* there, nor was any service held there. The Doctor met with a serious accident yesterday and was unable to preach."

"You misunderstand me," said Roe, resorting at once to his old dodge: he was always "misunderstood" the moment he was cornered. "I spoke of Doctor Campbell.

"I beg your pardon," replied the complaisant shopman; "I thought you said Doctor White."

"I couldn't well have done that," answered Roe, attempting his persuasive smile, but the big upper-lip refused to participate: "I couldn't well have done that, as I never heard Doctor White preach."

Certainly. Of course. And again the shopman man apologized for misunderstanding Mr. Roe.

"Ha! ha! ha!" said Traverse—only he said it in his sleeve.

CHAPTER XXVIII.

The boldness and extent of the jewel-robbery created a great excitement about the town. The amount of property stolen was estimated by the owners at forty thousand dollars; the selection having been made as skilfully, the proprietors said, as they could have made it themselves. And, considering the facility with which the thieves perpetrated the crime and made their escape, a feeling of alarm spread itself through the whole class of tradespeople. Nothing was secure against the depredations of such audacious villians.

Large rewards were offered by the owners and by the city authorities for the detection of the criminals; and additionally to the varieties of apprehension created by the incident, a general spite against the rascals, and a desire to see them properly punished, seemed to pervade the community.

This unusual excitement was natural and commendable, as among the citizens generally; but some ill-natured people were surprised at the action of the Common Council. "A set of men," said the cavillers, "who, without exceptions enough to prove a rule, are the most audacious and ravenous robbers on the face of the earth. And those that make them are like unto them: that is to say, those of their constituents who get office under them, steal as fast and as ravenously as they. Why should the members of such a corporation make a spasmodic effort to catch better men than themselves—men who have the boldness to steal in open violation of the law, while these sneaking scoundrels do the same thing under cover of the law?"

John Doe thought the action of the Common Council was the result of mere envy and jealousy. They claim, *ex officio*, either *per se* or *per alium*, to do all the stealing within the city limits. They are elected for that purpose and with that understanding. How can a corporation, so constituted, submit to have their dirty work taken out of their own hands, and performed by low-bred, unprincipled ruffians.

Mr. Gray thought, rather, that the City Fathers were desirous to make a show of their indignant virtue, of their abhorrence of crime, of their championship of honesty: and, by such demonstration, to silence the popular clamor against themselves. They wished to make an ostentatious display of their devotion to the public good—which good, however, they never by any chance promoted.

Richard Roe was more charitable. He disliked this readiness to dive into people's motives. Outward actions men can judge of; but God alone sees the heart. There are bad men everywhere: there might even be some in the church of Christ. But wholesale denunciations don't make them better. It's very easy for gentlemen to talk. It is easy for some men to speak evil of dignities. Richard preferred the example of Saint Paul.

Nevertheless, and in the meantime, the robbers seemed to have it all their own way. No traces of them could be found. The police had inducement enough to ferret them out, surely. First, here was a good opportunity to vindicate their professional credit *as* a police, which was just now running very low. A long time had elapsed since they had been known to do anything but help ladies through the omnibus-labyrinth of Broadway. And, secondly, and principally, the sum of money to be gained by catching these chaps was an irresistible temptation to vigilance and activity. The chances were, therefore, that the police, this time, would do all they could.

But mere human policemen cannot perform impossibilities. For example, they could not find Spring, because Spring, by long practice, had found a way of taking a fast train to Quebec, where he had a resident sister, with whom he had often before sojourned under the same comfortable circumstances as he at present enjoyed: a situation, indeed, not unlike Wilson's residence with the Pinches, except that the sister of Spring was better-to-do than Mrs. Pinch.

Then, as to Rabbit. Rabbit had no friend in Quebec and no facility for getting there; but he needed neither. He was in the disguise of a gentleman when he performed his part of the play, and the moment he returned to his old clothes, his old haunts, and his old vocations, he was as much out of the way of identification as if he had flown to the moon. He was, moreover, well aware of this: partly because Spring had told him so, at the commencement of his apprenticeship, and partly because his initiatory practice had proved it to be true. In fact, all that Rabbit needed as a condition of safety, was to keep quiet and mind his own business. He had cash in hand for all present emergencies; and, in due time, by removing a small diamond from its setting and putting the jewel up somebody's spout, he could replenish the sub-treasury: and so on, to the end of the pile. Masterly inactivity was, therefore, the sole and easy duty of Mr. Rabbit.

Unfortunately for him, his previously confirmed habits of intemperance and his coincident brutal treatment of his family, rendered his purchased wisdom unavailable; and, as has already been stated, he fell into the hands of the police on these last mentioned grounds, and through the agency of Mr. Jones.

Even under that arrest, he might have escaped any other penalty than what attached to the assault on his wife, if the policemen had minded their own affairs and not taken liberties with Rabbit's person.

To be sure, when a man is arrested on suspicion, or on a direct charge, of robbery, he may properly be searched, because the stolen goods, if found on him, are *primâ facie* evidence of his guilt. But suppose a man is arrested on an indictment for libel or perjury; has the officer any right to search him? So, when, as in Rabbit's case, a man is arrested for chasing his wife with a hatchet in hand, has the officer any right to search him? And, if he did search him, and found the hatchet in his pocket, what then? Is a hatchet a *corpus delicti?* However, not to pursue these obvious legal principles, the matter in hand is that, right or wrong, policemen are very apt to put their hands into prisoners' pockets; and Rabbit's pockets, though apparently offering no temptation either to cupidity or curiosity, were not excepted.

They didn't produce much. A jack-knife, a plug

of tobacco, a pipe, some shillings in small change, and something or other wrapped up in a bit of newspaper, completed the inventory. The articles were immediately restored; all but the bit of newspaper, which contained what was probably a mock diamond. But what was the use of wrapping it up in a paper? That seemed to indicate that the prisoner supposed it to be valuable.

"Here, Jack," said one of the men to another, "you're a judge of paste, having been a bookbinder; what do you say to that?"

Jack squirted an indefinite quantity of tobacco juice out of his mouth by way of clearing his visual organs, held the article to the light, and delivered himself of the opinion that a bushel of them things *might* be worth a dollar and a half, but he wouldn't like to be the purchaser.

"Where did you get this, my man?" inquired one of the officers.

"Found it on the pavement," replied Rabbit, with drunken gravity: which was the best matter and manner he could have hit upon.

"Give it back to him," said the last speaker.

"Hold on a bit," said another, "till I try whether it'll cut glass." And he applied a corner of the stone to a window, giving it a sliding curve across the pane.

"By Jupiter, it takes hold, though!" he exclaimed. Then, trying another corner on another pane, with the same result, he remarked that they had better not go too fast about giving it back to the man.

"D—n it," said one, "who knows but this is one of the stolen diamonds?"

"Sure enough," said another. "Keep it till to-morrow morning and find out."

Upon which, Rabbit was conducted to a sleeping apartment at the city's expense.

Rabbit was under the influence of liquor, as the Addisonian phrase runs; but he was not so far gone as to be unaware of the risks of his position. And the first thing he did, when he found himself alone, was to remove a small parcel of miscellaneous jewels which were sewed inside of his pantaloons; in order to have them always about him and always safe from ordinary observation; but not likely to be secure against such a search as he now foresaw would be instituted, so soon as the actual value of the diamond was ascertained.

The brief history of the case is, that he had intended the bit-of-newspaper diamond for the spout, but was interrupted in his trip by the little domestic episode of the hatchet. He had previously removed all the jewels from their settings and had hammered their gold attachments into a shapeless mass with the back of that very hatchet. That mass he stowed away under the hearth-stone. The parcel of jewels now cut loose was small in size—not larger than a piece of chalk—and it was easily hid in the bed of his cell, so that Rabbit could catch it up again in a hurry after he had been searched and before he should be removed. That done, Rabbit went to sleep.

In the morning, the little newspaper-stone was found to be a diamond of about half a carat in weight, and worth at least fifty dollars. This fact, coupled with the outstanding offer of rewards, put the whole department to its speed. They sent for the clerk who attended to the wedding-ring for Rabbit, to identify him.

At first, the young man said, *no:* nothing like

him. On a closer inspection, there was a resemblance in the face : but, don't you see ? the purchaser of the ring was a gentleman, and this fellow is a loafer.

"Better not be too sure on that account, if that's all that's wanting," said the more experienced officer, for the reward was floating before the eyes of the department, and each man's eyes were as large as saucers and as sharp as fish-hooks. "Here, some of you, fetch in one of those suits of detained clothes," he continued ; "we'll make a gentleman of him and then try the likeness."

This resulted more satisfactorily. The clerk saw his man. Hurrah for the reward !

Search him again ? Yes, of course. But they took nothing by that. Rabbit had been too smart for them.

"Some of you go search the house," said the captain, now fully awake to the importance of the discovery.

That, again, was successful. The mass of smashed rings, breastpins and bracelets, told a flattering tale. This was conclusive as to the man : but what had he done with the jewels ?

It is only the first step that costs. The official sharps had already taken the second step. Nothing, now, was impossible. Besides, it's easy finding the fox when you get sight of his tail. Rabbit had spent the night in the cell, and probably had not been idle. Search the cell !

———

Gentlemen of the jury, it's no use talking !

Rabbit went the way of his illustrious predecessors,

who had all taken their degree from the hand of Almus Pater Spring.

A man must be far gone, when the best thing that can happen to him, both on his own account and his family's—is a residence in the state prison for life. Such, clearly, was Rabbit's condition. A confirmed drunkard and a brute, what else is he fit for?

CHAPTER XXIX.

The Dusseldorf Picture-Gallery is a quiet place in the latter part of the day when visitors are few, and especially on a day when there happens to be a grand procession in Broadway, which brings crowds of idlers into the streets and keeps the better class of citizens out of them.

At such a time, an imaginative person, sitting in front of one of the fine pictures—the OTHELLO, for example—with a tin spy-glass in hand, may become so lost in contemplation as to fancy he sees a tear of mingled love and admiration twinkling in the bright eye of Desdemona: that he hears an occasional exclamation of wonder from the grave and reverend Brabantio ; and that he almost catches the perfume of the Falernian wine that sparkes in that flask: while over all, and pervading all, and dominating all, are the rich tones of the Moorish general recounting his travels' history.

The painter of that picture had the tact to antecede the action of the play and to embody on his canvas a portion of its preliminary history, as gathered from Othello's address to the Senate. It is the calm that preceded the tempest. A scene of domestic life for which, subsequently, the gentle Desdemona must so painfully have longed. One of the days of that romantic courtship when, as Bulwer has it, the cream and elixir of life were overflowing her cup and she had no foreboding of the wormwood at the bottom. A point of her history, in short, when her evil genius, Shakespeare's master-demon, had not yet begun to weave about her and hers that infernal " net which should enmesh them all."

The picture is a biographical sketch of the hero and heroine before the great magician takes them in hand. They are here acting their own parts, independently of his control. They are here free from the influence of those persons and incidents, with whom and which the action of the drama subsequently brings them in contact. If Othello and Desdemona could but have had the grace to wait until the heart of the father could be wheedled into following the heart of the daughter, and that his consent should supersede the necessity of a clandestine marriage; why, then, how much would the lovers have gained! Not as much, though, as the world would have lost.

Such thoughts as these may have been running through the brain of Mr. Jackson, one certain Thursday afternoon, about four and a half of the clock, as he sat in front of the picture referred to. Whatever were his thoughts, they, for the time being, had the mastery of his physical senses, for he was unaware of the approach of a light footstep. He knew not that within an arm's reach of his chair, stood a beautiful woman whose eyes were fixed on the picture almost as intently as his own.

His first consciousness of the presence of this fair neighbor, or friend, was occasioned by a gentle touch of a small, neatly-gloved hand on his shoulder. It is surprising how much more thrilling a light touch sometimes is, than a heavy one: how much more power to startle or to stay a man, lies in the hand of a weak woman than in that of a strong man. If a constable had laid his brawny grasp on the shoulder of Jackson, accompanying the action with a rude, blustering "I want you!" the young man would by no means have been so intensely moved as he now was by the almost imperceptible weight of that little hand and the almost inaudible utterance of—

" All alone? and thinking of poor Desdemona?"

"Not all alone *now!*" responded the happy man: " and not now thinking of Desdemona."

The gallery consists of two apartments, a large and small one, connected or separated as the case may be, by a door. As a matter of curiosity, the gentleman, on coming into the larger room, had peered through the narrow doorway, to see if anybody was there. And the lady, in turn, had done the same thing. Each, therefore, knew that they two were alone. But they had met there for a chat, and thought the little room the more cosy for that purpose. Thither, therefore, they adjourned.

They seated themselves so as to command a view of the door, and lost no time in commencing what they had to say to each other; but they conversed in so low a tone that no eaves-dropper could have caught a syllable. They soon became absorbed in confidences, or in explanations, and they gradually turned away from the door and waived their advantage, if it were such, of watching for new-comers.

They probably thought, if they had any thought on the matter, that there would *be* no new-comers so late in the day. And the ticket-seller and door-keeper, both capacities being united in one person, seemed to

be of the same mind : for he had thrown down his
everlasting newspaper, every word of which, adver-
tisements and all, he had read three times over ; had
also counted his tickets and balanced his cash account
for the day ; and, had fallen fast asleep. It was that
dreamy hour of the four and twenty when the sunlight is fading away and the gaslights, though coming, have not arrived.

People who occupy posts either of trust or danger,
if they do sleep on them, sleep lightly. Hence, the
footing of a man, though very gingerly developed in
ascending the staircase, sufficed to disturb the cat-
nap of the vigilant official, and he awoke to profit.
A quarter of a dollar, which he had not in the
slightest degree anticipated, was deposited on the dark
blue table cover, and a gentleman who may as well
be announced as Richard Roe, walked into the gallery with a flutter and a chuckle ; for, he expected
to make something more of his visit than the ticket-
seller had done. He expected to have his man Jackson snug under his thumb, henceforth, by virtue of
detecting him in an intrigue.

The first glance of the prudent and provident
banker gave him a cold chill. He had missed his
mark. The room was empty. There was no doubt
about it. Not a living person besides himself was in
the principal apartment of the gallery. And, with a
feeling aptly described by the word " cheap," he
began to stare listlessly about, perhaps with a dogged
determination of making up for his disappointment
by getting his money's worth out of the pictures.
His actual knowledge of, and taste for, the art of
painting, however, bore so small a proportion to the
expenditure he had lavished on it in decorating, or

cumbering, his own walls, that his chance of so getting his money's worth was very small. And a total want of interest in anything before him soon brought him so practically to that conclusion, that he would have gone away again at once, but for fear that the door-keeper would laugh at him for throwing away his money. In the emergency, he set himself down opposite the first picture that came to hand, ·and studied it with the most desperate determination.

He had hardly taken his seat and thereby ceased to impede his own faculty of hearing by the noise of his own motion, when the sound of a whisper in the adjoining room diverted his attention from the fine arts and concentrated it on the art of listening: an art which he understood much better than the art of painting.

Ah, Richard Roe! Richard Roe! *could* you but have heard!

But he couldn't. He waited patiently. Time was no object. He nearly caught a stray syllable. By and by something more distinct *must* come. Not so! Not a word. Not one solitary word. No matter, my fine fellow! You are in a trap, and you cannot get out. Poor Jackson! Ha! ha! ha!

The precise position of a sleeve when a man laughs in it, has never been defined. Nor do people generally understand which of a man's sleeves is referred to, in the popular phrase. Indeed, all that is positively known about the entire institution, is the fact that the sleeve is air-tight, so that no sound of the laugh ever goes through it. In the present instance this was proved, fully. Richard was enjoying the laugh in his sleeve at poor Jackson's expense, to an exorbitant degree; yet not a sound escaped. Besides, laughter, like jealousy, feeds on itself; the more Roe laughed, the more funny grew the joke; until at last, it became so funny that Richard forgot all about the sleeve and unconsciously let off an interjectional *snort* outside of it.

The sound, although Roe made it himself, startled him: and it also startled somebody else. For as Richard turned instinctively toward the open doorway, to see if he had alarmed the objects of his sometime listening, the face of Jackson appeared *in* the doorway to ascertain who was the listener. Before either man was aware of it, the eyes of both caught each other and held fast: and while for a brief breathing space neither seemed capable of doing anything *but* hold fast, the lady, who was mystified at Jackson's immobility and reticence, thrust her face into the *tableau*, a little on the right of Jackson.

The dead silence that temporarily ensued was impressive, expressive and oppressive. What a moment, as the novelists say, for a painter! Strange, that so rare an opportunity was lost on the spirits of those artists whose inspired pencils had peopled the surrounding walls! Strange, that not one among them all stepped forth from his glowing canvas to perpetuate on other canvas the conflicting emotions of that staring group! Surprise, terror, exasperation, jealousy, fury and hatred all flashed from those three faces, as under the spell of an exorcist; each distinct in itself, yet all so blended as no artist ever blended them!

In astronomical phrase, here was a conjunction of Mercury, Venus and Mars; and if perchance the exterior planet should be surprised out of his centrifugal force and fall within the orbits of the lesser globes, what a wreck of matter and crush of worlds might be looked for !

A pause, under these circumstances, was perhaps inevitable ; but it was growing long.

Richard Roe, so voluble in prayer, have you no words of exhortation appropriate to this season of trial ?

Joseph Jackson, cannot you hit upon some simple, plausible and credible explanation of what, on the face of it, certainly has a squinting toward the improper ?

Madame Helen Roe—brilliant, confused, dangerous—have *you* nothing to suggest ? Live long, my dear madam, live many years, and you may never again have so needful an occasion to color things equivocal with things of good report.

. The lady had a great deal of character—such as it was. Her attachment to Jackson had begun early and taken deep root, but it broke down on the money question; she having no fortune, and he being one of that class who, with a thousand good qualities, lacked the faculty of getting on in the world. About those days, Roe became smitten with the lady's personal attractions, which indeed were neither few nor small : Jackson grew jealous and quarrelled ; and the lady married Roe for money—and *got* it : the settlement of a fortune on herself having been a condition of the match. This might not have been the surest method to cure Jackson of jealousy and quarrelling ; yet it seemed to have that result, as the young people became friends again. Possibly ——

Things were substantially in this condition, when the three met at the Dusseldorf. The lady had hitherto taken pains to conceal her sentiments toward Jackson, because she thought, as most people think, that it is better to "save appearances;" but when, as now, appearances had taken to themselves wings, what was the use of trying to save them? At any rate, as to Roe her position was one of no trifling independence. She had a fortune of her own, she had no children, and she lived under the benign laws of the State of New-York, which allow married women with money in their pockets to do very much as they please. It was dangerous for Roe to attempt much exertion of prerogative toward such a lady, so minded: and he entirely miscalculated the force of his own authority, on the one hand, and the power of an unprincipled woman's recklessness on the other, when he at length broke up the magnificent tableau-for-a-painter, and advanced with the obvious intent of laying violent hands on his lady-wife.

Jackson was a splendid fellow, physically; altogether an overmatch for Roe; and whatever the rights or wrongs of the present case, he would have prevented such a personal collision as was now impendent, if he had taken Roe's life on the issue. But the lady needed none of his aid. The mere show of violence toward herself, had

> "Made each petty artery in her frame
> As hardy as the Nemean lion's nerve;"

and, withholding with her left hand the intervention of her champion, she stood forward against her desperate husband, confident in her own strength, towering, majestic; invincible at all points—except the justice of her cause.

King Lear says,

> " Thou'd'st shun a bear ;
> But if thy path lay toward the raging sea,
> Thou'd'st meet the bear i' the mouth."

At first, Roe instinctively "shunned" the athletic Jackson, and sought what he supposed to be a safer victim of his wrath. But when he beheld the dilating figure of this magnificent woman advancing upon him, instead of retreating; he found to his dismay that Jackson was only the bear, while the lady was the raging sea; and he incontinently turned to meet Jackson "i' the mouth"—that is to say, *with* the mouth; for Roe's physical fight was at an end when he quailed before his wife. It is one of the strange disabilities of cowardice, that the coward cannot play his game well, even when he holds all the honors in his own hand!

"Vile pander, begone!" cried Roe, attempting to be dignified at least in his language, but failing in that as in everything: for his pompous syntax, his cracked voice, and his ignorance of the meaning of words, combined to render his demonstration supremely ridiculous. He waited a moment to watch the effect of his demolishing remark, which in his judgment ought to have demolished anybody; but Jackson was insensible to its power. Roe, therefore, repeated the fulmination with increased vehemence: "Vile pander, begone!"

An exceedingly brief portion of material time had elapsed since this "scene" commenced: yet it had sufficed to moderate the first flush of passion with which each of the three parties had entered upon it; and to show them that, however these untoward circumstances might eventuate, the best thing for all of them was to " be gone." Each of the three seemed to have spontaneously reached that conclusion, as Mrs. Roe whispered something in the ear of Jackson. That gentleman hesitated; but she added, aloud,

"It is best, believe me."

He then bowed assent and was about to brush past Roe, when to the great relief of all, the door-keeper announced the arrival of his dinner-hour. An hour, he remarked, when it was too dark to see the pictures without gas, and too early to light up for the evening.

No interruption could have been more opportune. What took place between the Roes on their way home, never transpired. But at dinner, that day, Mrs. Roe was quite too radiant for any one to believe she was in the slightest degree subjugated; while the unfortunate banker, who had been for a week privately chuckling over the predicament into which he was about to plunge "poor Jackson," was proportionably out of sorts.

He made a demonstration or two on Margaret about the weather; but Margaret was too good a tactician to be drawn into quarrels other than her own; and, seeing matters ajar between Roe and his wife, although she knew nothing of the cause, she determined to let them fight it out, without her aid and comfort. Roe was thus reduced to silence; or its alternative, a few of his poor attempts at wit on Philip. Philip didn't see anything funny in Roe's jokes: and no wonder; nobody ever did see anything funny in them, though Roe had been practising them all his life. But Philip saw that he was expected to laugh, and it wasn't for him to judge of the quality of Roe's wit: therefore, he grinned and showed his ivory.

———

The next morning, Roe called Jackson into his private office.

"Mr. Jackson," said he, with severe majesty and majestic severity, "have the goodness to fill up a cheque for the amount of your account."

"Much obliged to you," replied Jackson, coolly; "no occasion for money at present."

"That's your affair," said Roe; "you can take your own time to find occasion for money. But before you leave my employment, I mean that you shall be *paid* in full."

"Oh," said Jackson, innocently; "that's it, is it? Before I leave your employment, Richard Roe," he continued in a different tone, "I intend not only to *be* paid, but to *pay* in full. At present, however, I have no intention of leaving your employment. The place suits me."

"Your occupancy of it, sir, does not suit me," returned Roe, with increasing severity and diminishing majesty. "Bring me the cheque, as I ordered, before I order you to quit these premises."

"Richard Roe," said Jackson, "we may as well understand each other. You speak as if you had control of my motions; whereas you are in my power; and, if you provoke me, I will ruin you. Don't fume, sir! Don't roll your eyes at me! Don't *flatter* yourself that my words have reference to any lady! I refer to your victims in this office, scores of whom you have ruined by professional robbery. Do you suppose that I am blind, and a fool to boot, not to

know the length and breadth of your dealings with
Hicks, Burton, Steele, and so on? They submit because they have no evidence of your rascality. But
I have full abstracts from your books of all those
transactions. Provoke me, now, with a word, or a
look, and I'll place the whole proof in the hands of
those men. You talk of ordering me to quit these
premises! Repeat those words, if you dare! I tell
you, Richard Roe, banker and church-member, you
are a villain. But it suits my convenience to remain
on a salary which I prefer to the restricted partnership you have often proposed. If I were half as conscientious, however, as you profess to be, I would quit
you of my own choice: for, after all, money received
from you is but the wages of iniquity."

So saying, and without deigning to wait for a reply, Jackson strode to his desk and resumed the
business of the day, which Roe had temporarily
interrupted.

As Jackson reflected on this interview, so unexpectedly put upon him, he was surprised at the ease
with which he had silenced his antagonist. But he
did not know how much he had been aided in the premises by a false impression in Roe's mind. Roe, in
his astonishment and dismay at Jackson's disclosures,
imprudently jumped to a further conclusion, namely,
that Jackson was the " successor" indicated in Wilson's postscript, and that Jackson therefore had
possession of that dreaded package of papers. Jackson had said nothing to warrant such an inference,
but—so prone are men to deceive themselves when,
with an over-estimate of their own sagacity, they once
set off on a false scent—the very fact of Jackson's
omitting any reference to the papers, strengthened

Roe's suspicions and apprehensions that he had them in his possession. Roe, therefore, in imagination had before him not only the successful intriguer with his wife and the equally successful spy on his business frauds; but Wilson besides with *his* knowledge and papers, all rolled into one person, and that person standing over him, in gigantic proportions, the very arbiter of his fate!

It is no wonder that Roe quailed before such an antagonist.

But, next to fear, comes hatred; and next to hatred, comes revenge. Look to yourself, Jackson! Roe has been crowded into a position where even cowards become dangerous. He would crawl through a very small hole to avoid a catastrophe; but when every avenue of escape is closed, the recklessness of despair may become a part even of his sneaking nature. Therefore, Jackson, look to yourself! You have pressed your man hard. But don't presume too far on his cowardice, nor on his religion!

CHAPTER XXX.

MARGARET AND SAM.

Sam Gray was a sad fellow. He belonged to that class of people who are counted in a census, or a crowd ; but who, in the qualities that constitute *a man*, fall so far short of any recognized standard, that they deserve no individualization in history. All that need be known about Sam, is known. He is the accepted admirer of Margaret Roe. Should the pair chance to be married, he would be known as the husband of Margaret Gray, *née* Roe. And when he ceases to be known at all, his epitaph would be, "He married a Roe." No great distinction, indeed ; but you can't have more of a cat than her skin.

How it came to pass that Margaret Roe ever descended to a passionate attachment—perhaps, more properly speaking, an obstinate attachment—to such a person as Sam Gray, is explained, so far as such a freak can be explained, in chapter VII., page 69, of this history—to wit : it cannot be explained at all. It is one of the strange facts of real life. It would never do in a novel.

Just now, Sam is ill ; and Margaret, silly puss ! is distressed ; and doctor Jenkins is in attendance. And Margaret, too, is in attendance more or less ; because that is one of the prerogatives of a young lady who is engaged to be married, and doesn't deny it. In that way it happened that Margaret and doctor Jenkins met one day in the parlor of Gray, senior.

"How is he to-day, doctor?" inquired the young lady.

"Very ill indeed," was the doctor's reply: and one might easily infer from the tone of the speaker that the fact gave him very little uneasiness.

"Doctor," pursued Margaret, "what is the matter with him?"

"A disease," answered the doctor, "which is the necessary consequence of his bad habits: it is neither more nor less than delirium tremens."

"Doctor," said Margaret, reproachfully, "I hope you will not turn against Sam, as everybody else does."

"Margaret," replied the doctor, softening his tone in deference to her real distress, "I have told you the simple truth from my positive knowledge of the case. And, as you intimate that everybody but yourself is of my opinion, I hope you will one day come to the same conclusion yourself."

"Never!" cried Margaret, passionately. "I never will!"

"I am sorry to hear you make so silly a remark," the doctor continued, but without any unkindness of manner: "you don't suppose, Margaret, that you are wiser than all the world?"

"I suppose," answered Margaret, "that Sam knows his own story better than all the world does; and when he tells me that all the world calumniates him, I will believe him against all the world."

"It is often the misfortune of young ladies in your position, my dear young friend," replied the doctor, "both to believe and to disbelieve precisely what they should not. I am entirely aware of the embarrassments of your position. I know its hardships and trials, at home and elsewhere. I make more allowance for your infatuation about that young man than others do, because my intimate professional relations with your mother, and my subsequent knowledge of your father and stepmother, have enabled me to understand the case fully. But for that very reason, since you now give me an opportunity that I have long sought, I wish to tell you plainly what you ought to know, and what so many of your friends have already told you, to no purpose."

" I hope," said Margaret, imploringly, " that you will not take advantage of this time of trouble, to say what I should not hear."

" Trust me, Margaret," returned the doctor, " I will say nothing that your mother would not say, were she here to see what she so truly foreboded. Her painful prophecy, thus far, is literally fulfilled : God forbid that the sequel should be so ! Possibly, this sickness was designed to bring you to a state of mind in which you will listen ; or, it *may* have been sent as the arbiter between you and the fate you are rushing on, to place such self-destruction out of your reach : a termination which, in my judgment, would be simply providential. But if the young man recovers, and you should join yourself with him previously to a thorough reformation on his part— which is utterly hopeless—you will have secured a life of such misery as all your home experience cannot aid you to conceive."

To this authoritative and solemn admonition, Margaret could reply only by tears and by broken asseverations that Sam's conduct would yet give the lie to his calumniators.

"So far, so good," said the doctor; "but in the meantime, why continue an engagement so fraught with risks and disadvantages to yourself? The probation you suggest will come to nothing: the young man will impose on your credulity in that, just as hitherto he has done in everything. And I may well transpose the scripture-text and inquire how much the better you will be, when you have gained such a husband and lost the whole world? We will await the issue of this illness; but meantime, Margaret, remember that what I have said comes to you, in effect, with the high sanction of your mother's authority."

And, as the doctor thought proper to leave the matter thus in suspense, other people must be content to do likewise.

There is no doubt that, if Mrs. Roe could have had a preliminary voice in the affair, she would have given it *against* being discovered by her husband at the Dusseldorf. But when the march of events took the question of privacy out of her hands, she was precisely the person, and in precisely the position, to make the best of the new order of things.

In the first place, she appreciated the advantage to herself of the limited character of the discovery. It made, to her, all the difference in the world, that no third person was present, to hear and carry the matter: and few things are more certain than that the three who *were* present would keep counsel. She felt refreshed by the novel circumstance of being involved in a family secret that *must be kept*.

In the second place, she enjoyed the full benefit of the paradox, that the discovery of her intrigue promoted its security.   There is no question that it did so, because,

In the third place, since detection must ensue, Richard Roe was the man of all the men, the person of all the persons, in the wide world, whom she would have preferred to accomplish it.   For, she was independent of him in property : she knew that his pride (the only vestige of a virtue that he possessed) would prevent his exposing her ; and *he* knew from her own mouth that she despised and detested him.   Why should she regret that he now had better evidence to the last point, than even her own declarations? What could he do about it?   How could he help himself?

It is a feature in domestic history, when a wife can set up her own private Gibraltar in the family mansion : her own rock of offence and defence against which a whole army of indignant husbands may blaze away, and welcome.   One's own Gibraltar is a great institution.   Conditioned, however, that the material is good.   Granite.   Not Soapstone.

When Mrs. Roe had finished this train of reasoning, and ascertained that *her* Gibraltar was made of granite, she felt very much as one feels after drawing a high prize in a lottery.   She was disposed to be condescending, liberal, magnanimous to somebody.   And, Richard Roe being out of the question for any act of her grace, and Margaret being next at hand, why, she would see what she could do for Margaret.   She therefore turned over a new leaf.   She became a non-combatant.   She took no notice of Roe, one way or another.   But she set about cultivating Margaret.   And Margaret, subdued by grief on Sam's account, and unconsciously mollified by the cessation of domestic hostilities, fell into half amicable relations with her stepmother, before she was aware of it.

It is odd, how things work together in this world! Margaret and her father not only never had any mutual cordiality, but there was no single point of friendly contact between them. Nevertheless, subsequently to the death of Margaret's mother, the father and daughter had got on quietly. They had lived peaceably. No friendly intercourse; but also, no quarrelling. The difference between that state of things and the turmoil of incessant controversy, is a difference that experience alone can fully comprehend; and that difference was developed in Roe's household immediately after the accession of Mrs. Richard Roe the Second. Hence, it is no calumny to say that *she* was the disturbing element in the premises. Roe was responsible for having placed her at the head of affairs, but she was responsible for the faults of her administration. Mrs. Roe, then, made Margaret's home more uncomfortable than it was before; and an unhappy home, in turn, had *its* effect in promoting Margaret's constancy to Sam— any change promising to be for the better, for her. She thought it safer to fly to ills that she knew nought of, than to bear those that she knew too much of. Nothing, therefore, could be more natural than that, while she was thus balancing contrasts, and while the admonitions and warnings of doctor Jenkins were ringing in her ears, a favorable change in the condition of things at home, produced by Mrs. Roe's change of tactics, should have led Margaret into reflections on her engagement with Sam, which were somewhat ominous for that young gentleman's hopes. And after all that had come and gone, if she could be brought to hesitate about that affair, the proverb would stand a good chance of being reversed. Thus—to repeat the first line of this paragraph—it is odd how things work together! The discovery at the Dusseldorf, which had no conceivable connection with Sam, led to a condition of things that might substantially disconnect Sam from his matrimonial prospects.

CHAPTER XXXI.

REUNION.

Phebe never made much account of her uncle Sam. She had, in fact, known her father, though she had very little recollection of him, and that knowledge, slight as it was, answered the requirements of Nature's statute, technically.

But Tom, who was somewhat in the predicament of Marryat's Japhet, having " lost " his father some months before he was born, had never yet had his bump, or sentiment, of filiation developed. That quality in him remained like the legs of a snake, indicated beneath the skin by imperfect anatomical articulations. But when the boy first heard of an uncle, a thing he had never heard of before as pertaining to himself, an undeveloped something under his skin sympathetically struggled toward a leap into the old gentleman's arms. Moreover, in the rare instances when he caught sight of this apocryphal relative—real, to him—his demonstrations attracted the notice of Wilson and produced a corresponding return. And when Tom learned his uncle's departure for Wisconsin without leave-taking, he had quite a turn of " homesickness," for which his limited knowledge of materia medica furnished no remedy.

Uncle Sam, however, did not leave his relatives without witness. He bequeathed to his niece, Mrs. Pinch, the furniture of his apartments, and the sum of one hundred dollars for pin money. He gave Phebe the sum of twenty-five dollars toward keeping her sewing-machine supplied with ammunition, whenever possession of said machine should be realized. And to Tom, he gave a like sum, together with his stock of cheap novels, magazines and illustrated newspapers.

Thus, with Phebe's prospects, and Tom's prospects and the widow's possessions, the Pinch family seemed to be in a fair way of not being pinched any more.

On finding herself thus comfortably established, Mrs. Pinch began to consider how she might do good to others; and she hunted up Mrs. Rabbit, her old friend and former fellow-lodger, whose story was soon told. It was another instance of the short and simple annals of the poor.

From the day when she was relieved of the intolerable burden of her husband, her health and circumstances began to improve. She gained much from the Society that first took her in charge, and more from the ladies connected with it, who found her skill with the needle could be better employed and much more munificently compensated, on their own finery. She was thus transferred suddenly from a state of great want to one of comparative affluence. Indeed, the change in her appearance and surroundings was so entire that Mrs. Pinch, who had not seen her for several weeks, hardly recognized her. And the baby, too, which was squalid enough at their last interview, was now as chubby, rosy and hilarious, as if it had been born with a silver spoon in its mouth.

On comparing notes, the two widows found that they could be of use to each other. Mrs. Rabbit wanted companionship, and a better location, and Mrs. Pinch wanted a tenant for uncle Sam's furnished apartments—which *being* furnished, could be rented cheaply to Mrs. Rabbit, and yet at a considerable advance over the landlord's price for the vacant rooms. Then, Mrs. Pinch could take part in Mrs. Rabbit's needlework which accumulated on her hands faster than her own hands could perform it. Again, by making common cause in the matter of housekeeping, they could secure innumerable little conveniences and economies. Moreover, the baby would be better cared for; and, in return, it would be a desirable acquisition to the circle—a real light in the dwelling. In short, the advantages of the plan were so obvious and manifold, that the women dropped the argument and set about moving energetically; and when Tom and Phebe came home to supper, they were equally surprised and delighted to find the pair of Rabbits permanently installed in uncle Sam's rooms, and a grand banquet of tea, chocolate, sweetmeats and waffles spread out in honor of the strangers.

Tom and Phebe both knew what was expected of them in regard to the supper, and both came up to Lord Nelson's order very harmoniously. But there was a strife between them for the possession of the baby, which seemed to have been kept awake for no other purpose. The difficulty was at length accommodated, just in time to save the young Rabbit from being pulled into two pieces, by the mother's decision that Tom must take turns with Phebe in holding it—the baby, meanwhile, manifesting the utmost impartiality between the combatants and being equally happy in the arms of either charmer.

The festivities were prolonged to a late hour—for

such a party. But as the clock struck eight, the youngster was cabined, cribbed, confined; the ladies withdrew to their gossip and Tom to his merchandise.

Jones also took a great interest in the new-comers. He had been directly instrumental not only in relieving Mrs. Rabbit's pressing necessities, but in actually saving the life of both mother and child on that terrible evening when the mother deliberately undertook her own and her child's destruction. And now that his good work was producing such good fruits, he seemed as much gratified as the party principally concerned.

One of the characteristics of benevolence is, that it always gravitates toward the objects which have once attracted it.

CHAPTER XXXII.

THE sober second thought of Richard Roe, as touching his purposes of vengeance on Jackson, was in no respect more favorable or propitious toward the object of his wrath, than his fiery first thought. But Roe was an old soldier, and was about the last man in these United States to act precipitately where, by precipitate action, he might break his own neck. He would use up Jackson. No mistake about that. But he would take his time for it. He would first survey the ground. He would see how the land lay. Perhaps he would draw Jackson into a conference with the ulterior purpose of drawing him into making a proposition. He might obtain from Jackson an offer to sell those papers which had been his bugbear for months, and would continue to be so until he got possession of them. No harm could come of getting Jackson to the point of offering to sell. He would see.

"Mr. Jackson," said Roe, in a tone which might be friendly, might be wheedling, might be dangerous, and might be almost anything, "will you step into my private office for a moment?"

Enter Jackson, conformably.

"Eh—Mr. Jackson," Roe continued, "you spoke to me about some papers—a—abstracts from books, which you have; and which you might put to use some of these days. Just for the curiosity of the thing, I would like to know your views."

" My views of those papers ?" said Jackson, not a little astonished at the suddenness of the application, but determined, nevertheless, to show a bold front; " my views are that those papers will secure me against any antagonistic action on your part for an indefinite period: and I hold them as a check upon you."

" But," said Roe, " supposing I contemplate no antagonistic action, as you call it: how then ?"

" You are rather an uncertain person, Mr. Roe," answered Jackson; " and a curb that I can rely on, is no bad thing for me to hold in readiness."

" Ah," cried Roe, with an unhappy effort at a sarcastic tone, " perhaps the curb you speak of is part of a harness of black-mail ?"

" If you wish to buy those papers and my silence along with them," said Jackson, feeling the reins and finding that Roe was champing on the bit; " if you wish to buy, you can mention your terms. For, after all, there is no great congeniality between you and me, and we might be better friends if a reasonable distance separated us."

" I said nothing of a wish to buy," said Roe, coldly.

" But you *have* such a wish, nevertheless," replied Jackson. " And if your diffidence prevents you from making an offer, you may find a friend who will make it for you. I wouldn't mind doing as much as that for you myself. I think I know your ' views,' and I will make myself an offer, on your account, conformably to those views. Then, on my own account, I will take your offer into consideration. I will manage the thing thus:

" 'Mr. Jackson, I am authorized by Mr. Roe to offer you for that entire parcel of papers and all the facts within your knowledge thereunto appertaining, the sum of ten thousand dollars.'

" 'Very good,' I reply, in my own person, 'I don't think I'll take it, Mr. Roe.'

"By the way," continued Jackson, interrupting his bantering and supposititious negotiation to throw in a side-winder, "I forgot to mention one thing which, to me, is superlatively indifferent, though you may regard it in another light. I have been sub-pœnaed in the case of John Doe *vs.* Richard Roe, on the part of the plaintiff; and, by coupling the sub-pœna with the order on you to produce the books on the trial, I imagine that I am to be called upon to testify as to my knowledge of those books: not only as to what they contain, but as to their disappear-ance—of which I know more than I have told! You must judge how my testimony would figure in that matter. All I can say is, that if you and I agree as to price, I will place myself in a position much re-sembling the books themselves, in one respect: I will be *unproducible* as a witness. And now, in view of this, *my* 'views' are, that I don't think I'll take your offer of ten thousand dollars."

Jackson had hit on that sum incidentally, and by way of feeling his customer. Yet the identity of amount with the offer made by Wilson had the effect of corroborating Roe's suspicion that Wilson and Jackson were acting in concert, and that Jackson really had possession of the dreaded papers. Rea-soning on this preconceived idea, he came to a sudden conclusion that he would make an *end* of the papers-question, all and singular, with Jackson's acquired information, and be thereafter in a safer condition to pursue his personal retaliation on Jackson himself. Vengeance was in his heart, but the time to strike with impunity had not arrived. One thing at a time, thought Roe. Negotiation first. Retaliation afterward. The papers must be got out of the way.

In pursuance of this thought, he replied to Jackson's last remark, that he, Jackson, need not be at much pains to decline an offer which he, Roe, had not made.

"No matter for technicalities," said Jackson. "I saw the offer in your eye; which, to me, is more conclusive than to have heard it from your lips. I understand your eye, Mr. Roe, and I can trust it. Your words are not always to be depended on. I consider that I have your offer under consideration."

"You may consider what you please, and carry your consideration as far as you please," said Roe, reddening, though he dared not exhibit much anger. "I have made no offer; but if I were to offer, it would be not only for the papers you have—*and all of them*—but for a supplementary affidavit, that whereas you spoke of having certain papers in your possession, you retract that assertion, and state, under oath, that no paper in your possession is a genuine account of any of my business transactions."

"If you multiply conditions," said Jackson, coolly, "I shall raise the amount of your offer. Meantime, if you are ready to commit yourself to a proposal for ten thousand dollars, you can't say so too soon."

"What answer do you make to the proposal for such a certificate?" inquired Roe; who was already insensibly carried beyond his intended stopping-place, first by his uncontrollable anxiety to get possession of the papers, and next, sympathetically, and by force of a habit that led him when he once began to "talk" negotiation, to carry his point to a practical conclusion—as children "play" fighting, and before they are aware of it, find themselves fighting in earnest.

"I have no objection to give you such a certificate," replied Jackson, "provided I carry my own points in the negotiation."

"And no objection, I presume," added Roe, "to discontinue all acquaintance and intercourse with my family?"

"My dear sir," replied Jackson, with a superb air of mock dignity, "don't embarrass our negotiation by references to any lady."

"It's all one," said Roe, stung to the quick by Jackson's sneering tone; "I can take care of that matter myself."

And he at once set about drawing up the requisite certificate for Jackson to sign. Roe prided himself on drawing papers and writing letters. He did them both very badly, because he overdid them. He conveyed in his letters either no meaning, or something opposed to his intended meaning, by his elaborate phraseology. And he made his "papers" so strong that they betrayed an over-reaching and dishonest purpose on his part; so that whatever their legal force might be, as against the signers, they proved rascality in the man who drew them.

"There," said Roe, as he finished the certificate to suit himself, "sign that and hand it to me with *all* the other papers, and I will give you a cheque

for the amount stipulated, including what is due you
on my books."

"At one o'clock," said Jackson, looking at his
watch, "I will be prepared to complete this. As
to the family matter—why, as you say, you can
take care of that yourself."

———

At one o'clock it was. Jackson presented himself
with a formidable package of papers, sealed and
addressed to Richard Roe, accompanied by the certificate, duly signed and sworn to, and a sworn affidavit that the package of papers herewith delivered
contained everything in his possession relating to
Roe's affairs. He also handed to Roe a cheque for
the money which Roe was to sign, the filling up of
which cheque was to be Jackson's last official act in
Roe's service.

It chanced, that Richard was prevented from
examining the sealed up parcel of papers, by the
entrance of the Honorable Thomas Snagg, U. S.
Minister and So Forth to the Hebrides, who was
about to sail for his destination, and was anxious to
pay his respects to the good banker. On this
occasion, Roe's weakness in affecting great men
prevented his making an examination of the
papers, and he signed the cheque on the faith that
Jackson was keeping faith—which, indeed, he was.

The loose screw in the business was the fact that
Jackson was *not* the "successor" indicated in Wilson's postscript: but Jackson could not be held responsible for that.

CHAPTER XXXIII.

"THESE papers," said Traverse, after he and Doe had carefully examined the documents obtained from Wilson, "show plainly enough that Roe is a villain, and they would legally establish our case, if we could supply legal *proof* of what they represent."

"The books of Roe will complete what the papers lack," replied Doe: "they contain the proof."

"Very true," said Traverse; "but how are we to get the books?"

"Surely," returned Doe, "the law on that point is compulsory?   On an order of the court, a man *must* produce his books."

"Doubtless, he must produce them, if they are *in esse*," Traverse replied: "but suppose Roe swears that he cannot find them, or has destroyed them?"

"That of itself would condemn him," said Doe.

"Of course it would, in the minds of all honorable men," returned Traverse; "but it would not establish our case with the court."

"Then," said Doe, "so far as this new matter is concerned, we are reduced to such power of intimidation as the papers in our hands possess."

"It would seem so," Traverse replied, "if the books do not come at our call.   When we have ascertained *that*, we must try the screw and the lever."

"Which," added Doe, "are not likely to prove

toys under our management, if we may judge of what they can do by what they have done. If the desire for those papers could send Roe to the Tombs on such an errand, what may not the fear of them produce, when *we* are playing against him?"

"There certainly is great force in that suggestion," said Traverse. "Now let us go over the case, and at some length, omitting what is already set forth in the pleadings. We can furnish positive proof that a little before three o'clock on the day of Wilson's escape, Roe bought a vial of chloroform at Scalpel's shop, and took Tom off on a fool's errand in search of a prescription that never was written; and then gave the boy the slip in the cars. Soon after, he calls at the Tombs and remains in Wilson's cell until the next morning; Wilson having in the meantime escaped in Roe's clothes under circumstances perfectly consistent with Roe's collusion, but not easily conceivable on any other theory. In the morning, *a* vial of chloroform is found in the cell, of the same size as the one sold by Scalpel, but not otherwise identified. No man can distinguish one vial from a thousand others just like it, when the suspicious fact of a removal of the label has taken place. I would like to hear Roe's explanation of his purchase of that vial of chloroform!

"Then," continued Traverse, "we have in Roe's hand writing a sketch or abstract of an account with Peters, showing a balance due Peters of one hundred and sixty five thousand dollars on the 1st of January, 18—; with a hypothetical memorandum in pencil that he, Roe, can probably wheedle your sister, as sole executrix, into settling with him and granting him a release on his paying her the odd fifteen thousand dollars; which is exactly the amount he *did* pay her. This abstract of account, Wilson says, exactly corresponds to Peters's account in Roe's books. We have also in Roe's hand writing the original letter from himself to Mrs. Peters—which letter she received about the time of its date, though she afterward unaccountably lost it—in which Roe boldly proposes to make false settlements with Peters's individual creditors, assuring her that such a course is necessary in order to enable him to secure the fifteen thousand dollars for herself, asking her to sign an enclosed power of attorney to facilitate him in concluding the fraud, and telling her *to destroy his said letter*, so soon as she has answered it. I would like to hear Roe's explanation of that!

"Again," pursued Traverse, "we have a paper in Roe's hand writing that at least very strongly indicates his complicity with Green in that old fraud of the Trust Company's bonds, by which the company lost a hundred thousand dollars, whoever gained it. The proof furnished by that paper is not conclusive of Roe's participation of that fraud: but if he had nothing to do with it, I would like him to explain how the paper comes to be in his hand writing!

"Finally," added Traverse, "we have the affair of the hat. I am not aware of any statute that specifically prohibits a man in Roe's position from going to the house where Snap 'spotted' him; but I would like to hear him explain to the vestry of Doctor Perkins's church what he was doing there! And I fancy, he would rather fit out a missionary or two to the Sandwich Islands, than have that question brought before the vestry. Now, these are things that can be proved: but how far they will help us in

the case, or in intimidating Roe into a settlement,
remains to be seen.   Of things that cannot be proved
in the absence of Roe's books, we have Wilson's statement of the transposed, altered and otherwise falsified
entries in those books—a statement necessarily true,
though incapable of being substantiated by us without Roe's compulsory aid. We may, however, by
presenting the items with Wilson's astounding expli-
citness, force Roe to believe that we have proof of
them, apart from the books, and we *may* thus gain
from his fears and his consciousness of guilt, as much
as by any other process.   In my opinion, when this
array of facts is placed before Roe, at a private interview, he will be frightened into an equitable adjust-
ment of your sister's claim : for, however such facts
may fail to reach his case in contemplation of law, an
exposure of them to the public would compel the
virtuous Richard to quit New-York ' between two
days.'   To be sure, this is a style of practice that no
lawyer would choose to pursue as a system : but he
may resort to it in an exceptional case where the
collateral and contemporaneous villainy of a defendant can be conclusively proved, furnishing presump-
tive evidence of guilt in other matters where the
proof halts. The only objection, that I see, to employing such machinery against Roe, is the possibility of his having dealt honestly with Mrs. Peters,
however improbable such an hypothesis is. But the
reply to that suggestion is conclusive: his books
must contain proof either of his guilt or his innocence : if he refuses to produce them, that refusal
becomes virtually a confession of guilt : and then,
all feeling of compunction on our part is entirely
swept away."

CHAPTER XXXIV.

On a certain day of a certain month in the year 18—, the case of John Doe *vs.* Richard Roe was called by the court, and the counsel on both sides actually answered " ready."

Traverse inquired whether the order of the court for the production of the defendant's books had been complied with ?

M. Demurrer, of the opposite counsel, responded that the order had not been complied with, for good and sufficient reasons. And he was about to add some explanation, when Traverse interrupted him.

" If the court please," said Traverse, " I will not trouble my learned friend to explain. But I will ask leave of the court to put the defendant on the stand and let *him* explain why the books are not here. The point is material to us ; and, in the absence of the books, we may be compelled to ask for an adjournment of one day, so that we can adapt our proceedings to the new state of facts."

Roe accordingly walked up to the stand. His complacent swagger, as he passed along, notified the audience that the individual now about to be sworn is Richard Roe, banker and church member. And to heighten their admiration, when the officer held out the Bible and asked Roe to put his hand on it, Roe took a step backward, bowed majestically and raised his hand toward the tabernacle already swept and garnished for his private accommodation on high—to let the officer know, and the judge know, and the assembled multitude know, that *he* didn't do his swearing like "these publicans."

Since there was no help for it, the clerk submitted to Roe's pomposity, and administered the oath, with the usual well-known solemnity, in the following impressive words:

"*You do swear in the presence of the ever-living God that the evid-you-sh-giv-t-mumble jumble gumble rumbletumblecourtandjurumblecourtandjuryevidtruth andwholeandallthatsortofevidhitormissandthetp, etc. etc. etc.*"

"Mr. Roe," said Traverse, "I will waive the usual preliminary questions as to your residence, calling and so on, which are getting to be pretty well known in New-York" (Roe bows, supposing Traverse intends a compliment!) "and ask you to explain your disregard of the order of the court as to the books of the firm of Richard Roe & Co."

"My explanation is, in brief, that I am unable to comply with that order," said Roe very blandly and convincingly, and attempting one of his persuasive smiles; but the big, meaty upper lip wouldn't answer the helm and he achieved nothing but a quivering 'grin.

"That explanation is rather *too* 'brief,' Mr. Roe," said Traverse. "May I ask you to elongate it a little? Will you inform us as to the nature and extent of your inability?"

Roe was, or supposed himself to be, a match for most lawyers in the game of "witness." He therefore took measures to let Traverse know that he, Roe, was not to be caught with the chaff of generalities, and he replied :

"I don't understand your question, sir."

"I think you do, sir," rejoined Traverse, quietly: "I think you do. You have stated your *inability* to produce your books; and you doubtless know what meaning you attach to the word. But I do not know your meaning; and I presume the court does not. My question is, what you mean by inability?"

"By inability to produce my books," Roe replied magisterially and with another useless attempt at the persuasive smile, "I mean that I cannot produce them."

"*Why* can you not produce them?" Traverse continued, patiently.

"Simply because they are not there," was Roe's conclusive answer.

"*Where?*" persisted Traverse.

"At my office," said Roe.

"Might they not be elsewhere?" rejoined Traverse.

"They *might* be anywhere, I suppose," said Roe, smiling in fact this time, upper lip and all; for his answer was not false, and besides, he was thinking of a funny story which turned on what a facetious old fellow once said his name "might be."

"Do you know of their being anywhere?" continued Traverse, steadily pursuing his point and not assenting to Roe's joke, as a joke.

"No, sir," said Roe, "not elsewhere than at my office."

"Have they ever been elsewhere than at your office?"

"N— not to my knowledge."

" When were they at your office ?"

" I can't remember how long they were there."

" That is not an answer to my question. But no matter. Were they there on the 1st of January, 18— ?"

" Yes."

" Ah, that's to the point : but how do you know that ?"

" Because that is the date up to which they were balanced and closed on account of the death of Mr. Peters."

" Did you then open a new set of books ?"

' I did."

" What became of the old books ?"

" They were put away."

" Where ?"

" On shelves, in the middle office."

." Were they ever referred to after they were put away ?"

" Occasionally."

" For how long a time ?"

" I can't say."

" For twelve months ?"

" I can't say."

" One month ?"

" Yes—probably."

" Two months ?"

" Probably."

" Three months ?"

" Perhaps so."

" Four months ?"

" I really can't remember."

" Did you ever miss them from those shelves in the middle office ?"

" N— never, until I received the order to produce them."

" Were there other and older sets of books on those shelves ?"

" Yes."

" Is any of those missing ?"

" No, sir."

" Sure of that ?"

" Perfectly sure."

" Were the books in question, I mean the missing books, plainly in sight on those shelves ?"

" They were."

" What were those books, severally ?"

" Leger, Journal, Cash Book, Day Book, Cheque Books, Letter Books, Bank Books, Ticklers."

" Were they all put away together ? all in one place ?"

" They were."

" Is every one of them now missing from those shelves ?"

" Yes, sir."

" Are you perfectly sure of that ?"

" Perfectly sure."

" Now, sir, will you tell me—could so many books have been removed from a place where you were daily accustomed to see them, without your missing them ?"

" I can't say."

" I wish you to say."

" I tell you, sir, I can't say."

" I wish you to say, however."

" I *can't* say, sir. They might and they might not."

Roe was growing nervous. He didn't quite see the

point, but Traverse's persistence showed there *was* a point, and he would just now have "paid handsomely " for an interruption that would throw Traverse off the scent and give him, Roe, time to reflect and study out a dodge. But Traverse gave him not a moment.

"Mr. Roe," he pursued, "I wish you to answer my question : Could so many books be removed from a place where you were daily accustomed to see them, without your missing them? Please to say yes, or no."

"I can't say yes or no. I can't say positively. I don't remember."

"I don't ask you to remember, sir. I ask you as to a matter of present knowledge. Could so many books be removed without your missing them?"

"I have answered the question, sir, so far as I can answer it."

"Do you swear, sir, that you cannot say either yes or no, to my question?"

"If the court please," interposed Mr. Demurrer, "this seems to me like trifling equally with the time of the court and with the witness. •The witness has said repeatedly that he can't answer the question. I trust the court will protect the witness."

"The court will *commit* the witness, sir, unless he answers the question !" said the judge peremptorily, his patience having been for some time giving way at Roe's prevarication, and now breaking down entirely at the attempt of the counsel to aid him in it. "There *is* trifling here, both with the court and with the time of the court, but not on the part of the plaintiff. Repeat your question, Mr. Traverse."

"Could so many books have been removed from a

place where you were daily accustomed to see them, without your missing them?"

"I suppose they might, sir," answered Roe : mentally reserving the point that, as he answered under compulsion, he was not responsible for the answer.

"*Were* they removed without your missing them?" Traverse continued.

"They were."

"Are you positive of that?'

"I am."

"How can you be positive of it?"

"Because they *were* removed, and I did *not* miss them."

"Why, then, did you so often say that you could not answer my question, when your last remark shows that you could have answered it at first?"

"I didn't understand your question, Mr. Traverse. I thought you wanted me to say when I first missed the books."

"Do you swear that *that* is what you thought I wanted you to say?"

"I do, sir"—(persuasive smile attempted. No use!)

"Mr. Reporter," said Traverse, turning to the stenographer, "will you read the question that I put to the witness?"

—"Could so many books have been removed from a place where you were daily accustomed to see them, without your missing them?"—

"How many times was that question repeated, Mr. Reporter?" said Traverse.

"Three times, sir," answered the stenographer.

"I would like to inquire," said Mr. Demurrer, rising with great dignity and directing toward Traverse one of those looks of withering superiority with which old lawyers so often demolish young lawyers, "I would like to inquire whether the Reporter has been sworn ?"

"You know very well, sir, that he has not," answered Traverse, not at all demolished, "and that there is no occasion that he should be. Every man present knows his report is correct. Mr. Roe," Traverse continued, turning again to the witness, "the question which the Reporter has just read was put to you slowly and distinctly three times, and you afterward swore that you didn't understand it. I don't ask you to explain that. I prefer leaving it to the consideration of the court, and to the recollection of all who heard your answer. I now ask you, sir, have you, or have you not, already sworn that you did not miss the books until you received the order of the court to produce them ?"

"I did not mean to say that," answered Roe, now completely bewildered.

"What did you mean to say ?"

"Well—really—I don't recollect, distinctly."

"Do you recollect indistinctly ?"

"I cannot be positive. My memory doesn't serve me on that point."

"On what point ?"

"I mean—that—I don't recollect."

Roe was at his wits' end; and it didn't help his embarrassment to observe that court, counsel and spectators were all on the eve of a broad grin—at the least.

"Mr. Roe," said Traverse, "I think we are getting a little foggy. I will change the subject. I will ask you, sir, whether you mean now to swear that you know nothing about the present condition and locality of the books in question—any of them, or all of them ?"

"I can't find them at my office," said Roe, delighted at an opportunity to touch bottom somewhere, though by an evasion; "and as to their present condition, I have not seen them for several years."

"That is no answer to my question, Mr. Roe," returned Traverse. "And besides, you might say *that* with perfect truth even on the extravagant supposition that a gentleman of your high character" (Roe bows again) "had inconsiderately secreted, or defaced, or destroyed those books several years ago. However, the court has heard my last question, and your answer to it. I am content to leave the matter there. He is your witness, Mr. Demurrer.".

But Mr. Demurrer seemed to be also content to leave the matter there; and not to appreciate the privilege of having Roe for a witness. At any rate, all the use he made of his witness, was to dismiss him with the stereotyped phrase, "that will do, Mr. Roe." And Mr. Roe stepped away from the stand with a swagger as different as possible from the swagger with which he stepped toward it.

Traverse now moved an adjournment until the ensuing day, to prepare for proceeding without the books. Nobody opposed the motion.

As the parties withdrew from the court-room, Roe whispered to Demurrer, inquiring how he thought the case stood?

"The *case!*" echoed Demurrer, testily; "the case doesn't 'stand' at all, that I can see. But I can tell you where *I* stand, if you wish to know."

"Where?" inquired Roe, tremulously; for the

tone and manner of Demurrer were anything but assuring to Roe's delicate nerves.

"I stand," retorted Demurrer, "where, according to the proverb, any man stands who is his own lawyer: I have a fool for a client."

Other whisperings took place. For instance, Doe said to Traverse,

"How does the case stand?"

"Just as we want it," said Traverse: "we can compromise now on our own terms."

Roe returned to his office, after the adjournment of the court, apparently in some doubt as to the wisdom of his having, years ago, hidden a part, and destroyed the remainder, of the books of Richard Roe & Co. It was a good joke in the time of it to put the books out of harm's way; but not quite so funny to be catechised on the subject under oath, before a court-room full of people, by a lawyer who suspected the truth and who, by his method of questioning, forced Roe into corroborating those suspicions. That was far more than Roe had bargained for. And now, a great point was to make sure that Jackson kept faith with him by keeping himself out of the way as a witness. *He* knew the story of the books, in part: and if he were to come under Traverse's examination, the suspicions would soon take the proportions of certainties.

While these thoughts were occupying Roe's attention, he had mechanically taken the evening newspaper and looked up and down its columns without heeding what he saw. Presently he caught a sus-

picion of Jackson's name; and, looking more carefully, he read in the list of passengers by the Persia,
sailed that day for Liverpool, "Joseph Jackson and
friend, New York."

"What's the meaning of that, William?" to his
second in command. Enter William. "William, I
see Mr. Jackson's name among the passengers by the
Persia. Is that our Mr. Jackson?"

"Yes, sir," William replied. "He called here this
morning to bid us good-bye."

"Where was I?" said Roe.

"At court, sir."

And the young man withdrew, leaving Roe "temperate and furious in a moment." Temperate, that
Jackson was out of the way of the trial: furious, that
Jackson had escaped his vindictive wrath. The
banker, therefore, went home to dine in a various
state of mind.

The appearance of things at home was not flattering. Margaret had walked out, or kept her room
with a head-ache; at any rate, she was not visible.
And as to Mrs. Roe, not only was there an ominous
"goneness" about herself, but also about certain of
her personal chattels. Articles of her toilette were
missing. Her wardrobe was empty. A little bit of
a note lay on Roe's dressing-table—some invitation to
somebody's—no; not the shape of an invitation—
what the devil?

"Dear Richard,—*Buy another Helen, for I have emigrated
into the heart of Paris.* Helen,
(*but not 'yours.'*)"

"Philip," said Roe, as the darkey announced dinner, "how came that scratch on the wall at the foot of the stairs?"

"Madame's big trunk, sir," said Philip; "the cartman slipped a-going down stairs."

"Then Mrs. Roe has gone"——

"Yes, sir, up the river, to Hyde Park," Philip replied.

"Up the river Styx to hell!" muttered Roe to himself. "*Joseph Jackson and friend, New York*, by the Persia. That's it! Helen *to* Paris. Helen *and* Paris. Helen *with* Paris. We are classical."

And Roe sat down to dine, all alone by himself, and nobody with him. It mattered little what he ate or what he drank.

When Richard had finished his dinner and his after dinner nap, and was considering how he would dispose of the evening, two cards were handed in by Philip. The gentlemen were waiting to know whether Mr. Roe was disengaged.

Mr. Roe was disengaged. The names on the cards were, respectively, John Doe and Alfred Traverse. Circumstances, domestic and private, and unknown to the two gentlemen, had combined to put Richard Roe in a mood even more pliable than they had counted on.

"You hardly expected a call from us, I imagine," said Doe.

"I cannot say I did, indeed," Roe replied: "yet extremes do meet, as somebody says."

"We have called on you, Mr. Roe," said Traverse, "to propose a settlement of this case, on what we consider an equitable basis. Are you prepared to negotiate?"

"I am prepared to hear what you have to say, gentlemen," said the cautious Roe.

"Then, without any preliminaries," said Traverse, "I will state, at length and in detail, exactly what we know, what we can produce, and what we intend to obtain from you in consideration of a settlement—if we can agree at all."

And in as plain terms as are used elsewhere in this history on the same subject, Traverse presented the matter from beginning to end. In short, he put the case *home*. The terms of settlement, he said, would not be made a subject of negotiation. He would take a fixed sum, secured to be paid within six months, or the plaintiff would proceed with the suit. He didn't wish to be offensively peremptory. But business is business. The fixed sum is one hundred and twenty thousand dollars, being a reduction of nearly one half from the total of principal and interest to which the plaintiff believes himself entitled.

"Gentlemen," said Roe, when Traverse had made an end of speaking, "as you say, business is business: and I have no remarks or comments to offer. To-morrow morning, in court, you shall learn what course I intend to take."

At the usual hour, on the following morning, a large crowd of people were assembled to hear the trial of Doe *vs.* Roe; and at the usual hour, the offi-cer of the day opened the court with his usual distinctness of articulation.

The spectators observed that the defendant was not present, in person; but he was well represented by the firm of Demurrer, Trover and Tort. They observed, moreover, that Traverse and Demurrer were in consultation; and when the two separated to take their respective places, the spectators fancied that Traverse was in much better spirits than his learned friend.

"Gentlemen," said the judge, "are you ready to go on with this case?"

"If the court please," said Traverse, "I have the pleasure to announce that this case is *settled*, by private agreement between the parties."

The judge half rose from his seat and leaned forward with comic incredulity in his face, saying,

"Do I understand you, Mr. Traverse? Is this case actually at an end?"

"It is actually at an end, if the court please," Traverse replied.

"Mr. Clerk!" said the judge, with an exuberant smile, and with irrepressible glee, "enter on the record that the celebrated case of John Doe *vs.* Richard Roe is taken out of the calendar and beyond the control of this court. And, sir," he added, as everybody was catching the joke and beginning to titter, "*adjourn the court to this day fortnight!*"

A jubilant roar of laughter was the requiem of

JOHN DOE

vs.

RICHARD ROE.

POSTSCRIPT.

An intelligent, but officious, friend—a man of some taste, too, in literary matters—who stood looking over my shoulder as I wrote those concluding words, remarked in an impatient tone,—

"That will never do! That is no way to end a novel! You must dispose of your characters."

"My dear fellow," said I, "don't get excited! I have fulfilled the promise of my title page, which is all any writer is bound to do. If some credulous reader has allowed himself to expect *anything more* than certain 'Episodes of Life in New York,' I may regret his disappointment, but I am not responsible for it. Besides, *que voulez vous?* The good people of whom I have given you some biographical sketches, are not under my control. They are not, as you intimate, at my 'disposal.' They will manage their own affairs hereafter, as they have done hitherto—just as they please. Moreover, my sketchy account of them, which you call 'a novel,' is nothing of the kind. It is a history; and, having brought my history down to the present day, I come to a stop as a matter of course. Not being a prophet, I have no power to proceed. I do not know how the elder and younger Miss Doe, Margaret Roe, and Phebe Pinch, will arrange their little matrimonial matters. They may all change their minds for aught I can tell; and, anyhow, there's many a slip between the cup and the lip. It will be time enough for *me* to

meddle with those things when they take place.
And so, of our young friend Tom: he may do well
or ill in his vocation; but I can't write his story before he enacts it.   I think I can *guess* what Richard
Roe is coming to.   But for the others, I can promise
only this: if they do or say anything hereafter that
is worth mentioning, I will endeavor to continue
their history in the style of the preceding narrative.
A promise, as you perceive, that is conditional—de-
pending necessarily on the acts of other people."

Meantime, I offer my acknowledgments for the
favor with which these sketches have been received
in their serial form; and I avail myself of *this* opportunity to express to my readers the assurances of
my distinguished consideration.

New York, *June*, 1862.

THE END.